ENTRY-LEVEL

A STORY BY
BOBBY CASELLA

coffeetownpress

Seattle, WA

Published by Coffeetown Press
PO Box 95462
Seattle, WA 98145

Cover design by Sabrina Sun

Contact: info@coffeetownpress.com

ISBN: 978-1-60381-058-6

I was pinned face-down in a pool of my own blood—in a bank vault. My cell phone lay just a few feet from my mouth, so she could still hear me if I projected my voice. "I just want some peace," I agonized.

"Can you see the bullet?"

"Yeah, it's over there in the corner. My skin's on it."

"I want you to stand up, honey, and I want you to get the fuck out of that vault. Then I want you to get out of there before the cops come. Do you hear me?"

"I do, Dawn. I really do. But the money, Dawn: it's sitting right here."

"Honey, a bullet went through you. You have an exit wound, and you need a doctor."

"There's a piece of my skin sitting on the floor. It looks like a strawberry."

"You're not thinking, honey...Am I losing you?"

"No...I feel fine. I just want to sit here and look at my money. I want to sit here and look at it a little while longer."

"Listen to me honey. You've got to get out of there. You'll bleed to death before the cops find you!"

"But I'm fine!" I snapped. I was delirious. I labored over to my back and I sat up. "See, I can put the blood back in."

"What are you doing?"

"I'm scooping the blood back in. I'm putting it back in the hole so I can escape with it." I was slipping hard. My blood wasn't really going back in the hole. It was just smearing all over my sweaty PVC suit. Ironic, the PVC suit. I'd suffered through wearing the hot thing throughout this whole ordeal in an effort to avoid leaving behind DNA. But now look. My DNA was a big puddle on the vault floor.

I wanted to tell Dawn how ironic this was—Dawn, the nice sex chat operator. But my mouth just fluttered. It made no sound.

"You there? Hello? Honey? You still there?" On Dawn's end of the line, there was a frighteningly long silence. I was

1

drifting. But I somehow managed to speak, "I'm still here, Dawn."

"Listen to me. You have to get it together."

"I'll be fine Dawn, I'm with my money."

"Honey, everybody in the world would want that money, but most of us are too scared to go after it. But not you: you went after it. I just met you, but I can already see that you have real courage. So all you need to do is pick yourself up and walk out of that vault, ALIVE, and a free man!"

I lazily rolled my head, enjoying the weightless feeling. "You're right. I think it's time to go. It's time for me to take my pill, and then I'm going to go. Thanks for everything, Dawn."

The cell phone rattled against the metal floor as Dawn shouted at me on the other end of the line. But I was not listening. My throat was so dry. My tongue felt like it had been cast in clay. It'd been hours since my last bottled water. Fucking details. I always overlook the smallest fucking details. I should have brought more water. Swallowing a dry pill wasn't going work. I couldn't even squeeze out enough saliva to help push it along. So I just chewed it, and let it soak in.

I lunged over and shut the cell phone, ending the call with Dawn still screaming. *Thanks Dawn.*

The speed burnt its way in, working its way in through my gums and cutting me like razors as I ran my tongue across the front of my teeth to catch a taste of the grains. It felt like a mouth full of broken glass, but my mind was coming back. The lights were back on. They were blazing.

Part I

Graduation (a Blackout) and a High Speed Chase West

*One year earlier...*All I can *clearly* remember from that day is loading my already drunk roommate into my Volvo station wagon that was parked in front of the house we rented that year. He wore pajamas, and I was still dressed in a white linen suit and rubber sandals from the night before. It was eight AM.

College graduation at eight A.M?

It had to be the earliest I'd ever gotten up during college. And it was way too early to get up, still drunk, to go to an auditorium and listen to the Governor's wife talk about how important she is.

But the ceremony wasn't actually in an auditorium. It was in the sweaty basketball arena, which is nowhere near as intimate as the ass-smell that permeates from cheap cloth seats in the state university's auditorium. But nonetheless, it was still a ceremony...to get drunk at and ruin.

We showed up fifteen minutes after the multi-denominational prayer, about twenty minutes late. Aware of our advantage, we knew that smug academic types on a state wage weren't willing to wrangle two revved-up punch drunks. So we rushed the place like we owned it. Spotting some open seats near half court (actually *on* the court!) we plopped down to graduate.

The instant Mrs. I-Used–to-Fuck-the-Governor-Before-He-Starting-Cheating-on-Me walked onto the podium, my roommate and I began choking down the flasks we'd packed under our outfits. I used the breast pocket of my sport coat, and my roommate stuffed his down into his sweatpants, covering the bulge with his nightshirt. We stuck out sorely, the two of us, he under-dressed, and I over, in a sea of black robes, literally thousands of them—a Big Ten graduation. We were the only two bright spots in the black puddle.

We arrived that morning knowing very well that we were special. Out of the entire lot of soon-to-be graduates, we were the only ones that had learned anything during the eighty-eight thousand dollar party. We, and only we, had any reason to be honored amid the surrounding tide of lechers. For we had developed our brains enough during the past four years to make this one sound judgment:

Don't drape yourself in a black sheet to receive a lecture from some twat whom couldn't give two fucks about you. If you haven't learned how to be a rebel, then you've learned nothing. Rebels are not people that get up before eight AM to wear the same damn thing that seven thousand other people are wearing.

The Blackout

I briefly emerged from the blur that was the ceremony to find that my roommate and I were stumbling around the parking lot looking for my car. Good thing Mother spotted us before we had to take the bus. She tugged at my father's sleeve and screamed, "Bob, look at your son!" Then she unloaded a stack of ceremony programs on Father and gave instant chase; to hunt me down and use her camera to capture a photographic record of my misery.

"Quit running!" My father shouted.

The inebriation worked against me. It betrayed me. Fleeing my parents, I tripped over my rubber sandal and fell—flat on the gravel. "Shit!" I screamed. Looking up I saw my beet-red father hovering over me, ready to lasso me and jerk me to my feet. "What's the matter with you?" he snapped. He then *smelled* a better understanding of my state. "Oh," he said.

4

Being terribly drunk, this wasn't the
to take pictures, a habit of hers that ha
There was no way in Hell I wanted thi
college graduation, to be documented
Hell I wanted to stand out in the hot
and pissed off, and swirled in a suffocating cloud of p
lot gravel-smoke. I wanted to get the fuck out of town
immediately and never look back—*this was a hard breakup.*
Smiling for a camera in this condition was NOT what I had
in mind. But I guess Mother forgot to realize that I hadn't
majored in theater because there was NO way I could fake it.
To make the situation worse, she even thought to bring
along a black robe and pizza box hat. She somehow knew
that I wasn't planning to wear one.

"Since you're never going to do this again, here," she said,
handing me the outfit. I backed away from the vile costume
as though it was radioactive radium. "You're obviously not
accepted to law school," she screamed, waving the pizza box
hat in my face. "We drove seven goddamn hours for this!"

"Elizabeth!" my father scolded. "You wonder where he
gets *his* mouth?"

"Oh Bob, would you just look how drunk he is!"

"Mom, just take the picture!" I begged.

"You need to smile," she ordered. "You need to *look*
appreciative of the education *I* paid for!"

"It must be real hard to sit back and sign a check, Mother.
Real hard."

"Bob, listen to how disrespectful your son is being?"

"Boy's got a point, dear."

"Full of excuses," Mother snapped. "Just like his father."

Father placed his fists in the small of his back to massage
it. "Please just take the picture honey—my back hurts, and
I'm hungry."

"Yeah, snap to it, Elizabeth!" I laughed.

Mother drilled the camera, smashing it against the gravel
surface. "Don't you dare speak to you mother that way."

ther shook his head with disappointment, "Good going
, you ruined your mother's graduation."

Mother kicked the poor camera. "That's it, Bob. We're
going home. Your son can find his own way back home since
he's grown up and turned into his father."

On the way back to the apartment, my roommate threw
up in the van.

The deal was, if my parents dropped us back at the
apartment, I wouldn't drive my car completely smashed.
Mother was mad as a two-assed wasp, but that's just the way
she gets—Italian. And what really set her off was Italian
food; that my reservation at Puccini's had NOT been
confirmed.

"But I DID confirm Mother! Those scoundrels are trying
to sabotage *your* graduation. And I won't stand for it. We
won't stand by and live this day without a proper
celebration! I'm ordering pizza and kegs...on, Father!"

"I think it's time that you and your disgusting roommate
go home!" Andy's eyes fluttered. He'd heard his name but
had no clue the context. Soon I was helping him out of the
van and herding him back inside the first floor that we
rented of the big three story house. Mother yelled at us from
the van, "The two of you need to go inside and dig deep into
the sources of your demons!" Then the van pulled away.
Mother and Father left town.

Twenty minutes later, when they were good and far out of
town, I received the expected phone call, the one that
females feel they must always throw in for *last words.* She
revealed that it was not so much the pictures, public
drunkenness or lack of law school offers that pissed her off.
That much, she said, she had only expected. *"I know what a
drunk looks like, I have your father. And that ceremony
was the ugliest thing I've ever set eyes on. All I wanted was
dinner at Puccini's. You'd think for eighty-eight thousand
dollars I could at least have a piece of tiramisu with my
son."*

Like most college campuses with rich sports traditions, there was a designated area for riotous gatherings before passing out in a puddle of boozy vomit. On this particular campus, a large fountain was situated in front of the stately auditorium (where they should have held a respectable graduation ceremony in small shifts, cordoned by college).

There were probably forty orphaned lunatics already debauching in the water when I arrived. The drunken mob was prying loose the statues of bronze fish surrounding the pool. They were a heathen pack, crazed on hallucinogenics because they had no parents present to tell them otherwise. Our reasons for being there were varied. But I assume that mental breakdown from the brain damage caused by four years of heavy drinking and drug use was at the root of the problem.

So there I was, enjoying soaked handfuls of titties and splashes of jungle juice. Was I finally enjoying this awful Graduation day, or was I just living another raw moment of college life?

DRUNK GIRL: "No more fucking class!...Fucking history class. Fuck!

DRUNK GUY: "Fuck you, history class."

ANOTHER DRUNK GUY: "I'll make this beer history!"

ME: "Put that in your history books. Stupid history department. Fuck you!"

DRUNK GUY: "Yeah, fuck, whoa!"

I chugged from my beer and dumped the rest on my head. Then I spit a beer spray, soaking the crowd in the pool.

DRUNK GIRL: "What the fuck, man!...Richard, that jerk spit beer on me!"

RICHARD: "Fuck yeah!"

Then Richard spit beer on his girlfriend too.

DRUNK GIRL: "Richard!"

RICHARD: "What Julia?"

ME: "Take off your shirt, Richard! Gross everybody out with your body!"

Richard took off his shirt, and everybody started spitting beer on everybody. It was heathen now. Even Richard's stuck up girlfriend with her Toucan nose was spitting beer now.

MAJOROITY OPINION: *"Hell Yes!"*

But that's when campus police arrived to our nakedness.

The fraternity house fire across campus was under control, making campus-wide crowd control the new priority. I shot out of that fountain, fast. My soaked white suit clung to my body transparent: you could see my boxer shorts. No way was I going to get tossed into campus jail to be held against my will at that miserable university any longer than I had to be. But since I wasn't already naked like most of the other people, I wasn't pursued like their sleazy asses were.

I returned to the apartment somewhat sobered up by the pool party. There I found that my roommate's family had come to pay respects to his accomplishment—surviving a school year of living with me. I plopped down on the couch and started telling his white-haired octogenarian aunt about pizza.

"I sure am going to miss college," I eventually admitted.

"Do you have plans?"

"No. Not yet." ...I thought a minute... "No wait...I actually do have plans. I PLAN to have a cocktail...*Cocktail?*" I offered.

"I think maybe you need a change of clothes and a nap."

I stood up from the couch, leaving behind a puddle of water. "I THINK I NEED A STIFF COCKTAIL, and I know what's best for me! I'm fixing us *both* some nice cocktails." I stumbled into the kitchen to slap together some drinks. But what I found was a girl of about nineteen packing someone's pots and pans neatly into a box.

"I didn't know we had pots and pans!" I announced in astonishment. "How did they get here?"

"Uhh...I just found them," she replied. "Like, what should I do with them?"

I sized her up. "You must be Andy's woman...He likes 'em young and eager to please!"

"Fuck you."

"Hey, have you seen all the vodka?...Oh there it is." I grabbed the bottle with compulsion.

My roommate burst into the kitchen for intervention.

"Leave my cousin alone, man."

"Cousin?"

"Yeah, she's my cousin, and you're not making your bed this early," he said. "It's like one o'clock."

He then poured my drink for me, a teeny, tiny pathetic excuse of a shot, and confiscated the rest of the bottle. I accepted the drink and leaned back on the counter. Smiling at my roommate's cousin, I goaded, "Andy likes his women just like his whiskey: aged seventeen years and mixed up with coke."

She flipped me the middle finger and stomped out of the kitchen. "Pervert."

Andy laughed but distanced himself with the bottle. "I'm rationing your booze." Then he realized I was soaking wet. "You asshole. You didn't tell me you were going to the fountain!"

"I'm sorry man." I gave him a hug. "But I don't know how I got there. I was just *there*. And everybody was drinking and getting naked. I just *got* there somehow. I don't remember."

Another round of the unexpected drunken sobbing fits came on. They had been coming intermittently ever since Mother had ruined Graduation. I wailed into Andy's shoulder. *"I really wish you could have been there man. I feel like I left you behind to die. Man down!...I love you man!"*

"It's alright," he whispered. "I went out to eat with my family." Then he took my arm and walked my pathetic mess of an ass back out to the couch. "Look at the ice skates I stole off the wall at Applebee's!" Lying on the floor in the hallway was a pair of old fashioned skates. "My mom totally freaked out." He was so proud.

I sat down on our living room couch and taking my jacket he said, "Sit there and chill. I'm going to finish packing. Then we're getting trashed!"

"Andy!" His aunt snorted. "What kind of filth did you learn at this place? What's the matter with you?"

He shook his head in disagreement. "*You're* the one with the problem, Aunt Mary!" Then he slumped away to continue packing and left me alone with poor Aunt Mary. I began sobbing...

"And she just never shuts up. Every day has to be her day. She just can't let me have my moment. It always has to be about her. Her, her, her. Well, someday I'm going to have my day. These were the best four years of my life. MY LIFE. And she had to show up on her broom and ruin it. I'm going to miss college so much. Life after college isn't the same, you know. It's all work, work, work, and you can only party on the weekends, and people expect you to show up places not drunk."

Extremely alarmed, Andy burst out of his room and rushed down the hallway to muzzle me. But not before I could add...

"I sure am going to miss college. I sure am going to miss all this pussy."

After the Blackout

Watching a college campus pack up and move out is like watching a whale give live birth: a messy affair with lots of floating debris. The street corners around my student neighborhood piled high with dinged up furniture. Lines of cars scooted out of town, filled to their roofs with crap and shit and people, and more crap and shit and people piled on the roofs. It was as if the Beverly Hillbillies had won scholarships instead of hitting oil.

The next few days after Graduation was contemplative inactivity and living off what was left of the frozen food. I had some time to try and level out. Time to burn my school papers and other bad memories in the charcoal grill. With time to spare, I also said goodbye to the people I'd met during my four years. The people were the only education I had gotten, and I'd never see most of them ever again. It pained me a great deal—like surviving a bloody crisis and losing everybody.

Added to the depression was the backdrop of a trashy Midwestern town. The manufacturing concern, an elevator company, had moved to Nogales, Mexico over a decade before. Most of the workers were either displaced or relegated to the service industry. Those that remained became more visible once the college kids left for the summer. For a few months it became the towns-peoples' town once again. A number of them crowded around street corners fighting over the piles of debris: desks, lamps, chairs, etc. I contributed a metal warehouse desk to their cause. I had used it for homework once or twice, so it still had some years left.

On the third night we went out for the final toast of final toasts, to empty our wallets and fill our stomachs, to soak our sorrows; to drown further.

Seven of us debauched in a corner booth the campus' world-famous English pub. Our reason: a last throw of Sink the Biz. Like most drinking games, losing a round of Sink the Biz meant drinking more beer than everyone else. We were all accomplished losers.

Fat Dallas sadly withdrew his eyes from his empty glass of beer. "This is ridiculous. Dollar beer should be all night, or at least until they run out of beer.

"Then it wouldn't be Bladder Busters," Crazy J pointed out.

Shakes distributed pills to everyone at the table. "Here, everybody take one of these." He always had a different pill for every occasion. "It'll cause your bladder to shut down," he claimed.

The Snake, on his way to law school asked, "Should we be taking these with alcohol?"

Shakes thought it over. "I wouldn't eat any spicy food," he suggested. "You'll burn your asshole out."

A muscle-bound bouncer was staked out at the bathrooms to monitor the lifespan of the Bladder Busters drink special. The first person to enter the bathroom ruined the dollar beer special for everybody else in the bar. Pissing in the alley wasn't a game plan. Once you left the bar, you weren't allowed back inside until after the special was over. So hold it in, or go in your pants.

A sneaky bitch was already trying to make her way to the bathroom. "Traitor!" I screamed. I pointed her out to everyone and screamed again. "Traitor! Bladder Buster Bitch!"

The barroom became a maddened pit of buzzing aggressors. Everyone started screaming at the girl, calling her *Bitch!* and *Dyke!...plug the Dyke!* But she was headstrong, and the Bladder Buster Bitch shot past a shooter girl and continued urgently towards the bathrooms. She only gave a fuck about her own selfish need to pee: she did *not* give a fuck about dollar beer happiness for everybody else in the bar.

Crazy J detonated. She shot out of our booth and chased Bladder Buster Bitch through the Birth Canal, a famously crowded squeeze between the rear of the crowded bar and the bathroom doors. "Man up, Bitch!"

Four more girls also realized what was happening and joined the chase. "*Stop that bitch!*" It was like seeing the Bears defensive backfield chase down a loose ball. Only slightly different, in that this was a frenzied scrum of swinging Mardi Gras beads and belly shirts.

"I can't make it!" Bladder Buster Bitch screamed. "I'm going to piss my fucking pants! So fuck you all!"

Crazy J shouted over the uproar, "Hurry! Buy more rounds! Quick!"

I sprang from my seat and chased down our waitress, "PBR me ASAP!" Oney stood up from the booth and spoke deliriously into oblivion, "Hey Bladder Buster Bitch." He had a gigantic soaked spot on the front of his pants. He'd pissed himself and was proud. "Yeah, that's right...This is how we do's it!"

Fat Dallas slammed his fists against the table. "This is ridiculous. What kind of bar allows their customers to drink uncomfortably in their own urine? Why can't they just extend the special throughout the night?"

Sperman, a Long Islander, had enough of Fat Dallas' bitching, "Then open your own damn bar!"

"I will," Fat Dallas snorted. "Dallas is a metropolitan city. Trashy beer specials in divey holes like this would never be accepted in Dallas!"

WHISTLE!

That was it. The special was over. Bladder Buster Bitch crept out of the bathroom. Crazy J pointed and screamed at her. "THERE! THAT'S THE CUNT THAT PISSED!"

The Snake sunk into his booth laughing, "Very classy pun, Sugar."

The bouncer handed Bladder Buster Bitch her trophy, a beer mug shaped like a toilet. Now she got to drink for free out of that mug for the rest of the night. Everybody in the bar laughed and pointed at Bladder Buster Bitch. It was so funny that a girl peed and ruined the drink special for everybody. Now the special was over. It was so funny. And now the lucky girl got to drink for free out of a toilet-shaped mug. So funny. Our table cleared. My friends bolted to the bathroom. Why not? The special was over, might as well pee.

Crazy J went to get more beer, and Shakes probably took a different pill to turn his bladder back on. I left the bar. The special was over, and so was this nonsense—college—it was over too.

Within a few minutes I was walking through an empty quad of limestone lecture halls. I was heading home alone and in desperate need of some advice.

"Gimme a hot sorority sister."

"Please hold"

Buzz...click..."Hello."

"What sorority are you in?"

"Which one do you want me to be in?"

"One where they do fat circles. I want you to tell me about the fat circles."

"Fat circles?"

"Yeah. That's what I'm paying you to talk about. Fat circles. Now get to talking."

"If that's a lesbian thing, then you'll need to buy another line for two girls."

"Quit trying to up-sell me..."

"Then what the hell do you want?"

"I want fat circles. I want to hear about how the sisters make the pledges strip naked and stand on a table in front of the whole sorority. Then they circle all their fat parts with a Sharpie and make them feel worthless."

"That's sick."

"But it's what I want."

"That shit's awful. What kind of sick bitch would do that to her friends?"

"Sorority Sisters."

"So why do you want to hear about it?"

"Because it's repulsive. And I want to hear about all the stupid shit that college kids do. Like beer specials that end when the first person in the bar takes a piss."

"Hello! You called a phone sex number."

"But it's my fantasy."

14

"Well, it don't sound too fantastic."

"I want you to tell me about fat circles. Then I want you to tell me how proud you are that I graduated. Nobody else has told me that yet."

"So that's what this is about... another one of these college graduation messes."

"What do you mean?"

"I get tons of you fuckers about this same time every year. You get all depressed, and you all call in and want phone sex operators to solve all your problems."

"Yeah, well what can you do for me?"

"Fuck! I can't tell you what to do with your life, college boy. I ain't even got a high school diploma. You're the college boy. Go get a job. Get married, have a family. Do whatever. I don't give a fuck. That's not what I get paid to do. So if you want me to touch my cooch, that's one thing, but I ain't gonna sit here all night and tell you what you should already know."

Maybe she had a point I figured. Maybe this time I actually needed phone sex and not therapy. "...Okay, I'll settle for you telling me about how we're going to fuck...but at least tell me how proud of me you are."

"Get your parents to tell you that shit. That ain't my job."

"I pissed my parents off and they left town. You're all I have. So please, just help me figure a few things out."

She breathed hard, yawned, rather. She was relenting..."*Okay, what are your options?*"

"Options?"

"Yeah, options. You got a degree, so you must have some options."

"Let me see..." I hadn't seriously considered my options yet. I had been way too busy recently, completing my College Bucket List, to have considered options. "I guess I'll just have to live with my parents for a while."

"That ain't no option! Be a man and take care of yourself."

15

"I'll contribute!"

"No you won't, lazy ass. So come up with something better."

"Okay, what if I head out west, to California. I have a friend that just moved there. He said I could crash with him until I find a job."

"Now that's a start. But what do you want to do?"

This prospect was exciting me. The West. The possibility. "Wow, you're right," I cracked. "But I can't think of anything...I've never really through about this until now."

"Come on, just start thinking."

But I couldn't. I was deadpan for ideas. Safety and security are big adversaries to the modern collegiate. Dollar beer specials and dorm food. Pledges to do your laundry. You can get smashed for ten dollars in college—ten dollars. A ten-dollar party is a mighty fine value—hardly a quarter tank of gas. It is also a mighty fine way to tune out from the world. You can spend four years of your life getting drunk for ten dollars a pop and ignore reality. But someday you're going to realize that it's over. Whether it be sobbing to your roommate's octogenarian aunt or walking across a podium, it *always* comes to an end—the greatest party of your life—and to me, that is no day to celebrate. "Thanks," I said sadly. "But I can't think of anything right now."

I hung up the phone and began thinking about *Options*. Yes, California was my best *Option*, and I had a long drive ahead of me to think about it.

Minor Interstate Distractions

Seamus McCaffrey's Irish Pub and Grill was everything an Irish bar in Arizona could be. Unlike the World's Largest Trading Post, a huge lie that I stopped off for in Oklahoma, this Irish pub properly tricked you into thinking that you were actually in a different place and time. The bar tricked you into thinking you weren't in Arizona, but in Ireland, drinking with poets and farmers, the Irish, in the mid 1980's. And though the bartender wasn't very convincing with her fake accent, it would begin to work on me if I stayed a while.

The Irish bar had long been a crutch of mine while traveling and miserable. I first used it at 18 years of age while on a six-day Roman hostage situation with Mother. I hate churches, and I refuse to wear pants just to go into St. Whatever. But if you're wearing shorts, they refuse to let you through the door. This sent Mother raging into an unholy conniption fit. A pack of Priests had to initiate an emergency exorcism. They too wanted her to shut the fuck up, and as a fluent speaker, Mother was quite able to comprehend "Shut the fuck up you crazy woman" in Italian.

"YOU'RE ruining my vacation," she screamed at me. *"I can't go into the cathedral because YOU refuse to wear pants. YOU have to wear shorts for everybody to see your hairy, camel jockey legs!"*

I finished lighting my cigarette and I screamed back at her, "They never said YOU couldn't go into the cathedral, only me...So have fun."

"But I brought YOU here because I wanted YOU to see the cathedral."

"I'd rather see my own knee surgery. BYE!"

I found myself snared in my vices: the best Chinese restaurant in Rome, and a world class Irish bar right across the street—nothing Roman about either one. I couldn't have been happier to take a vacation and get out of Rome, a stinking, hot, miserable, overpriced city full of tightly wound Catholic Americans like my mother. It's a wonder the place doesn't crumble to the ground during tourist season. In addition to the already yelling and screaming Italians, the additional yelling and screaming tourist mothers is enough noise to crush stone.

So how the hell did I end up in a Monday-through-Friday-happy-hour Irish pub in the middle of Phoenix, Arizona? How the hell had my life brought me here?

That's right...*Carlsberg on tap.*

"Hey there Las, can I get another pint?" I tipped my glass with droopy eyes.

"Whoots ye pleasure?"

"Another Carlsberg."

"Why noht tlye an Irish beer?"

"Because your fake accent killed the mood."

"Hey pal..." I heard someone say from down the bar. A drunken golfer wanted my attention. He was hunched over a bowl of peanuts, fresh off the course and brightly sunburned. But he was about to close in. "What was that you said?" he asked. He got sidetracked on his way towards me. "Imme a second." he said. He queried the bartender, "Matches?" and she handed him a pack. He sat down on the stool next to me. "Smoke?"

"Two please. I'm traveling."

"Have four." He dumped six on the bar. "Where're you heading?"

"San Diego."

"Great. Fucking. Town. I have a half brother in law there. A florist. But he still fucks my half sister, so he's not fag...Where did you say you were headed?"

"San Diego."

"Oh that's right. I have a stepsister there. You parked out front? I'm going with you!"

"Aye, shut your tlap." The bartender snapped, "Ye cab's coming to fetch ya."

The drunk ignored her and continued, "Three times in my life, I've packed nothing but a suitcase and started over. Three times. Is this your first?"

"Yes, this is my first start. I'm only a few days out."

"Well good for you, son. You're going to San Diego. Good for you. Good luck finding a job! It's tough there. But you could have a job in Phoenix by Tuesday."

He was right, why not just stay here? This guy, so he says, had already packed up and moved three times. Now his hat was hung in Phoenix.

The bartender set the bar phone back in its cradle, "Cab's here." The golfer then pulled himself up from his stool and got to his feet. "Good luck out there," he said. We shook hands. "But here's some wisdom for you: That girl was born in Cork. She may have a speech defect, but she has a heart of gold." He paused a moment and narrowed his eyes on me. Then he spoke as soberly as anybody can. "You're going to have a much better life if you can learn to start paying more attention to what's around you. Appreciate the simple things and don't be such an asshole." He threw the rest of the cigarettes on the bar and walked out the door to his cab. I deflated into my seat, and a fresh beer sat in front of me.

California

I hadn't been in San Diego for five minutes before someone asked me if I would sell her some drugs. As soon as I got out of my car, at the exact moment I first set foot on Californian soil, a Jewish American Princess approached me and asked if I had any pot that I could sell her. "Out of my sight," I snapped, "and get your designer purse out of my sight too!" forgetting my lesson at the Irish pub.

Alarmed at my outburst, she changed her mind and backed down. "Welcome to California, fuckwad." She flipped me a middle finger and stomped off, "Get fucked."

But I couldn't blame her. I knew why she chose to approach me. Ten days into my journey, standing beside my boxy Volvo, tacked up with obscure band stickers, I indeed looked like I would have pot. *Good* pot.

My beard was thick. I was dirty and suntanned almost black. I was emaciated from the booze/caffeine rollercoaster and lack of food. I was wearing some punk band's t-shirt with the drawing of a skeleton riding cowboy on a miniature rocket ship. I looked high. I'll give her that much.

The excitement aroused my liver. I climbed into the backseat and dug around in the trash where I had an empty beer can stashed for just the purpose. I didn't want to piss all over something so beautiful—this city.

The skyline was enchanting company. A halo of green and purple neon created a smoky backdrop of light that bounced off the thick ocean fog and lit up the city. The planners had obviously gone to lots of trouble to erect the most wonderful city in America, right next to that toilet, Mexico, to rub it in their faces.

* * *

Mid-stream, that's when Sion buzzed my cell phone. He informed me that he was parked behind me and had a good idea as to what I was doing in the backseat of my car. So I got out of the car with my pants around my ankles. I held my hands above my head like I had just gotten pulled over and was asked to step out of the car. Then, just like the drunk guys do on *Cops*, I clutched the beer can over my head, holding it like a torch. "What's the problem officer?"

* * *

It couldn't have been too soon: the journey was over, and I was sleeping well in Sion's Little Italy apartment with an ocean view. But at 1:30 AM, I could hear Italian-American screaming coming from the streets below. *Was it about tiramisu? Had somebody graduated?* Mortified, I plugged my ears and hid under my sleeping bag. I dared not to think that she might have followed me to San Diego.

The terrible bout of screaming commenced once again...This time I was ripped up out of futon. It was like panic at gunpoint. Madness led me to imagine that Mother was terrorizing main street in Little Italy, shrieking and hissing, and beheading newborn babies.

Morning finally came, and Sion found me in the bathtub, wrapped in the shower curtain and clutching the shower rod where somehow I'd managed to doze off. After he was able to find his camera, he kicked me. "Wake up!"

I leapt up to my feet and defended myself with the shower rod, "Who goes there!?"

"It's Sion."

"Did she find you?"

"Who?"

"She! Did *she* find you?"

"She!?" He croaked.

"Mother! Dammit. Has she poisoned you? How long do you have?" I marched out of the bathroom with the shower curtain trailing behind, "Hurry!...We must find the antidote!"

"When did you start having nightmares?" Sion laughed.

"Hurry...There's no time to waste. We need that antidote!"

Sion and I were founding fathers of the Brew Crew, the most wicked pirate league of binge drinkers to ever brutalize the Big Ten. And now I was acting like a pussy in front of him. I took him by the shoulders to explain.

"Sion. Listen to me. She's out there. She knows I'm here...Mother...She knows. She was...last night...screaming. Like a crazy person. It's only a matter of time before she storms the building. She's probably barricaded outside."

He rolled his head back and cracked up laughing, "That's just the crazy old drunk lady. She's out there every night."

"DECEPTIONS! Get a hold of yourself, Sion! We have to investigate."

Sion faithfully followed me around the apartment complex, capturing my every move with his digital camera. "Dude, these are going to be great on Crazyroommate dot com." He followed me behind the dumpster. "Come on, there's no way your mom's hiding back there. But keep up the excitement. Let me get another shot of that."

"Sion, it would be great if you could quit worsening this situation with your negative energy!"

"This situation really couldn't get much worse," he responded.

"Chi, Sion. Chi. You need to center your Chi, pronto."

But Mother wasn't in the dumpster.

She wasn't hiding under any of the cars in the parking garage either.

"We take our search to the streets," I announced.

We entered the nearest hotel, La Pension, in the heart of Little Italy, the perfect base camp for Mother.

"There is no Elizabeth Casella on our register," the desk clerk affirmed.

"Go back a few days. I know she's been here." I felt it was necessary to update Sion on the situation, "She's trying to give us the slip. She's hopping around, shifting her operations because it's harder for us to track her that way."

"How about you try the Best Western," the desk clerk suggested.

"That's a great idea. Mother would never stay at a Best Western."

Seconds later we stepped out of La Pension when Sion grabbed hold of me, "We're *not* going to the Best Western. We're going to get some breakfast, and you can calm down with a few Valium."

"Good thinking. We need proper nourishment to continue. We must re-fuel before canvassing the entire city."

Attached to La Pension is Caffe Italia, a sit-down style Italian café and deli. "This was an excellent idea, Sion. Mother will walk through that door any minute. It says ITALIA on the window! She won't be able to resist."

"Shut the fuck up about your mother and order something. The breakfast panini is pretty good," he added.

"Then it's settled." I approached the counter and placed our order. "We'll have two of the breakfast *Panineses*.

Chasing the Valium with a double espresso killed any benefit of either substance. "Sion, here, take a few of these," I said, offering him some Valium. "I don't think it's going to work for me. You'll need them to tolerate me."

He got up from his seat, "I think I'll just go and talk to that girl." A So-Cal cutie sat alone at one end of an otherwise empty sofa. She must have been produced in a tittie factory—stacked. Sion approached her and whispered something to her. She compliantly ended her cell phone conversation, so whatever he communicated must have been right on the money, but creepiness crept up.

It *was* Mother. She *was* in San Diego. Seated in the corner, facing the wall. I couldn't see her face, but I knew it was her. With the over-dressed ladies suit and volumes of dyed black hair, it had to be her. She was talking on her phone...and...talking with her hands; flailing them around and mimicking her words—Italian talking. Yes, it *was* Mother. A son knows when his mother is out in the neighborhood looking for him, to hand him a *Baccalá* for running off.

I called Mother's cell phone to test her.

She didn't shift position to take the incoming call. Instead, she continued her animated rant, complaining about me to a friend of hers, there, across the café, sipping her tea, freezing me out, anticipating my haphazard approach. Cunning tactics. *Haphazard approach she'll get.*

23

I threw my hands up into the air and marched in her direction. "BULLOCKS!" I shouted.

Sion was interrupted in his conversation. "I have a situation," he said, calm and collected. "My patient is having an episode." He glided across the room to intercept me, "*Yes. I'm a doctor*," he explained over his shoulder.

"Let's get one thing straight Mother...OPPOSITE COASTS!...I will not have you barging..."

The over-dressed woman spun around. It was NOT Mother! It was an olive skinned Asian lady that I'd never seen before. Misfire. Possible embarrassing situation on my hands. I had to think quickly...

Turn the situation around...Make it funny—Quickly— There, yell into that decorative mirror hanging above her table. Act as if you see an image in it—a haunting of sorts. Yell, deep, into the mirror like a psychotic person! Like it's possessed by evil.

"Quit barging into my life, Mother. Wait until father hears about this!"

Surfer Girl spoke up from across the room, "It's okay, lady. That's his doctor."

Sion grabbed me by the shoulders, "There, there buddy. Come with Doc Sion. Let's go sit down and have some coffee cake."

"But Mother!...She's followed me. This place is unclean. It's soiled with her presence. We must go to McDonalds, where she will not venture."

Sion addressed the Asian lady, "Sorry ma'am. Just a little outburst, but he won't hurt anybody."

The lady seemed convinced enough. "Well if he's your patient."

"Can't you see Doc? It's Mother!" I interrupted. "She's following me!" I stepped towards the mirror and waved my hands erratically. Speaking into the mirror, "Mother's insulting me! She's hiding in the mirror. Can't you see her?"

24

Sion let go of me. "Schitzo. Guy's a complete schitzo freak."

"Ugh!" Asian Lady gasped. "That's no way to speak about a sick person. You should have your license revoked!"

"Oh, come on, you know what I mean."

"No, I *don't* know what you mean!"

The Barista looked up from his work at the espresso machine, "Yeah man, we don't serve insensitive people. You're going to have to leave. But your patient can stay if he chills."

Sion defended himself: "I didn't mean it that way!"

Surfer Girl folded her arms across her heaping chest. "I can't believe I even talked to you, you jerk!"

I rode the favorable momentum, "Doc's a real quack," I announced. "He shocks me and assaults me with cattle prods."

"You should call an attorney," the Barista suggested. "Your doctor isn't right, man."

The Asian lady dug into her purse. "Sir, here's my card. I'm an attorney. I can put you in touch with someone that will help you get legal help and *better treatment.*"

We spilled out the front door of Caffe Italia, "Goddamn, you're in for it," Sion half laughed and convulsed. He inspected the business card trying to get himself together. "Connie Wu," he read the name off the card.

The intense excitement of my mistake-turned-prank sent shivers through my body. The aftershock felt like a lead cannonball was rolling around at the bottom of my stomach.

"Give my card back." I snatched the card from Sion.

"You haven't changed a bit."

"It's only been a few weeks since graduation."

"Yeah, well what have you done with yourself?

"I drove to California!"

"So did I. But now you gotta get your shit together. Your shit was cute in college, but you're going to have to grow up if you want to crash at my place."

"Fuck you. I'm employable."

"Well you'd better hurry up and find a job. I'm done with training in a month and I'm getting relocated."

"Relocated?"

"Yeah. Relocated."

"To Laguna Beach, I hope."

"Chicago."

"Too cold. You should stay here and maintain an extra futon in the comfort of this beautiful sunshine."

"No way. I'm out of here, and I'm taking my futon with me."

"I can fend for myself, fuck face."

"You have less than thirty days."

"I drove through Oklahoma to get here, Sion. Oklahoma! A state so awful that it's even shaped like a gigantic middle finger!...I at least owe myself a decent shot at California."

"Surprise us."

Job Search

San Diego, Santee, Irvine. On up the coast to Orange and Anaheim. Then back down again to Chula Vista, Mar Vista, Costa Mesa, Kearney Mesa—Mesa Vista, Mesa This, Vista That.

Banking, Real Estate, Astronaut, Hired Gun, Estate Planning. Sales: knives, Craftmatix, Insurance, Insurance, Insurance, all kinds, all issuers. That racket will hire anyone with a pulse. Stocks, bonds, mutual funds. All scams, yet you need a state license. Cars, trucks, snowmobiles (in Southern California), Boats, kites, prepaid legal services. Sales, Sales, Sales. Join the Army?

San Diego was a sellers' job market. That's because it's a place people go to die—a retirement town and gigantic military base. The only good jobs are selling shit to old people or joining the military. So if you're not a bedpan cleaner or a jarhead, you have to sell things or else go to law school.

I had to move to a bigger market, a smug, smelly, smoggy market to the north.

LA

The Volvo pulled into town around noon. By five o'clock, I had been turned away from every known youth hostel in Hollywood proper. As it turned out, you have to be foreign to get a room.

Fucking racists.

I finally found a firetrap promoting itself as a hotel, situated on the corner of Franklin and Vine. It allowed US citizens to crash for up to twenty-eight days. After that time you had to vacate for three days time. But then you could come right back for another twenty-eight day sentence of shared bathrooms and bunking with scumbags. They gladly accepted credit cards.

After claiming a dingy bunk in one of the many six-men rooms, I decided to go across the street and get a six-pack, also on my credit card of course. I'd need plenty of booze to handle these conditions. Then returning to the hostel with some beer, I decided to join the party in the lounge area and introduce myself.

Spanky was an S&M *thing,* and her specialty was letting people beat the shit out of her for an hourly fee. She had an unfortunate face that looked like a traffic accident, and as a commercial sex worker she was a real retreat from anything sexy. She obviously had a raging alcohol problem, too. She was in the lounge watching television and getting sloshed on Makers Mark—practically topless—her shirt had slipped down around her waist. Yet there she went, half topless, cramming her mouth with enough whiskey to cure a sore a throat.

That's when Chester arrived with a jug of pink wine.

Chester earned his living by renting out his own fleet of motor scooters to tourists and geeks. Much older than the rest of us, he was like a gay Danny Glover. "Watcha ya'll bitches doin'? Who wants some wine?"

Spanky raised a hand. "This bitch!"

Chester observed her condition and curled his lip. Spanky had two swollen black eyes behind her sunglasses. "Damn sweetie, who beat the fuck out of you with a sack of nickels?"

"Fucking high school teacher—two hundred bucks!" She responded. "Then he made me fuck his..."

"Spanky!" someone quickly cut her off, "cut the fucking details." His name was Will, and he was a loser from the *Aspiring Actor Crowd*, the majority of the hostel's population.

"Fuck off, vanilla," she barked back. Then her attention returned to the jug of pink wine. "Give me that." She shoved the jug into her mouth and went bottoms up. But as soon as the wine touched her mouth...*"Oh my God,"* she gagged. *"What is this shit?"* Pink wine spewed like a jet stream from her mouth.

So what's she do?

She scoops up the bottle of whiskey and fights fire with fire. She sucks back an eye-popping injection of whiskey-booze. I ran. I got the hell out of there before the bitch exploded and doused me with Gonorrhea.

Then she slings the jug of wine, spilling it all over the floor; an improvement. The alcohol wiped out two or more epidemics cultivating on the linoleum.

Chester covered his face, horrified. *"Oh Spanky, you crazy ass cracker!"*

So does she barf at this point?

Bourbon + pink wine = barf, right?

No...She does *nothing*...Not one damn thing.

She just settles back onto the couch as if nothing
happened and lights a cigarette. *"Chester, don't ever bring
that goddamn shit in here...ever again!"*

"Like that's the worst thing you've ever put in your
mouth?" Will noted.

"I'd rather eat a bag of dead assholes," she assured him.

As this happened before my eyes, I quietly sipped my beer
and made a mental note of where she sat on the couch. I
vowed never to sit there, ever. Then I realized I ought to not
sit anywhere in the hostel. I knew this much after only being
there for a few hours. This observation led me to go to a
hardware store. There I bought a heavy plastic tarpaulin to
cover my bunk to ward off the infections.

Settling down to sleep that night, on the clean plastic,
after an overdose of Valium, I made this pact: *Hence forth, I
will only change clothes and sleep at the hostel until I find
gainful employment and my own apartment. Once I find an
apartment, I will douse it with bleach and examine the
walls with a black light. Then I shall clean myself from
head to toe, for no less than three days straight in one
continual shower, or until my skin begins dropping off in
chunks. I shall become clean again before venturing out to
find my fortune.*

It took almost four weeks after I'd make that pact to get a
job offer. I didn't have to sell anything or deal with the
uneducated public. I was hired as an accountant for a
reputable firm that sold plumbing supplies throughout the
United States. Independent Plumbing Distributors—secret
corporate motto: *We Keep the Shit Moving.*

With two weeks until my start date, I had thirteen days to
find a place to live, and one day to learn the accounting skills
fabricated on my resume. But most important, I needed to
find a neighborhood to settle into; a place to hang my hat
until my derangement called to flee Los Angeles.

I was prepared to sign a one-year lease.

PART II

Wrecking Balls—a Woman and a Credit Union

My gang of co-workers was seated around a conference table at IPD's corporate headquarters. "I don't like that idea at all," I snapped. Our mission was to come up with a viable project for our department's quarterly community service requirement. "Only people that already own houses should be building houses for other people."

Krissie, a competitive tri-athlete, was the Chair of the Community Service Club. She gasped, "That's why it's called community service!"

My peers, all young, all deranged, had been locked inside the miserable conference room for almost an hour. Community Service was IPD's clever way to market the company without having to pay for real advertising. But that did not explain the motivational platitude poster hanging next to our blank dry erase board. Printed in bold block letters at the bottom of the poster was, *"Giving Back...Because not all Work is Business."* Above the message was a photograph of young, attractive professionals. They were sharing a picnic lunch with a happy group of senior citizens.

"Now, hear me out," I continued. "People that already own houses are too busy shopping for decorations. So they don't have time to build houses for people that don't have houses. It's easier for them to leave the work to poor people like us that have to live in studio apartments."

Lenny slapped the conference table with the palm of his hand. "He's *right!*" Lenny was the department's *Attention-to-Detail Japanese-American*, as well as the token

Recovering Addict. "There's no way in hell I'm building a house unless I'm building it for myself. I have dignity."

I laughed at the statement's absurdity. "Like we even know *how* to build houses? You have to go to construction school for that, and they would probably want us to pass a drug test."

"No," Krissie contradicted. "They already told me that there will be no drug test. Lenny's fine." Then she thought for a moment, "Lenny, I thought you got clean?"

"Passing a drug test wouldn't be a problem," Lenny stated proudly. "But I still get toasted drunk on the weekends."

Krissie rolled her eyes, "We're not actually building the house, Lenny. We're painting it. You know how to paint don't you?"

I was once again annoyed by this whole idea of painting houses. "Let the poor people paint their own houses. I don't even have time to paint the bathroom in my studio apartment. And again, why do poor people have houses in the first place?"

Krissie beamed me with an ice cold stare. Tall and buxom, it was intriguing. "If you're not going to cooperate, you can leave," she hissed. "I didn't ask to head this stupid committee, so I can do without your flak!"

Winston, the department's token *Chinese Immigrant with Hideous Americanized Name* tossed in, "Lenny can't be near paint! It's an inhalant."

No one thought that Winston's comment was very funny, and note wads were thrown at Winston in support of Lenny's recovery. This meeting was going nowhere. I wanted to get out of the office and get to Chili's for lunch. I could still catch the tail-end of the game, I hoped. So I decided to intervene. "Alright guys, I have a solution...I'm serious. Everybody quit throwing their notes at Winston and listen to my solution." I tapped the desk with my pen. "I wish to propose a solution to the committee..." I was getting no response. *Okay*, I thought... "I move for everyone to SHUT THE FUCK UP!"

Silence.

Apparently it had been a while since someone said "fuck" in a committee meeting.

"Now that I have your attention," I continued, "I know of a soup kitchen on La Brea that is in constant need of volunteers to serve Sunday dinner. I think this would be a great opportunity to get Katie off our backs about the community service requirement."

Looking around the room, it appeared as though I was getting some buy in.

"Go on," Krissie said.

"I used to occasionally eat at the soup kitchen when I was living in a youth hostel. That is, before the benevolent Independent Plumbing Distributors took me in off the streets and gave me a paycheck and health insurance."

"You probably still eat there," Winston joked.

Lenny jerked up. He was actually interested in what I had to say. "If you were born in China but your name is Winston, shut up."

"Okay *Lenny*, from *Ja-pan*," mocked Winston.

"Hey guys! Knock it off!" I ordered. "This is real simple—stupid simple. All we have to do is call in before three o'clock on Sunday and tell them how many people we're bringing. Then we have to show up by four, sharp."

Winston raised a pointed finger, "The homeless prefer to be fed promptly at four. They don't have time to be kept waiting."

I rolled my eyes, "No, actually Winston, if you're late, they run out of volunteer slots and we'll have to go build houses. Companies all over town send their people there because it's a known pushover for easy volunteer hours. I got two numbers from 3M salesgirls in *one night*."

"Pitty-fakes," Krissie mumbled.

"No, Krissie, they were real numbers," I said, "and all you have to do is show up and not sneeze in the soup. And they even give you a hair net and a facemask. It takes two hours, and we're out of there with a signed certificate to bring back to Katie. It's that easy."

"And you said you know of this place because why?" Krissie asked.

"I told you, I use to eat there when I lived in a youth hostel," I said with conviction. "I was practically homeless back then."

"*You* were practically homeless?" She narrowed her eyes on me and smiled. My Bohemian history was turning her on in a mysterious way.

"Well it sounds like a scam to me," Winston piped in. "I'll bet departments all over the city operate the charity as a front to get easy community service hours. I'll bet dozens of companies are in on it. They probably transfer siphoned funds from just about everywhere to bankroll it. It's a collusive corporate scandal. I think we should go in and audit!"

Krissie stomped her foot. "Do you want the hours or not, Winston?"

"Do we get to eat for free?" he asked.

I was left shaking my head, fed up with Winston. "It's a soup kitchen, dumb fuck.

The Youth Hostel

I was thoroughly charged about the opportunity to return to the old chuck wagon, my once sole and civil source of nourishment. I was so excited in fact, that I decided to visit Will, my one time roommate at the Youth Hostel.

Will looked like a troll and had come to LA, via northern Florida, to pursue acting. Of all the people living in the Hostel that wanted to be actors, I'll admit, Will had the best shot of any to make it. He really *did* look like a troll. I'll guarantee to you, Reader, right here in print, that the next time a low budget feature needs a troll and can't afford the makeup, they'll call Will.

It had been over a month since I'd left the Hostel. Not that I missed it, but I decided to drop by after work and tell Will that we were having a dinner party on Sunday. But the first person I wanted to tell was Spanky. I wanted to make sure that she was there to show her off to my co-workers. I wanted them to see living proof that I was not the most fucked up person in the world.

At first, I felt guilty about being in the company of the pond scum that I once shared a roof with. I had made something of myself, and they all still lived in the Hollywood House of Halitosis. I had my own 500 square feet of a studio apartment in Westlake Village, a new mattress, a second hand mini-fridge, and a coffee pot. They were still under constant threat of infectious disease, and shoddy bunk beds on verge of collapse, and likely fatality.

Chester was in the lounge, as usual, trying to make passes on one of the new Europeans. I decided to spectate. But I also wanted some pink wine.

"Oh look! It's the Deranged Young Professional, come to see all us hoodlums down here at Chateau Misery!"

I bowed.

"Here honey, pour yourself some wine." He slid the box of wine across the tabletop. "You come here to rent a scooter? Chester needs some money. Look..." He held out his plastic cup of boxed variety Franzia wine, indicating that he had expensive thirsts that could not be provided for at the moment. "The new Russian roommate owes me two hundred dollars for what he did to the yellow scooter."

Enjoying my first sip of pink wine since moving out, I sat down to catch up on all the drama. About half of the people I remembered were still left, including Spanky. The others had moved on or gone back home because LA ignored them just as much as anywhere else. Some had gone to rehab because they were hookers.

"They're tearing this mother down at the end of the month," Chester told me.

"You're kidding. What the hell is everybody going to do?"

"I was hoping I could move in with you." He winked and poured everybody another round from the box. "All us crazies will be turned out onto the streets just like during the Regan administration."

"It can't be," I croaked. "This hostel is one of the most historical landmarks in the city."

Rumor had it that in its heyday, the property was an enclave, a boutique of rental villas that catered to Rat Pack types when they needed a place to lay low for a couple of days. I could believe it. It had multiple buildings running up into the Hollywood hills. At one time, each structure was a pristine miniature estate with balconies and a private garden overlooking the historic Boulevard. There was a time, during the golden age of the property's life, when on a nice evening such as this one, there would be dozens of tiny, discrete parties—evening gowns and champagne flutes, starlets' distant laughter riding on the breezes.

But now the Spanish Mission architecture was worn down to the nubs. Like its once notable guests, the property had died. It was in the state of unstoppable terminal decay, soon to be tilled under the earth.

In the seventies, the property fell into disrepair after the Hollywood posh spot moved westward towards Fairfax, closer to Beverly Hills. Other well known hotels, heavy hitters like the Ambassador, had fallen off the A-list and become nothing but memories.[1] The well-kept secret places

---

[1] The Ambassador Hotel, home of the Coconut Grove nightclub and site of the Robert Kennedy assassination, was demolished in 2006 at the hands of the fascist Los Angeles Unified School District. Pitiful they are at educating, swift and certain they are at destroying irreplaceable history.

like the former hostel fell out of fashion and couldn't hold
on. A whole new breed of big spender fled to West
Hollywood to places like the notorious Chateau Marmont.
Out of the former property's ashes rose the Hostel; a
nobody. A place for nobodies.

These days, upwards of ten vagrants were packed into
each of the hovel villas. The gardens were filled in with
cigarette butts, broken glass, vomit, and Spanky's abortions.
It became a place where we transients could come in off the
streets for twenty-eight days at a time.

Rumors had even perpetuated far enough to insist that
Matt Damon and Ben Affleck had stayed at the Hostel when
they were struggling. It's hard to believe they'd ever step foot
into such a place, so I saw the rumor as more of a story of
hope for the current residents. I would imagine that Matt
and Ben were swept up into stardom the minute they arrived
in Hollywood. Yet, per the rumor, they too sought shelter at
Hotel Dumpster on the corner of Franklin and Vine. And if
it's true, they must have sucked every bit of soul out of those
walls that was left there by the Rat Pack. Not the soul the Rat
Pack left *on* the walls, but the kind of soul that fills up a
room just knowing that someone important once stood
there. I didn't see any more success stories walking out of
that building; Matt and Ben took the last of those with them
when they moved out. But at least Will still had a shot; in
Troll Country, he's King.

Will returned to the hostel after his shift as Lead Parking
Lot Attendant. He extended me a warm greeting. "You
motherfucker. Getting drunk and wondering over whether
or not to let Chester suck your dick. You dirty fuck."

"He already said no," Chester confessed.

"You look important in that parking attendant hat," I said
to Will. "It's good to see your deformities haven't improved
in their condition. You wouldn't want to spoil your acting
career."

"So what do want, asshole?" Will asked.

"I came here tonight to invite you guys to a dinner party at our favorite place."

"The Soup Kitchen!?" Chester squealed.

"Yes," I replied "Our beloved banquet hall."

Chester raised his cup. "We'll be there!"

We gave cheers. "I have to volunteer for my company on Sunday, and I thought it would be fun to reunite the Disciples for a last supper."

Will's thick eyebrows pushed together like two candy bars, his "mischief look." "Oh we'll be there. We'll make it the best showing ever."

"Let's make it a costume party," Chester cheered. "I want to play dress up!...I want to be a dock worker!"

Anne-Laure

At first, I thought the neurotic brunette in the jogging suit was one of those horrible newspaper subscription scumbags, the breed that haunt high turnover apartment complexes. I watched her approach two girls getting into a car and they blew her off immediately. So when she made it to my car I had a remarkable defense prepared.

Fuck you! I don't want your damn newspaper, you newsie tramp.

But thank God I didn't use it. The poor girl's car needed jumped and none of the other bitches in the parking lot would help her. She was as cute as the day is long, and *French*. She was athletic with long, black hair, bright blue eyes, and light skin—and *French*, shit you not. The blond bimbos must have gotten jealous, and that's why they blew her off. That, and now the blondes probably thought that cars could jump.

"I sorry to bother you. But I must hurry. I have *tee-nis* match."

She'd caught me unloading an embarrassing mess of yard sale furniture from the Volvo. My jaw dropped. My hands shook. I needed to get it together if I was going to talk to this angel.

"My car eez dead. I leave light on and eet not starting."

"Your car's dead? Did you forget to water it?"

"*NO!* eez battery. I need you help...we must hurry."

She jogged in front of the Volvo and I followed behind, watching her backside do the "look both ways." That's where a girl's ass goes from side-to-side like someone's head will do when they stand at an intersection and look both ways. I could have driven around all day watching that ass—I was hoping that she'd forget where her car was parked so that I could enjoy it a little while longer. But unfortunately, she led me directly to her tiny red convertible. I went right to work. In just moments I gave her the go ahead to start the car.

"I *sank* you so much. Just throw in," she said in regards to the jumper cables.

She was already backing out and about to drive over my foot. Without much choice I tossed the cables in the trunk, where the battery was located, and I closed the lid. Everything *looked* disconnected.

I returned to the apartment, and Will called. He told me to get some sleep because the next morning we were going to a fall-down-drunk-during-the-day party at a beach house in Santa Monica.

"Who do you know that has a beach house?" I asked.

"I met some people doing extra work...It'll be full of wannabe actresses. A total gold mine."

"I won't be partying in somebody's broken into vacation home. Who lives there that you know?"

"What's the big deal? So I know someone that lives at the beach."

"You still didn't answer my question, Will. One, why would someone invite you to their party, and two, why are you inviting me?"

"I'm trying to be nice."

"Again, Will. Why?"

"I need a ride."

Anne-Laure came knocking at my door a few hours later. But it wasn't on account of my tractor beam of sexy that could stun the pants off any young French girl. It was because I'd caught her car on fire...

"I'm smelling this horrible smells. Eet smell like coal. And I see smoke from the back of de car. So I stop. I call the 911 because I think eet might combust. And I run away as fast as I can and the car eez smoking. And the police arrive and they stop all the cars. And everybody is angry and they are honking horns and yelling. And the police man, he yell 'everybody shut up or we sit here all day.' And then he open trunk and there is no fire, it just *melty plas-teek* and the Police, he say 'Okay everybody go now.' And all the cars, they going, and everybody showing middle finger and yelling *'beetch'* at me, and I was crying and I wanting go back to France. And the Police, he pull cord you use to *feex* car and it touching battery and it *melty* and that was smoke. It was *plas-teek!* And I crying and then the fire truck come and eet so loud and I so nervous. I think I go to jail or loose my visa and then the fire man he inspect car and he say eet fine for me to drive. And the police man he say 'alright you can go now.' And then the ambulance coming and eet so loud and the police man and the fire mans they so mad and they screaming 'Who send ambulance? Nobody call ambulance. Tell ambulance get out.' And the ambulance stop and then the doctor, he running out of ambulance with table and they yelling 'where is *veek-tim*?' And the police start laughing, but the fire man, he is mad and he screaming on he radio, 'No *een-juries* were called in...who send medic?' An then they tell me go get car inspected on Monday, an then everybody just leave. And I standing alone and I crying, and I miss *tee-nis* match and I so embarrassed. So I come back, and now I so excited. My heart beating and I just want to relax."

Her eyes had been darting around my apartment as she'd ranted, curiously eying the bachelor indecency of the place. The apartment seemed more intriguing than the story of her own disaster. Finished, her eyes met mine, *"Eet smelling in here. You come to my apartment...I next door."*

Daytime Keg Party

The house party the next afternoon was on Ocean Avenue, on the boardwalk, facing the Pacific Ocean; far from poverty. We were soon kicked out.

The hostess, a sexy, elusive *Japanther*, came rushing Will and me screaming, *"You fucks get the fuck out of my house."*

"I can explain," I tried. But she cut me off...

"Which one of you fucks did this?" She pointed at the urine soaked carpet in the corner of the bedroom. Will himself had placed the spot.

I stepped forward to meet her and explain the situation. "My patient apologizes for the mess he has created," I said calmly. "But I can assure you, that as this man's attending physician, he has since taken his medication and there will be no further incident."

Apparently being a doctor is not enough to get someone laid in LA—it doesn't even allow you to stay a while longer at a keg party under such circumstances.

We were tossed out onto the streets. But at least that gave us the rest of Saturday afternoon to continue blacking out and terrorizing Santa Monica. We proceeded to get kicked out of two bars, a Starbucks, an omelet bistro (Santa Monica's version of the diner), two more bars, a Starbucks, and then a Starbucks. This was all before we got tossed off a city bus, *Downtown*, miles away from where we started, and in the pitch black of night.

Vernon is an incorporated city next to downtown LA that is zoned industrial only. Hardly anybody lives there, so there aren't any shops or restaurants—it's a dead zone at night.

The thirty-six people that do live in Vernon are city employees, and they live in one of the few city-owned residences. This is considered a privilege, but that depends on your concept of privilege.

As late as it was, past eleven, the entire city was cleared out for the weekend. This meant that Vernon was the first place we wouldn't get kicked out of. But something was amiss. One of the senses—sound, a critical component of the feeling you get when you're in a strange place—was gone. The silence was like standing in a crowded airport terminal with earplugs jammed in your ears; it was excitement and silence at the same time. The silence made me feel miles from nowhere. The Valium warmed me. In front of me was the illuminated skyline, and among it, the tallest building on the West Coast, US Bank. It was all right there. I could almost grab it. Yet, with the lack of sound, I was far, far from the moment. I was immediately drawn to this Vernon. It was different. It was an adventure where there's not a damn thing around except for forgeries, factories, and warehouses. There's not a damn thing in Vernon other than that. Not a dry cleaners or a barber shop. Not a restaurant or even a gas station. There's not a damn thing in Vernon, not even a bar... There's not a damn thing in Vernon...There's not a damn thing in Vernon...Except for a credit union. And I stood there in front of it wondering what the hell it was doing there.

The next morning, I was in my apartment, doubled over the toilet in my Sunday morning prayer position—swearing to God. The stomach demons lurched. They punched and kicked but wouldn't quite fight their way out. Cowards! My poor stomach was a roiled bowl of acid, unprocessed beer, and bitter coffee: vomit. If those assholes at Starbucks hadn't kept kicking us out, I would have stopped making a game of it. I would have stopped going into different Starbucks just to get thrown out between the rounds of Santa Monica bars.

My face was inches from the blue water in the bowl. The water was calming and therefore wasn't giving me the motivation I needed. So I tore the lid off the tank, ripped out the blue cake, and slung it into the shower. Then I flushed. Twice. Clear water. Time to go gonzo. Finger down the throat. I tapped on the wall. "Anne-Laure!...If you're in there, I wouldn't be. I'm gonna hurl, and it's gonna to be gross."

"Hello," she said through the wall. *"Are you seek?"*

"Hungover."

"Drunkard."

"Eurotrash."

"Eet serving you right."

Though we'd only just met, we'd already hit it right off. We were already busting each others' balls. "This is your last warning, Anne-Laure. I'd get outta there if I were you."

"I get ready for date. I need to do make up!"

My head shot up, the demons kicked. My stomach screamed. Then I screamed, "Date!?" But unfortunate was the timing, because my head dove into the bowl. *Uuggh.* The first flood of beer barf came up like my water broke and I was birthing twins out of my face. The backfire stung in my eyes. "With who!?" I demanded to know at once.

"You sounding terrible...I coming over."

Second wave. Another set of twins.

I sprang up from my kneeling position and sprinted towards the front door. I had to lock it before she could barge in and see me in such a state. We'd still only just met. But too late! She was already inside my apartment.

"Why you do theese to you self?" she asked.

"Why are you all dressed up?"

"I having date."

"With who?"

"With boy. I not like girls you *ee-diot.*"

"What boy?"

"Eez not your *beez-ness.*"

"But..." I choked before she cut me off.

"Where eez your toaster?"

"I don't have one."

"Then how you make toast?"

"Why should you care?"

"I trying to help you."

"Don't you have a date to get to?"

"You want help or no?"

"No, I don't want your help!"

"Okay, I go on date then."

"Good. Go."

"I will," and she started for the door.

"Anne-Laure, can I come over and use your toaster?"

"No. My date eez coming."

"But I need some toast," I whined.

She shook her head, "You should go very far away from apartment building. Buy toaster een another neighborhood and not bother me." The door slammed and she was gone. But the idea that she was going on a date was not.

The Dinner Party

We gathered around the stove in back of the kitchen, where the soups boiled on gas burners. Krissie wore a loose fitting jogging suit as per my instruction. The vagrants' shameless thirst for young flesh might provoke unwanted harassment, I told her. Lenny and Winston were just *there*. That was liability enough, and Lenny was already drunk. We were supposed to wait until *after* volunteer duty to go out for drinks, but I could tell by the way Lenny was pouring white wine into the French onion soup that he had forgotten that part of department meeting. "I'm just classing it up a notch," he said. "*We serve to serve the public.*"

Jen watched Lenny with a critical stare. "I wish you would get yourself completely clean."

"One habit at a time," Lenny smiled.

44

Winston shuffled up to a pot of soup and dipped in his finger for a sample. "So I bet these chicks are easy, right?" he asked me.

"Probably," I agreed. "They usually don't have plans after dinner. Most of them are available to party."

"But where would you take one, Winston?" Lenny asked. "You live with your mother, and you obviously can't go to the homeless chick's place because it doesn't exist!"

"Why don't you show up drunk at community service, Lenny." Winston chided.

"I did!"

"That's enough!" Belinda, the sweaty Kitchen Manager scolded Winston and Lenny. Then she tossed a pile of old hairnets onto the cutting table and studied Lenny, "Are you a *guest*-volunteer or just a volunteer?" she asked.

"What's the difference?"

"If you're a *guest*-volunteer it means that you *live* here too. And if you live here, you can't be drunk."

"Why would I live here? I have a job."

"You look like shit. That's why. And you stink too. Here..." She shoved a facemask into Lenny's face. Then she turned towards me and warmed up a little, "Hey, I remember you. You're one of those bums that comes in with the hostel freaks."

"Today, Belinda, I'm a *volunteer-volunteer*. I live in my own studio apartment."

"That's nice to hear. But we haven't seen your friends for a while. Is everything all right over at the hostel?"

"Oh you know. Staph infections, lice, nothing new."

"That place is a dump. We even call you guys the Flea Farm around here."

My laugh was interrupted by an ear-shattering cacophony erupting in the dining hall area. Winston looked up from typing a text message on his cell phone, "Does that mean the 3M salesgirls are here?"

"No. I'm afraid not." I casually stepped towards the door to enter the dining hall. "Excuse me, but I must go. My dinner guests have arrived."

Outside in the dining hall, Chester, dressed as Cat Woman, had leapt onto a flimsy folding table and was defending himself against an attack by Soily Schmitt, a regular diner and delusional. Chester swatted at Soily Schmitt with his plastic Cat Claws. "Nay you miscreant!" Schmitty, the attacker's real name, had always thought that homosexuals were space aliens and that it was his mission to apprehend them for the Republicans. "I'm getting you this time! I'm hauling you in. You Thing!" he barked.

Reinforcement arrived when Spanky, dressed in a Nun's outfit, swooped in and threw a bowl of lettuce at Schmitty, hitting him in the face. "Sit down, old man!" Schmitty spat roughage from his beard and leapt at Spanky. "Speak your blessings, Sister! He grabbed at Spanky, "It's only God that can save us now!" But he was soon intercepted by one of his companions, a lesser-deranged old wino, Peaty. "Sit your ass down, you old fool."

Even though professional obligations at the parking lot had interfered, Will somehow managed to round up a majority of the *real* whack jobs from the hostel. There were ten in all, including Spanky and Chester, wearing everything from hospital gowns to flight suits. But the guy in the hospital gown, whom I had never seen before, had probably just escaped from a mental ward and checked himself into the hostel before stopping to buy new clothes.

My cell phone rang, withdrawing me from the spectacle. The pizzas had arrived. "Get these lunatics sedated!" I shouted. "The food's here."

Belinda met me by the back door as I paid the delivery guy. "Are you out of your mind?" she asked. "You'll turn this place into a circus." I shrugged her off and began setting my haul of twenty pizzas in the serving window. On Sundays, New York style pizzas are buy-one-get-one-free in

Hollywood. An urgent panic swept the diners once the fatty smell found its way into the dining hall. Like a massive Wall Street sell off, a wave of consternation exploded outside the kitchen. My co-workers quickly deployed to the buffet table, where they transferred pizzas from the window to the table as fast as they could keep up. "I sure hope there's some sausage and pepperoni left over!" Lenny cried.

"Not today!" Soily Schmitt grabbed an entire box and danced away from the crowd with the box held high above his head. That is, until an angered bag lady smacked it out of his grip. She scooped up the fumbled box and ran it over to a safe corner where she fortified herself.

Amid the chaos, I found my hostel companions patiently awaiting my arrival at a cozy rear table. I was greeted like royalty, and Spanky extended me a European greeting, "Our gracious host." She hardly looked religious in her patent leather Nun's cassock and black eye. As I sat down, Winston sprinted over as instructed to attend to our every need. "What can I get everybody to drink?"

Spanky tapped me on the shoulder. "Is that the Chinese guy you want me to fuck?"

Franklin Vista

After wrapping up with our volunteer hours, we made very damn sure that Belinda signed our forms. I said goodbye and thank you for the opportunity. With the satisfaction of a job well done, I stepped outside the back door and into the urine soaked parking lot for my car. There was Will, camped out next to the Volvo.

"Thought I'd drop by after work," he said. "Let's get a drink."

That was his coy way of bumming a ride off me, and probably a drink or two. So I figured that if I stood there long enough, silently, he'd go away...

"Just open the door," he griped. "I have some something for you."

We head a few blocks north to The Lava Lounge, a place that is supposed to look like the *inside* of a volcano. It's a windowless cavern of red neon lights and walls made out of lava rocks. Sitting in this place and sharing a table with Will, a guy that looks like a troll, I had the overwhelming impression that I *was* in Hell and not just LA.

"I see an opportunity to score big with that office of yours," he began, "community service, right?"

"Yeah, we do at least one project per quarter."

"They tear down the hostel in a few weeks, and it's going to take Rhanja's crew at least a few more weeks to clear out the rubble. I bid twenty grand for one weekend to clear out the site and he accepted."

"Krissie would never go for it. It's too much work."

"Bring in more departments. Your company's big."

I thought about it for a moment. *Yes, it could be done.* The troll was right about that. But first I would have to remove Krissie, and yet still, the job itself was too much. A whole weekend was too much time to snare my co-workers. There would definitely be extreme resistance.

"What about just one Sunday?" I asked. "I could probably get them to volunteer for a Sunday. How much do you think Rhanja would pay us for that?"

"The building gets razed on a Friday, and Rhanja wants the whole site cleaned by the following Monday. It's a perfect gig! You just bring in your crew, keep them happy, and Rhanja will pay us twenty large."

"What's your cut?"

"Half, of course."

I shot up from the table and slammed my fists, "If you think you can con me into buying you a drink and then try and fuck me with some bogus offer, you're one dumb fuck."

"Sixty-forty."

I sat back down. To insult Will, I snatched his drink off the table and gulped it down.

"So you want me to risk my job on some con? When it's my workers? Then I have to split almost half the score with some dirt bag like you? Will, that's just crooked. I could only feel right about it for one thousand dollars your way."

"Feel right!? Who's the slimy fuck now? One thousand? You're a crack head." Will reached across the table and snatched *my* drink. Then he insulted me as I had insulted him, and sucked mine down. "Five grand...I'm going to need at least one grand to move into a new apartment, and I owe four grand to my ex-girlfriend. So that's five."

"I bet she's a real prize...*if* she exists."

"Come on, you have to understand that I'm on the streets when that building falls. I set the deal up with Rhanja. It's my plan. So that should count for at least a quarter."

"Thirty-five hundred and *you* cover expenses."

"Expenses?"

"YES EXPENSES. A fake charity... t-shirts, buttons, pens...*A fake charity!* We require a scale model of the future site to present to my boss. Are you a fucking idiot? You don't just con your entire workforce into working on a fake charity project without first guaranteeing that you have a believable fake charity!"

"Bump up my taste to five grand and I'll get you a scale model. But I can't do anything else."

"Okay. But in lieu of t-shirts and buttons I get that promotional video. I need to have a video when I pitch to my boss."

"Can you give me a couple of days?"

"I go to my boss on Wednesday," I said quickly. I was becoming excited. This project. This moment. This was an *Option*. This was my first opportunity to hit big.

Will could tell that I was satisfied with the deal. "Let's drink one to Rhanja then," he said.

I rolled my head back and yawned, "You're just trying to bilk me for another drink. So fuck you. You don't really want to toast to anything."

That Wednesday morning, I was pitching Katie in her office. "And as you see, Katie, the existing site is a complete eyesore for the neighbors and taxpayers. The Renaissance Hotel, three stars, and the Methodist Church have had enough. Not only will this project clear the way for a much needed senior facility, but we will also be cleaning up a landmark corner of our city."

"Does Krissie know about this? The committee is hers you know."

"Katie...I'm unhappy to be the one to tell you this, but Krissie has grown bored with the committee...She lost her interest once she was accepted into an MBA program."

"What?"

"That's right, Katie. I'm afraid that she was only using the committee to serve for her own selfish gain."

"Well that's it. It looks like you're the new chair. Especially if she's unhappy with it."

"Extremely unhappy. But I also want you to know that Krissie's MBA is just a bogus online program. What I just told you is confidential, right?'

"Right."

"So let's redirect our attention back to the video for a minute. I want you to meet the CEO of the non-profit that is responsible for this *necessary* project.

I pressed the play button, and Chester appeared on the screen. He wore a pleasant smile and an ugly knit sweater, a look that screamed philanthropist. As a set they used Rhanja's office, which coincidently looked like the unpresumptuous headquarters for some pitiful humanitarian organization.

"Why hello there, and thank you for your time in considering Franklin Vista Assisted Living Community as part of your charitable giving program. With over twelve

*percent of the US population already being retired and an
additional four percent set to retire over the next fifteen
years, assisted living is a crucial part of the solution to
provide comfortable, affordable aging to our seniors.*

"Wait, let me fast forward to the model.

"But I didn't get to hear what he had to say!"

"Katie, I don't want you to hear what he has to say. I don't
want to ruin your day...Can you imagine how many seniors
live below poverty level?...On the streets or in squats? If we
continue to listen to that man, Katie I assure that you that
the rest of your day will be ruined. Lunch. Dinner.
Everything. I bet you didn't know that every year, in the LA
area alone, over a dozen seniors are kidnapped and sold into
forced labor." I pressed fast forward. Beyond the
introduction, Will's video wasn't very convincing until the
part with the scale model. "Yes, it's better that we just forget
about that. I have something I want you to see."

I pressed *Play* having arrived at the desired section,
"This, Katie...this is what I'm talking about. This fine
building, as depicted in the model, is what Franklin Vista is
all about. This is the closest thing to Heaven you're ever
going to see...Assisted living at Franklin Vista is the last stop
before heaven, the perfect place to kick it before you *really*
kick it."

"Wow. It's beautiful," she said in awe of the model.

Our fictional senior center was an *actual* architect's
model. It was a scale replica of a new high school that was
about to break ground in the up-and-coming neighborhood
of Hancock Park. Will was working as a temp for a catering
service and stole it during a PTA fund raising dinner. After
chopping away two thirds of the model, pared down, it
actually looked like something that might fit on the site of
the old hostel. "You like that Katie?" I continued. "That sure
is a beautiful building. It sure is better than talking about
senior abuse. Talking about senior abuse is never a good
idea. It's always better to just ignore issues like that."

"It really is going to be beautiful."

"You have good taste, Katie."

The video wrapped up with a slide show of live action photos of seniors doing all sorts of activities:

Drinking dinner through straws,

Watching television game shows,

Discussing bowel movements,

Wheel chairing,

Medicating, and

Aching and paining.

"Katie, the evidence is over-whelming...We *must* incorporate this project into our community service program. But I need your help, Katie. Only *you* can make this possible...you...So I ask, are you on board with me Katie?"

"Of course. This seems like a noble cause."

"Great Katie, but in order to make a project of this magnitude work, I need the project to count as community service hours against the next three quarters. It means that in order to get cooperation from my people, I have to promise that this project pays them up for the next nine months.

"Okay."

I also need more manpower. I need to make this opportunity available to other departments at IPD on those same terms.

"Okay."

I scrawled a figure on a scrap of paper and slid it across the desk. "And I'll need a budget of this much for incidentals."

It was a week and a half later, Friday night. Anne-Laure and I were beginning to spend much of our time together, even going next door to each other's apartments to *check* on one another. Together, we watched the first pass of Rhanja's wrecking ball smash through the rotten stucco of the old

Hostel. The wall shattered it into thousands of unidentifiable chunks. My rickety bunk bed once stood behind a section that was now a gaping hole. A second pass came and the mighty crane's hydraulics flexed their might against the feeble structure. Breaking it down was as simple a motion as sweeping paper wads off an office desk. One more swing and, the very wall that was once my sole protection from the horrifying streets of Hollywood was no more.

Anne-Laure had never had an opportunity to watch a building be torn down. In France they like to keep buildings around a while, or at least until the Germans drop by. When I asked her to join me watch it be razed, she insisted. With each strike of the wrecking ball, she'd grab my arm and writhe with recycled excitement. She didn't know that I once lived inside that place.

The next day, Saturday, was the first day of our fictional volunteer project. Groggy IPD employees moped around clearing the job site, dragging rubble and dragging their feet.

"Coffee!" I announced. "Who needs coffee?"

"Un café au lait." Anne-Laure also insisted on *volunteering* to clean up the debris. I didn't have the heart to tell her that it was a scam, but it seemed like she was having fun. Her hand was bleeding, and she'd already skinned a knee. But that just comes with the territory in the destruction business. I was proud of her.

When I asked Lenny for his coffee order, he asked me, "How much petty cash did Katie give you?"

"That's none of your business."

"I bet she gave you a shit load."

"I have to document everything."

"Why don't you go and meet my guy under the 101 overpass at Chuenga. I'll call ahead."

"You're buying."

"Bullshit. We're spending IPD's money. And I won't tell her about how you haven't lifted a goddamn finger this

53

whole time. So you'd better start doing something, like buying cocaine."

"I'm keeping things in line, Lenny. Projects of this scale just don't happen by themselves."

The only thing you're lining up, is behind that French girl's ass every time she bends over to pick up a rock."

"Don't objectify my volunteers!"

Lenny held his hands out, inviting me to take a look. He'd lost two whole fingernails, and a third was hanging on by a thread. "I just wanted you to see that. I wanted you to see what a goddamn asshole you are. Now get me a coffee from Starbucks, you asshole, I like caffeine when I'm high."

Lenny wasn't the only IPD employee with an abusive, exploitive attitude towards my offer to make a coffee run. There were over fifty others present, and they all figured that because it was the company's money, I couldn't wait to drive around Hollywood picking up whatever they wanted.

Between an eight ball for Lenny and about fifty of the most expensive coffee drinks on the Starbucks menu, I was fiercely burning through the incidental dollars Katie had given me. Fortunately though, I got Will to agree that we would cover any significant overages out of our twenty grand to keep suspicions low.

When I arrived back at the site, I expected to be received with heartfelt open arms. Instead, I was met by an upset line of about fifty unappreciative co-workers shouting obscenities at me.

"Wipe that stupid smile off your face. Nobody's smiling but you, you horse's ass."

"But you won't have to do community service for nine whole months!" I reminded them. "Nine months is a long time!"

"That still doesn't mean that I have to be nice... I said Americano, you retard. This is drip. I oughta throw this in your face."

Volunteers can be so rude, especially when you fuck up their coffee order. For some reason, they have this unrealistic expectation to be treated well. Like Winston, who approached me to claim his frozen macchiato. "I said extra whip, you fucker." He dug his finger into the mound of cream and scooped out a fluffy white ball. It looked delicious until he licked it off his dirty finger. "Oh yeah, and Krissie's in the hospital...You're fucked."

Will entered Presbyterian Medical Center through the main entrance, coming in from the street. He took the bus because he didn't own a car to park in the garage. But wearing a moderately priced navy blue suit, the troll-like public transportation user looked somewhat respectable. The yellow 8x11 envelope that he clutched gave the added impression that he was on official business.

He found the room where Krissie was recovering and knocked softly on the door.

"Yes?" a male voice called out abruptly. It was Krissie's fiancé, who'd come to make Will's job harder. But Will stepped inside surefooted as any. "Reverend Will Williams, representative of Franklin Vista."

Winston had stopped working. Completely. He was sitting on a curb, slouched over and chain smoking, refusing to move.

"Winston, it's not like I don't have enough problems already. Krissie went completely blind." His eyes found mine, his were concerned. That's a look I'd never seen out of him before, *concern*. "But let's not start assuming things," I said. "It's just what I heard."

"It's not like it's completely unbelievable though. This *is* back breaking labor. Mexicans wouldn't even do this shit." Other IPD volunteers were starting to notice Winston, and soon they too would all be assuming that this was *take a break* time and not *work* time. "Nine months, Winston. You won't have to lift another finger for nine months."

"Krissie's in the hospital for fuck sake."

"What's it going to take to get you to get back to work and set a good example for the others?"

"You're pretty fucked, you know that?" Winston's assessment was cold but accurate. "The surveyor came by and we spoke. They're building a hotel here."

* * *

Will poured a glass of ice water from a pitcher on the medicine table and returned with it to Krissie's bedside. The fiancé remained fixed on the muted volume of the football game. Will kindly offered the glass to Krissie and she accepted it with a shaky arm. "How are they treating you in here?" Will asked. He brushed her hair aside, like he owned it, like he was *allowed* to touch it, and took a peek at her wound. It was nothing more than a cat scratch. Duly, that's why the finance was none more concerned.

"All wounds heal in time," Will assured. "I've seen burn victims, Krissie. *Burn victims*. It's the most intense thing. It's the greatest damage the body can endure. But I've seen the worst cases heal." Will placed his stubby hand over Krissie's heart. "In here."

Krissie nursed up some water from her glass as if doing so was necessary to save her life; as if life were quickly slipping away. As she drank, Will took the opportunity to obtain Krissie's chart from the foot of the bed. He walked it over to the window where he drew the drapes to let some Saturday sunshine in. "Los Angeles really knows how to make some sunlight, does it not?"

Krissie squinted. The intense light poked at her and made her jerk. "It's nice," she whispered.

"It *is* nice. Very nice, Krissie. But I want you to know something about the sun Krissie. I want you to know about how 'the sun' can mean different things to different people."

The fiancé burst up from the bed, "No good! It's no good!" Then he plopped back down as quickly as he sprang, plunging back into his preoccupation, the muted football game.

"Avoid burning, Krissie...*Expose* yourself to the *Son*...The *Son* of God Almighty." With that, Will folded his hands in prayer and dipped his head, inviting Krissie to ponder. It gave him some time to review her chart:

Minor head trauma. No other signs of complications to patient. Patient complains of headaches and fatigue. Observe patient for symptoms of fatigue and recommend treatment if needed. Review for immediate release at 14:00. Refer to OBGYN.

Will pulled his eyes away from the chart and looked directly into the scolding hot sunlight. "Have you *exposed* yourself Krissie?"

"Exposed what?" the fiancé snapped.

"Have you exposed yourself to the *Son*, Krissie? The Son of God Almighty."

Krissie could see Will's darkened silhouette against the screen of intense light; framing him, emboldening him patriarchal. What she saw was as man of reverent self-sacrifice out, to serve senior citizens. But what she missed because of that blinding light was Will's troll-like wicked grin melted into his square head.

He returned to Krissie's bedside, away from the sunlight.

"Krissie, are you feeling better?"

She smiled and stretched but maintained her feeble antics. "Yes."

"Well good. Because before I tell you this, I want to make sure that you feel well. And that you feel...right about this."

"Yes. Much better. And right."

The fiancé rolled his eyes.

"Krissie, see that bright sunlight out there?"

"Yes."

"Los Angeles really knows how to make sunlight, doesn't it?"

"It does."

"Well Krissie, it might seem bright and sunny to us, but for thousands of senior citizens out there, in Los Angeles and beyond, even a day like this *isn't* so sunny. See, there are people out there, elderly people, in suffering. Suffering right now. And it's our *duty* as Jesus' children to care for these people. Krissie...I need to tell you about something. There's something that you need to know about...It's called senior abuse.

* * *

I studied the surveyor's business card Winston had given me, *Eastham and Associates*, and called the number. Someone picked up."Hello there," I began. "I'm the foreman of the cleanup crew at the site on Franklin and Vine. One of my workmen said that someone from your outfit stopped by this afternoon."

"Yeah, I dropped by around noon."

"So you must be," I consulted the card, "Chief surveyor—John Eastham."

"Yeah that's me. But say there, that's not your typical cleanup crew is it?"

"No it isn't John. We're just a bunch of students out to earn a buck...So let me tell you why I called. I was just curious, what are they going to build here?"

"It's going to be a hotel."

"Oh that's weird. We were told that it's going to be a senior retirement home."

"No. I'm sure. It's going to be a hotel."

"Who's building it?"

"Rhanja Seth is the owner. Pegasus Construction is the general contractor."

"Okay John, thanks for your time. We'll have the site all squared away some time tomorrow."

I couldn't dare laugh at Winston's shit-eating grin. I had to act surprised or else the cat would be out of the bag. "Winston, I think somebody fucked us," I shouted. I beat the pavement with my heel. "FUCK." Then I grabbed Winston and shook him by his shoulders, "Somebody fucked us Winston!"

His eyes opened wide, scared, "You're not going to tell Katie are you?"

He tugged at my shirtsleeve, "Nine months with no community service! Don't you realize? If she finds out you fucked this up we might have to do more community service. Who cares what they're building here?"

"Those bastards!" I lowered my head and paced around like I was contemplating heavily. "Winston, what are we going to do? I let you guys down."

Winston met me at eye level..." Nobody knows about this but us. So I get to drive the bulldozer, and you can't stop me, asshole."

* * *

Will returned to the pitcher a second time and poured another glass of water. Krissie was crying, and Chad, the fiancé, was no longer seated quietly at the foot of the bed watching the game. He was dashing about the recovery room looking for something to break. Will was the immediate option. "I think it's time you got the fuck out of here."

Will took a deep breath and whispered, *"Jesus bless this child, for he hath breathed sin."* Will offered the glass of water to Chad.

"I can get my own, goddammit."

"Chad!" Krissie scolded. "Reverend Williams is a *representative*."

"This man is none more than a con artist; here to take *your* money that *you* need to pay *your* deductible."

"Now let's not go around accusing folks, Chad," Will responded. "He who throws rocks breaks windows, verse ten, chapter two..."

Chad cut Will off, "These people sent this smooth talker to wave a thousand bucks in your face and get you on their side. And now they want to try and talk you out of accepting it. It's a bait and switch. This guy's a con artist."

"Sir, that's a broken window," Will injected. Then he whispered, "*Jesus bless this child. For he not knoweth the power of his damning rock throwing verses...chapter nine, section B.*"

One thing Will learned during his days as a Floridian used car salesman was that making the sale never had anything to do with the man in the relationship. It was always about the woman—because she'll always half the money and *all* the pussy. So it's always the woman you're selling to. And Krissie was obviously wrapped up in the do-gooder holy show that Will was selling.

Chad pointed towards the door, "You need to get the hell out of here. And take your hush money with you, because we'll see you in court. We're suing for damages."

Krissie waved the quit claim agreement in one hand and a pen in the other. "We're not suing anybody, Chad. *We're* not even married."

Will, realizing his elevated position, patronized Chad by smiling, "I'm afraid this is between your fiancé and Jesus. So perhaps it's time to go watch your football game in some heathen sports bar of iniquity."

Chad just shook his head, having given up, "I'm meeting Curtis at the Beanery, and I'm getting shit-faced until the Bruins can learn how to win a game. Which might be a while." Chad gave Will the middle finger and shouted at Krissie on his way out the door, "This is your mess now."

"How am I supposed to get home then, Chad?"

"A church van!"

Per the quit claim agreement, the injured party would release Franklin Vista and IPD from any liability. However, Will continued to close the deal, "Krissie, I want you to do what is right for Krissie. But I also want you to remember that Franklin Vista is going to be the savior for a lot of needy people. So be mindful of what is best for your elders. Krissie, sign this blessed document and agree to not hold Franklin Vista responsible. And please consider pledging this one thousand dollars to Franklin Vista's going concern."

* * *

I sat alone in the Volvo waiting on hold to place an order for pizza delivery, the crew's dinner. The respite gave me a quiet opportunity to chew some Valium and regroup. Winston's outing of the truth, stacked on top of the Krissie incident, was about all I could handle. Fortunately, though, I was able to talk Will into delivering the money order and quit claim agreement. No lawyer in their right mind would try and sue given our documentation, meaning that no lawyer could potentially drop the dime on this to Katie, and knowing this was somewhat of a relief.

Tap, Tap, Tap.

It was Winston. He wanted to get into the Volvo with me. I waved him off, "A minute please...I'm ordering pizza."But he let himself in anyway and got in the back seat, which immediately tipped me off that something else was wrong. Sitting in the back would make it harder for me to strike him.

"I've changed my mind. I want a massage instead of driving the bulldozer."

"What kind?" I asked the pizza guy on the phone, having missed what he'd just said.

"Rub and tug, Thai," Winston interrupted, again.

"Ssh. I'm talking to the pizza guy...I need ten cheese and ten pepperoni." Then it occurred to me, "Wait a fucking minute, who's driving the Bobcat then?"

"Lenny."

"Lenny!? Are you out of your fucking mind? You're letting a drug addict drive a bulldozer?"

"But..."

It was the pizza guy again. "Wait...how much did you say that was?" I had to think... "No, no. That's too much. Make those all cheese." Then, returning my attention to Winston, "You get that guy off the bulldozer right now before I have to shell out to have half the block rebuilt."

"You pay for me to get a massage or else I'll tell Katie that you shit the bed on this project and that we all volunteered for nothing."

"Why would you do that, Winston? What's it fucking matter *who* you volunteer for? Just think about those nine months where you don't have to do jack shit. You said it yourself!"

"What about my massage?"

The pizza guy returned with a new total, "Whatever, that's fine. Just get it here," and I closed the phone.

"What about the bulldozer?" Winston asked again.

"Get Lenny OFF the fucking bulldozer before I allow him to run you over with it."

"He's being aggressive. He ripped me out of the seat and took over. I tried to fight him, but he kicked me in the shin...It fucking hurts man. I think he's coked up again. You're going to have to handle this one."

"Here's forty dollars for your little happy ending. Now go. I'll handle Lenny."

"It's fifty."

62

"Bullshit. It's forty. Go on the corner of Melrose and Vine. It's just as good as the fifty dollar ones on Sunset. AND LASTLY...you're going to keep your mouth SHUT about this to Katie. You got it?"

Winston counted the bills. What I was saying was going in one ear and out the other.

"Winston! Do you hear me?"

"Sure man."

"Winston! *Look at me.*"

He finished counting and looked my way, but not exactly *at* me...."Krissie?" He said.

Then Krissie let herself into the back on the side opposite of Winston. Great. Now I had my two biggest problems of the day sitting directly behind me, where they could have an even better angle to continue to fucking me in the ass.

"Winston, get out of here. Remember what we talked about?"

In one ear, out the other.

"I'm back!" Krissie cheered.

"We can see that!" I acted genuinely happy, even though it was Krissie. "What happened? I was picking up lunch and when I came back..."

"I'm pregnant."

"What!?" I cried.

"That's great!" Winston sneezed.

But Krissie and I both shouted at the same time, *"NO IT'S NOT!"*

For her, it meant she wasn't ready for a baby. For me, it meant that I'd spent a thousand dollars on shit. She'd gone to the hospital for something that had absolutely nothing to do with me. I didn't impregnate her, and I didn't hit her over the head with a fucking board.

"So Krissie, did someone from Franklin Vista come by to see you?"

* * *

You cheap bastard...cheese pizza! Hey, somebody order some real pizza. Somebody order some pizza with some toppings on it and get this shit out of my sight.

The outlook was bleak. Each new shift of IDP volunteers got snarlier. When the late shift showed up at six, most of them reeked of booze—they were tanked. They'd met to watch the game and had been doing shots after each touchdown. It must have been a fascinating game, judging by how drunk they were.

Fuck you, I come to volunteer and you feed us shit. B. Double E. Double R.U.N.—BEER RUN, bro. You go and get some cases, or we call this shit off.

"Did you not listen at the meeting?" I screamed. "This project pays you up for the next three quarters. So if you want to be an asshole, then I don't give a shit. It means I don't have to sign off on your attendance sheet. So if you want to spend the next nine months painting houses with the new hires that didn't have access to this great opportunity, keep being an asshole!"

The rest of dinner went much like this until I found my relief, Anne-Laure. She was still there. Ten hours, she was still there and still helping. "I no eating pizza. It fat. Look at Anne-Laure arm." She flexed her biceps. "I no want to be fat like Italian girl."

"Hey, I'm Italian!"

"And you fat." She poked my gut and laughed at her own joke. "Like all American, just a little bit fat around belly." She poked it again.

"You gotta build a big shed to protect a big tool," I said.

"When we going? I so sleepy."

"You're the one that wanted to come...I told you twelve hours."

"But I so tired. Look..." She gave me her hand. The nails were battered down to the nubs. "Is no sexy, no?"

"Very provincial."

I dropped the Volvo keys into her palm. I wanted to kiss her on the forehead. She'd been the only person all day that hadn't given me any grief. I wanted her to be able to go home if that's what she wanted. I'd figure out a way to get back home on my own. She was the only true volunteer among us.

Except for Lenny.

Coked up, he worked like a madman clearing debris by the ton with the Bobcat mini-bulldozer. He wasn't just some alcoholic drug addict with nothing to do on Saturday—he was great at this. The project was about complete—a day ahead of schedule. I would be on time and under budget!

"Get me a fucking sandwich," Lenny shouted. "Another hour and I'll have this place cleared. I deserve a fucking roast beef sandwich!"

"Winston, get Lenny a fucking sandwich," I delegated. "I don't have my car any more. My hot, French friend took it."

"That's not my job."

"Winston. Dumb ass. You used pencil on the sign in sheet. We have about one hour left here and then no more community service for the next nine months. But not for Winston. Because Winston didn't show up." I started erasing Winston's name on the sign in sheet.

"Fuck you, man," he said.

"I'm still erasing!"

"Fine," he said, stomping his foot. "But I'm getting a sandwich too! And I'm NOT bringing you one."

* * *

The entire department was seated in a booth at TGI Friday's; it was Monday. We were gathered to welcome our new hire to the department, Dave. Dave was a cocky son-of-a-bitch from Orange County, educated at University of Florida, wiseass by birth. We became good friends from the start.

"Wing Dingers anyone?" I asked the table. "I feel like celebrating." This *was* a day to celebrate. I'd moved out on my own six months ago to the day. I was six months into this drunken mess, my adult life, and I was still alive and fourteen large in the black. Bring on the boneless chicken wings!

So I ordered a round for the table. But I reserved the right to the celery sticks and got more and more depressed. Constipation seemed more appealing than eating chickens born without skeletal systems. I wondered, *Where on earth does TGI's find these poor beasts? Is there a specialized farm for these handicapped birds that exploits them for their profitable deformities? How despicable it is to devour a being that does not even have a sporting chance to defend itself for lack of a skeleton. I surmise the poor birds wallow around, a fat bag of muscles, blood, and skin until the fatal ax comes down upon their boneless necks. Their squishy heads roll flatly across the chopping board for lack of a skull. The head is dented with dimples and the brain is mushy. It's a quite miserable and squishy situation to ponder, but seems to be appetizing amongst the kids and sports fans alike.*

My hatred for life and its boneless chickens was growing stronger with each wheezy breath. We were celebrating a young man's first day on the job, while opposite the table was me, fuming at my poor showing over the past six months. By now I should have accumulated at least six hundred thousand dollars to be on pace, yet I had barely just squared up with MBNA. How could they sit there chewing up physically retarded chickens as if everything were alright?!

"You haven't touched your celery," Katie pointed out.

"It's undercooked," I responded, revealing my true nature as a jackass, "maybe I should send it back."

Her expression told me to *"Quit acting like a jackass in front of the new hire."*

I really wanted to tell her: *"He'll learn soon enough what a jackass I really am, Boss. Because in about four hours from now I'm taking him to a stripper bar, where I'll teach him how to consume the perfect mixture of jalapeno poppers and cheap beer to ensure the biggest farts to queer up a lap dance. And it's Monday, so lap dances are two for one."*

Luckily, our entrees came before I could finish preparing my statement and deliver it to Katie. There were seven different variations of a chicken tittie sandwich being passed around: BBQ, fried, Dijon, roasted, poached, dildoed, and finger fucked. Then there was my lettuce wedge with blue cheese vinaigrette drizzle. On top of already being pissed off, having to eat a head of lettuce because I don't eat chicken made me want to gut everyone at the table. But I wanted to save my boss for last—to skull fuck her to death on an altar of chicken titties and wing dingers. Luckily Lenny cracked the iced over tension, "You don't want your lettuce wedges to get cold!"

That was it. I signaled that I was going to make a phone call and crept away from the table without looking back. My rude behavior was sure to be discussed in my absence, but I didn't have any other options. By walking away and *not* doing my boss and co-workers in a crowded restaurant, there would still be a chance that I would have a job when I got back.

* * *

"Tell me how sexy my studio apartment is," I told the sex chat operator.

"Is that where you are? Are you comfy?" She had a raspy alcoholic's voice.

"No, I'm in a stall in the men's room at a TGI Fridays. But let's just pretend that I'm in my studio apartment, alright?"

"What are we going to do in your studio apartment?"

"We're going to eat burnt ramen in my studio apartment. Then I'm going to suck your old toes. But only after you walk all over my filthy, dirty carpet." With the "mature" chat lines you can say anything. Let it all out. Share and be as self-loathing as you want, because they've heard it all. At two bucks for the first minute and ninety-five cents for each additional minute, it's the cheapest therapy money can buy. You don't have to make an appointment, and it's accessible round the clock, even in the middle of a departmental lunch.

"What's your name? I want to call you Ramona. I bet you have a fat camel toe, Ramona."

"You aren't finished sucking those toes. Suck 'em, loser."

"That's right Ramona, or whatever the fuck your name is. I like it when you call me a loser."

I heard someone enter the restroom... "Is that you?" they asked. It was Winston. "Are you taking a shit and calling it a loser? That's right dude, *talk shit* to your shit."

"Yeah, it's me. Real busy in here. Lots going on...Why don't you just tell the others to get started without me."

He started washing his hands, "I thought you left to make a phone call?"

"I was trying to be polite, *Winston*."

"Okay! I understand. But I'm still mad at you about Saturday night, so I'm going to tell them that you were talking to yourself and taking a huge shit."

Performing Arts

Tradition in our department calls for the new guy to be taken to the tittie bar immediately after the close of business on his first Monday. So Lenny, Winston, and I took Dave to the *Center for the Performing Arts*. It's located in a scant converted warehouse in the bowels of the San Fernando Valley. Accommodations include discrete parking, a full bar in an adjacent building, and a yeasty pole to enable the visual decadence of every Deranged Young Professional in The Valley.

But it's California. You still have to smoke outside. There's a room full of eighteen year olds displaying their buttholes for dollar tips *inside*, but you still have to smoke *outside*. And outside smoking a cigarette, I met Pete. He claims to have been a major drug trafficker in the seventies, and through his adventures in that occupation, he claims to have met and befriended John Holmes (the mass murderer with a baker's dozen in his pants). He also happens to be the biggest, meanest sixty year old on the face of the earth. He's also completely full of shit.

I was chatting with Pete about our favorite places to get tacos, when a Chevy pickup whipped into the parking lot. It was Chad, Krissie's fiancé. His eyes beamed trough the window, and they were cold-locked on me. He looked like Blackbeard's beardless, twenty-five year old ghost piloting a phantom vessel, gliding ominously through the parking lot. I was fucked. "See that guy?" I said.

"Yeah...He looks like a bitch," Pete figured.

"He's here to kick my ass."

"Well, if you're banging his girlfriend, that means you have something he don't."

"I didn't bang anybody!"

"You owe him money?"

"No."

"Then what's up?"

"You know people, right?"

"I know lots of people."

"Do you know people that kill people?"

"I kill people."

"Well, kill *that guy*...I'll be inside getting a lap dance."

Her name was Luna. She smelled like flowers and feet, and she was visibly drunk and pregnant. But that's not what the strip club meant by *two-for-one Mondays*. It meant that

Luna would dance for twenty minutes and not just ten. It just also happened that on this night, Luna brought her baby along too.

Outside with Pete:
Pete stepped in front of Chad. "You aren't bringing any trouble in here! What's your beef with that guy?"

"Who the fuck are you?"

"I'm your bus driver to Hell if you don't watch your tone."

"That guy scammed a bunch of senior citizens."

"He fuckn' did what?"

"He's a scumbag! He fucked over a bunch of old people! He took their money, and now he's in there stuffing it down panties."

"Well fuck him up then! That bastard." Pete opened the door. Chad walked right in.

I pushed Luna out of the way so that I could peek into the club from behind the curtain. I saw Chad seated with Winston and Lenny at a table next to the runway. Luna sat beside me and was having a conversation on her cell phone in Spanish. A drunken pregnant smoker is one thing, but Luna was the kind of stripper that gives up. She'd quit dancing. She had a quitter's personality...and that is not sexy.

Chad offered up a handful of cash. It went right onto Dave's bare chest where the strippers had removed his shirt and bound him to the pole with his necktie. The vultures danced around their offering, dipping their stinky parts to obtain the bills. Dave was just Chad's bait—Chad was using him to get to me.

My twenty minutes was up, and Luna pushed me out of the booth, "Mericone!"

"Pregnant stripper!" I shouted back. But I had no choice but to get moving. The gangster-looking bouncer at the end

of the hallway eyed me through his sunglasses. Bouncer.
Sunglasses. Toothpick. Dark strip club. Fuck.

He stopped me, "We was watchn' you on the closed
circuit. You wasn't feeln' that hoe was you?"

"She smelled like barf. Get me another hoe."

"Na man. Yo boys is lookn' for you." The bouncer pointed
towards our table. "Yer boy got bottle service."

"I'd rather have another lap dance."

"Na man, hang out witcha boys for a minute. These hoes
like to get down after hours. I'll hook you guys up." Without
much choice he pressed me towards my co-workers,
thinking that he was doing me a favor. "Don't be a faggot,"
he said.

I ran as fast as I could out of the strip club. "Pete!" I
slammed right into him like a brick wall.

"Hold it, asshole." Pete grabbed me by the collar. "That
guy says you scammed a bunch of senior citizens."

"Not true."

"He seemed pretty fucking sure about it."

"Let go of me."

Pete let go. But he slammed me against the wall and
pinned me instead. "I'm a senior citizen, you suit fuck."

"I would never scam a senior citizen. Never."

"I'm also on head full of Oxycontin and my trigger finger's
dying to slip on some suit fuck college boy like you. I've been
waitn' all day." Pete dug his middle finger into my forehead
like it was a pistol.

"Pete, chill. That guy's crazy...Hey...I'll pay you! Just calm
down."

"That's not going to cut it. My mind's made up, I'm going
to fuck you up."

The door blew open beside me. It was the huge gangster
bouncer from inside. "Pete! What the fuck's yo problem,
man?"

"This asshole's my problem."

71

"Nah old man, they was just fuckn wit you. His boys is gettn' fucked up and they be lookn' for him. Let him go back inside."

Chad waved me over, "Right here man." He clutched a liter bottle of Grey Goose in one hand and a stripper in the other. "Celeste...I want you to meet my business partner."

I got a sinking feeling in my gut, *business partner?*

"We have some business to talk about," Chad continued. "But first, DeShawn, please take my friend to have the full-service with Celeste." The bouncer grinned, his toothpick rode between his lips. "Quit being a faggot and come with me," he said to me. My heart was about to climb out of my chest not knowing what was going on. I tripped and almost fell over my own feet as my legs lost their strength. DeShawn caught me and kept me on my toes. "What the fuck's yo problem, man? It's just a mouth."

"Can't we talk about this?"

"Why don't you just shut the fuck up and sit the fuck down." DeShawn pushed me through the curtain.

* * *

Back at the stage:

The strippers were doing a birthday stage show. They had yet another Deranged Young Professional bound to a chair and gagged with his necktie. Dave had been used up and was on the bench, watching from the table. He along with the others, Lenny and Winston, each had squirt guns, and they were soaking the strippers with offerings of tap water and dollar bills. Lenny offered a joke to the young men whom had privilege in their upbringing—college educations and no Daddy issues. "How many strippers does it take to screw in a light bulb?"

"Trick question," Winston answered. "Strippers don't screw in light bulbs. They smoke meth out them."

* * *

I saw the curtain stir out of the corner of my eye. I assumed DeShawn was returning to tune me up—I assumed. I jolted from the surprise, and my zipper caught Celeste's lip. "What the fuck!" she barked. "You fucking cut me!"

But is wasn't DeShawn, it was Chad. Having seen what he walked in on, "Sorry dude. Come get me when you're done. I'll be next door."

"What the fuck do you want, man? Are you here to beat my ass or act like we're fraternity brothers?"

"That Reverend Williams owes you a thousand dollars."

Chad sat across the room and was getting his lap danced on by Luna, the pregnant stripper whom I was ignoring at this point. Celeste was working my lap, and I peeked around her abdomen to speak to Chad. "Luna smells like barf, doesn't she?"

Chad poked his head around the mass of pregnant belly and titties, but he ignored my comment. "So that friend of yours went right to Pink's Liquor and cashed the money order after he left the hospital."

"Fucking figures."

"I want a cut on what you guys scored."

"What are you talking about?"

"I know who Rhanja is."

"Did that fucker Will tell you!"

"No. I went to the courthouse and checked the deed. I'd hate to have to show it to your boss."

"I'll give you Will's thousand."

"Times five."

"Since when did I start looking like a fucking bank?" I consulted Celeste, "Hey honey, do I look like a fucking bank?" and I stuffed a twenty into her garter.

Chad came back with a counter offer, "You're going pick up tonight's tab and peel off two thousand to me. Consider it an early wedding present to Krissie and me.

I wrinkled up my lips as sort of a grin and bear it gesture. If Chad only knew how much we really made, he'd have asked for more. I pushed Celeste's hair out of the way. "You know, this extortion shit really pisses me off, Chad. But for some reason it's not bothering me that much right now." Then I smiled at Celeste.

But later that night, at three AM, it did bother me. Two thousand dollars worth of booze and strippers and two grand in hush money really bothered me. It bothered me a whole lot. It was during that lonesome time of night when the stoplights go from timed to blinking—in the deadest of hours on abandoned industrial streets. Vernon is only five square miles, but I must have driven 77 miles without encountering another living soul.

I got out of the car and stepped foot onto the dew-covered pavement. Crumpled underfoot was the trash and debris from the workday past. Only ghosts lurked where earlier, thousands of workers traveled the streets. But that's thousands of paychecks. Cut and cashed on Fridays. Stockers, loaders and un-loaders, packers and un-packers, crane operators, drivers, and maintenance men. All the different players in the wholesaling, shipping, and manufacturing concerns that are situated in one of America's few all-industrial communities. Where the welcome sign says, "Welcome to Vernon—A City That Works."

The hardworking men of Vernon eat out of lunch buckets and keep themselves going on cups of strong black coffee they pour from steal thermoses. Their blistered feet are covered in steel-toed boots and their broad shoulders are cloaked in heavy triple-stitched overalls. It's their isolated industrial fraternity hiding out in the middle of one of the most glamorous cities on the planet. It's a caged monster that sweats and pounds his chest by day but hibernates like a cold stone at night. And now it had a trespasser.

Part III

Derangement, Valium, Donkeys

The rapture of accounting wore me down bit by bit. By lunchtime, it had manifested into full-blown Monday morning eyes, glazed over and sunken in. The clock on my computer screen claimed that I had at least four more hours of this—to me, that seemed an eternity. But it was Friday. There was no looming workweek to be terrified of. I was simply coming down with a nasty cold, perspiring, and suffering a nervous twitch. *Perfect.*

I tapped gently on Katie's door. "Katie?" I whispered.

"Yes." She said, looking up from her magazine.

"I have a doctor's appointment."

"Yeah, you don't look so well."

"It's my sleeping, Katie. My sleeping is being interrupted by respiratory complications."

"My dad had sleep apnea. Maybe that's what it is?"

"I sure hope not. That would be awful." I placed the back of my hand on my forehead. "I should swing by Human Resources on my way out...and have them update my life insurance."

I hustled out of the office and made a straight shot for the credit union, wanting to get there before they closed. Making it in time, I could immediately tell that First State of Second Rate Credit Union was a cash house. It was a congested mob of workmen who had just punched out. They had checks in hand and that three o'clock Friday buzz to give them an extra jolt. They had just enough reason to wait in a long line before retreating to the haven of the weekend: cash. I watched as they would mechanically approach the teller windows with the rickety rhythm of a worn assembly line machine. One man would reach the front of the line, disperse to the first available of four tellers, and slip his rectangle of white paper under the window. Another man would immediately follow. Almost instantly, a stack of green paper would shoot under the window to each man, and two other men would soon be on their way to fill the already empty spaces.

The job would have to be pulled on a Thursday because by the end of business on Friday the vault would be full of the worthless checks. This meant the cash must come in via armored car before Friday morning to meet the demands of Friday's payday. By Friday afternoon, it was all handed out and in the temporary custody of the workmen before being handed over to their wives or barkeeps.

I cashed a twenty and returned to the Volvo. There I waited—like Chuck Norris: eyes peeled, mouth slightly agape, ears porous, soaking up sounds that were *too* quiet. Stocking fluids in tandem to fight my fever. Shots of orange juice. Doses of Gatorade. Heater, full-blast: baking my skin under a hooded sweatshirt and sucking out the poisoned sweat. Fever lifting. Twitching tapering. Delirious, but health slowly returning.

Four tellers retreated with horny steps to their parked cars. Friday five o'clock-eyes: weekend free. A cleaning crew, two ladies with latex-gloved hands, traded places with the tellers and entered the bank. "Ola." "Buenas noches." Once inside, the cleaners doused the toilets. Shook the crumbs off the floor. Kicked around the dust. Smiled at job well done. Then headed home to let down their hair, wash themselves, and fuck their men. One more person left in the bank: Yvonne.

Chocolate, long and luscious, she looked tastier than a brown wet bottle of cold beer. Her first meaty thigh poked through the front door, pointing her toe like a striptease. Her pantsuit was pasted on tight. The second leg followed.

That's two leggy fantasies leading up to ass that was stacked like a palate. She turned around to lock the door, lifting her heels off the ground and leaning into the stubborn lock. The ass flexed. You could have seen that ass in a dark hallway, sticking out like an end table. However, she seemed like the single type. Another week had passed, and she said goodbye to her beloved bank.

Yvonne was heading towards her car, trying to get herself excited about another lonely Friday night of a bubble bath, some lotion and a robe, but her momentum stopped. She noticed the green Volvo station wagon with its engine running and she must have thought it odd. It was. A road-worn college car sitting idle among this land of work vans and tractor trailers signaled that either someone was lost or up to no good. But she wasn't going to get far with a description of the stolen dealer plates. I smiled, studied her, and looked right into her eyes. Yes, there she was, Yvonne—the gatekeeper. She was like the stacked blonde's protective girlfriend at a nightclub, the one that gets in your way. Yvonne was my first obstacle.

WEEK ONE

Anybody Got a Nice Party Van to Sell?

The Volvo steamrolled like fuck-all into the muddy field as if *the car* was the hell-bound lunatic and not me. It was as if the car had a demented mind all its own. Mud smeared my windshield, and the wipers spread it out like I'd hit a peanut butter truck head on. I could not see. I was totally fucked. So I cut the engine and let the Volvo coast to a plodding stop in the sinking mud.

I stepped out of the car and sunk my feet into an expanse of newly overturned field. It smelled like shit. Scores of workers poked at the earth with seeding devices. They smelled like shit too, but I envied them. They were hard at honest work. *"English!?"* I hollered in their direction.

A weathered Latino fellow approached me. "The interstate is that way, my fren." He pointed in the direction from which I came.

"You know anybody that's got a nice party van?" I asked. "It doesn't have to have air conditioning, but the windows should work. I just want a nice party van."

"How much you wan pay?"

"I have one thousand. Cash."

"Whey here, Senor." He meandered over to the field like he had all day. There were literally families of people busy at work in the veggie patch. Maybe I wasn't so envious of these people after all. I could never work alongside my family.

He returned with another weathered Latino fellow.

"My fren say he want two tousan, Senor. No negosee-ason."

"Will you deliver to Westlake Village?"

"No pro-lem. You ha de money?"

The men discussed the deal in snappy Spanish.

"So what are you guys growing, broccoli?" I asked.

"Lechuga!"

Then I noticed a towering billboard rising out of the corner of the field. It said "Mother Lettuce."

Later that week in Katie's office...

"It's congenital...My bad genes are up to their old tricks."

"Now what is it exactly?" Katie asked.

"It's called Ondine's Curse."

"Really?"

"Yes, the name comes from a Greek myth where Goddess Ondine put a curse on her unfaithful lover. If she ever found him *knowing* another woman, then when he fell asleep, he would forget to breathe...That's some pretty heavy stuff for just knowing around."

"That's terrible, you can't breathe at night?"

"It's troublesome, but I count my blessings Katie, it's treatable. It's a severe form of sleep apnea, just like you mentioned, except there are complete respiratory arrests during sleep. I literally can't breathe. So I have to go in for a ganglia smear and they're going to do something with my dysphagia and look for some agenesis in my pupilla. I wanted you to know that I won't be making it to work on Friday...that's all...more tests."

Friday

I was parked in the van, in the lot opposite my side of the apartment complex. But girls have a knack of finding you when you don't want to be found...*KNOCK KNOCK*...I could see that it was Anne-Laure on my new monitor.

I stayed perfectly still and quiet. Using the remote control camera I'd mounted underneath the van, I took a look around and observed her returning back to her car. She fetched her cell phone, and knowing who she was calling I hurried to turn mine off. I defeated her.

She came back to the van and peered through the driver door. She was wearing those damn tennis shorties under her skirt, obstructing what would have been a good view. The driver door opened. "*Hello...Isa anybody een here?*" I couldn't see her on the monitor anymore, and there was a cardboard barrier installed between the cab and the bay. I could hear her studying it with her fingers, running them along it, looking for a spot where she could reach in and pull it back. But it must have been too much hassle because she let herself back out and the door slammed.

She stepped back into my frame on the screen, and I followed her with the camera until she wandered out of range. The rear doors jolted. She was trying to get into the back! "*I know dees you van...I see you driving eet.*" At this point, all I could do was jump behind the couch where she

81

couldn't see me. I was just in time before an intense blast of daylight poured in to shed light onto my vast array of monitors and surveillance equipment surrounding a second hand couch.

"Oh," she mumbled.

The door slammed and all was quiet once again.

The Next Friday: "asdfdfowmefq afdafdfdsa"

I managed to deflect Anne-Laure's inquiries for a whole week, staying busy and out of the way. Telling her, *I have a major project going on at work.* But I had to be the only guy in Corporate America that could get a case of the Fridays. That's because I was the only guy in Corporate America that was staying out all night on Thursdays, camped out in the back of a van. I only got two hours of sleep after my Thursday shift, and I still had to go to work. Then after work, I planned to grab a quick nap and go right back to Vernon to collect more data.

Not going to happen. Impossible.

When Katie dropped by my desk, I didn't have time to hit the boss button on my internet browser. I was completely asleep and had no clue that she was standing behind me.

"How did the tests go?"

I awoke like a bomb went off and I started typing immediately. The computer screen was open to a sports book website. I placed an erroneous bet for "asdfdfowmefq afdafdfdsa."

"Oh well, you know," I said confidently. "It's sort of a hard disease to diagnose."

"You mean curse?" she laughed.

"Right, curse...But they need me to come in next Friday for some observation. I have to spend Thursday night at the hospital while some doctors watch me sleep and then run tests all the next day."

"I think you should go home. You're obviously not feeling well."

"I feel great...You know me...I like hard work."

"I want you to know that I did some research on your condition and I have to admit, I don't know how you're able to make it."

"It's the challenge, Katie. The daily challenges of this job keep me going..." I began cleaning up my desk and shutting down my computer. "But if you insist."

I was poked between about a million cars in mid-day Highway 101 traffic, and I was fumed: *Don't hesitate to speak up...I'm really concerned. I looked on the internet and found out that you're not full of bullshit...I think you'd better take off your pants for an oral exam. Then you should rest your sleepy head on my tits and take a nice nap too. I feel terrible for you. You poor thing.* I raved like this during the entire drive home to the hideout. That fucking Katie was fucking with me. I knew it. She'd probably been tracking my internet traffic and was suspect. I'd done too much research at work. Now she knew that I was casing banks and was probably already cooperating with the FBI. *I don't know how you make it? Take an energy squirt off my big jugs for a mid-day boost. That's it sweetie, pucker up like a poor little baby...*

* * *

IPD was quieter than Vernon is at night—Friday night—cemetery quiet in a corporate headquarters. Earlier in the day, when Katie cut me loose, I immediately went home and got involved in some cocktail hours. I had decided to give up on the back-to-back stakeouts. Now I was a little buzzed. It was one AM, and I was bumping into things in her office.

The first thing I did was allow myself behind Katie's desk to view her infamous collection of photographs. The other workers in the department could only speculate as to what those photos were of, because in all their years *nobody* had *ever* ventured into the Forbidden Zone, behind Katie's desk. As far as I knew, I was the first employee to sneak back there. So I decided to unzip my pants and leave a pube.

The photos: assorted family pictures. But then, there was *The Picture.* The almighty boss picture of Boss Pictures. It was Katie at the beach, smoking a cigarette and looking foxy in a bikini. *Nice.*

I returned from the copy room and replaced the picture precisely as I found it. Then I went for the file cabinet. It's California, so lax corporate culture dictates leaving file cabinets unlocked. Soon enough, I was digging through the perm files. Lenny had a police record, big surprise. Winston had taken a leave of absence for mental health after getting mugged and ass raped during a trip to Mexico. Dave, well, Dave had something on his record that I can't even tell you about here. Let's just say that Dave shouldn't be left alone with twisty ties. Lastly, there was me. Nothing. Just a copy of my resume and some shit about Ondine's Curse. But I was not satisfied. So I continued digging.

Okay. Check elsewhere. She's obviously hidden the documentation because the situation involves the FBI.

I found it! A lock box in the bottom drawer.

Key? Where's the fucking key? Look in her pencil drawer. Envelope that says "Keys!" Okay open the box. Shit. This is just the petty cash box. No signs of confidential FBI memos.

Getting sleepy. *Make a pot of coffee in the break room...No way!...SCORE. There's a bottle of Ritalin in Katie's pencil drawer. "Tanner Sandburg." Do 20 milligrams off her desk. Shit, 20 milligram pills! Her son Tanner must be a total spaz! But watch out...Do your lines on the side of the desk where there aren't any of your pubes.*

A little over-excited about the Ritalin, I walked off with a few souvenirs. Then back at the Hideout at about 7:30 AM, still wide-awake Ritalin bombed, I sat at my computer and did some surgery on the schedule. A week of Thursday and Saturday stakeouts was designated as "A." A week that was a Friday night only stakeout was a "B." I laid out my weeks at random. It looked like this:

ABBABAABABBABBABABAABAAB

Twenty-four weeks! No way. I backspaced twelve times:

ABBABAABABBA

Then I changed it up a little for the sake of randomness. This, this is what the next twelve weeks of my life would look like:
ABBABAABAABB

* * *

I decided to handle the Anne-Laure incident. She obviously knew that I was up to something because she'd seen the van. I didn't want to put off clearing things up any longer. So I took her on a proper date. The restaurant of choice featured a casual patio overlooking the calm waters of The Lake at Westlake. The man-made body of water is nestled in a bowl-shaped valley below the jagged cliffs of the Santa Monica Mountains. Topping those cliffs are stunning mountain top dwellings that overlook the shimmering lake to the east, and across the misty horizon to the west is the Pacific Ocean. Lazy electric boats purr around in the calm lake water. The residents each have a private dock attached to their property. Instead of walking, they board their quiet, electric boats and float around the lake visiting friends and socializing on the water. Anne-Laure and I shared our desert and observed this well-kept secret of a community.

"Did you open the door to my van the other day?" I asked.

"I not know what you talking about," Anne-Laure replied. She drank deeply from her cup of tea, hiding her eyes in it.

"I'm hoping it was you and not the people that I'm investigating!"

"Who a you investigate?"

"Bad people."

"Are you police!?"

I took her by the wrists. "No, I'm not with the Department...I'm actually conducting an internal investigation on one of my company's warehouse managers. He's suspected of running an operation...an illegal operation."

"Ooh! And dey aska you to spy?"

I forked a piece of chocolate cake and fed it to her. "Yes. This is a big promotion for me at work."

"Mmm...eeez good." She smiled as she chewed. "An you promotion eez good too."

"But this is serious, dangerous stuff, Anne-Laure...I thought the other day that you were one of *them*. One of the bad guys. That's why I hid when you came to the van." She made a surprised, guilty expression. She did not know she had been caught snooping. "But after I checked the video, I saw that it was you...I'm sorry I have to tell you all of this. I hate to put you in danger."

"Isso fun...you are spy!" She looked at me and then down at the cake, still shy about having been caught. I fed her another piece of cake.

"Anne-Laure...listen to me. I need you to stay away from that van. And when you see me drive away in it...forget about me...I don't exist. Got it?"

She smiled with one side of her mouth and her eyes narrowed on mine, giving me some old-fashion indication. "You so dangerous," she giggled.

"You must really want me right now," I said.

WEEK TWO

Not Peace—Piece

I needed to decide whether or not to up-size this caper to an armed robbery.

And the answer was YES.

Carrying a piece is a stupid idea because it turns what could be a non-violent crime into a violent one. But walking around downtown LA in the middle of the night with millions in cash and no gun is an even more stupid idea. I wasn't going through all this trouble to risk some asshole sticking me for my take. They could try, but they were going to get shot—in the face. Two or three times—lesson learned. And once in the chest—review session.

The decision to arm myself meant driving to Bakersfield to go "antiques" shopping. It was the closest place I knew of that was certain to have white trash, and therefore a likely place to find a flea market. No background checks, no questions. Just prompt service and a slightly used heater—and I could also get some fried cheese and a velvet Elvis wall hanging for my apartment, or *hideout*, as I was calling it since I'd become an aspiring bank robber. So Bakersfield it was, boyhood home to Merle Haggard, regional flea marketing hub of note.

I found a good one not far from the freeway, and once inside I approached a dingy, skinny guy with some missing teeth and a distant burnt out look—a straight up Southern Rocker. He wore a Jack Daniel's racing hat, and I figured that if he were hayseed enough to broadcast that he liked whiskey and fast cars, then he was probably hayseed enough to have a gun to sell. But he engaged me first, asking me, "You know anybody in-ersted in a nice pocket knife?"

I looked him square in the eye and adjusted my speech to match his, "What about a crossbow? You have a crossbow, Mister?"

He attempted to scratch his head. His fingertips just slightly grazed the top of his cap. He was burnt out as fuck. "Crossbow?" He asked.

"Yeah, you know. Like a bow and arrow. To shoot them A-Rabs with the next time they come attack us in our own damn country...A fuck-em up cross bow. That's what."

He raised an eyebrow and shook his head, "Ain't no crossbow gonna set no crazy A-Rab on eez ass."

"So what should I get then? A ninja sword?"

"You mean a katana?" He shook his head again, "No you don't want no katana." Then he made a dumb, blank expression and started laughing. Brown spit soared between the gaps of his rotted teeth. "I got sumpin."

From behind his wares table he lifted a milk crate stuffed full of old *Penthouse Letters* magazines. He carefully placed it on the table next to his inventory of Dixie Flag and marijuana decaled cigarette lighters. "Now if you really wanna fuck up one a dem A-rabs..." He lifted the stack of magazines out of the crate. Resting at the bottom was plastic handgun case. A big one.

"What's that?" I asked.

"That's for sale, is what that is."

Troll Hunt

Will's pathetic parking lot domicile was tucked amongst the crack alleys and tranny hand job nooks of Hollywood's filthy east side—close to where we used to live. The clubbers had parked their cars and jammed out for the night, not to be back for hours, which abandoned a leisurely chunk of time where no one would be watching.

The fluorescent light from Will's attendant's shack cut a sharp line against the black night. His back faced me and he was busy rehearsing lines from a script so he couldn't hear my footsteps over the thunder of his voice. I had a well lit, clear shot at the back of his hairy neck—his fucking brain stem. And I had all night. But my heart was beating too fast. My hands were shaking: buck fever. I was finally able to shake it off. I pulled down my hood and got moving again.

Will recited a line, "As I told thee before, I am subject to a tyrant, a sorcerer that by his cunning hath cheated me of an island."

What the fuck is he talking about?

"Thou liest, thou jesting monkey, thou! I would my valiant master would destroy thee. I do not lie."

I can't do him like this. There's no honor in this.

"I say, by sorcery he got this isle. From me he got it. If thy greatness will revenge it on him..."

Oh, fuck it. I drove all the way down here and that bastard stole from me.

POP!

I drilled the troll fuck right in the melon leash, where the neck tendons grip hold at the base of the skull.

He dropped instantly.

"I brought you some ramen, loser."

He slowly made it back to his feet, still a little stunned from the shock. "Well you didn't have to throw it at me!" Piping hot noodles clung to his neck and the collar of his uniform. He futilely dashed at them with his troll mitts.

"What do you want, Will? I come down here to bring you some dinner and I find you raving like a lunatic."

"I'm getting ready for the biggest audition I've had since I got out here! And all you can do is throw ramen at me?"

"Yeah."

"Well fuck your ramen."

"That was actually *Pasta Barata*, which is Spanish for 'drunken pasta.' It's Fiesta flavor ramen prepared with a shot of tequila and a squirt of lime.

"I should come to *your* office and attack *you* when you're in your cubicle jerking off to all your little spreadsheets."

"You're being awfully nice considering that I just threw a bowl of hot soup at you"

"Whatever."

"No man, seriously. Why are you in such a good mood?"

"I told you. I could care less about your stupid ass. I got this huge audition. This play runs for months and if I get the part, I'll be making enough money to quit this fucking job and buy a car."

"Sounds good, man. Best of luck to you. But how's the new apartment? How much did the security deposit set you back?"

"I've been wanting to tell you. Ranjha has our money."

"That's good. But how's the apartment? How much were the move in costs...like one thousand dollars?"

"Did you hear what I just fucking said? Ranjha has our money. We're fucking rich as soon as we drive over there and get it."

"*We're* rich?" I questioned.

"Yeah, *we're* rich."

"No, *I'm* rich," I corrected him. "I'm getting sixteen thousand and you only get four."

"We agreed on a fifteen-five split."

"You know what I'm talking about. Sixteen-four. That makes us even."

He threw his parking attendant's hat at me, "You're out of your fucking mind." I snatched the hat out of the air. I was about to whip my pecker out and urinate on his hat until...*Wait a second...He said audition...He said enough money that he could quit the parking lot gig and buy a car. This is a big break for him. A dream come true...A dream that can be crushed!*

This prospect settled me. "I was just fucking with you, man." Then I brushed the remaining noodle off the hat, and handed it back to him, "Let's go get our money."

WEEK THREE

"Teenis" Match

"*Qweet* driving like you drunk!" Anne-Laure shouted.

"What if I am?"

"Could you just be serious for one *mee-not?*"!"

"I don't want you to be late for your match, honey."

"I not honey."

"Sugar."

"Stop eet!" She flipped the disk changer. Loud music erupted from the speakers. *Irritating Euro-pop!* My eyes rolled.

"Don make dat face! We leesin to you stupid screaming music all the time."

"I didn't mean it that way. We'll listen to whatever you want, just relax."

STOP SIGN. *Stomp the brakes!*

Her racket bag jettisoned out of the back seat and landed between us. She slung it back like she was fighting off a buzzard, "What eez de matter wis you!"

"Stop signs aren't *suggestions*, Anne-Laure."

"Is stupeed idea letting you bring me." She cranked the nauseating Euro-pop even louder. I reached over to turn it back down but she slapped my hand away. "I not even want to hear you breazing right now."

Calm her down, fast...Blank face. Engage her eyes. Don't move a muscle. We'll sit at this stop sign all day if we have to.

"You going to move or not!" She barked.

HONK. Cars were beginning to pull up behind us.

Keep staring at her. These LA drivers can fuck off...

HONK, HONK, HONK.

"What eez the matter? Why you not driving?"

She's unbuckling her belt. She wants me to think that she's getting out.

SCCREEETCH. An asshole pulled around us and snuck past between our car and the curb. The brazen driving maneuver scared Anne-Laure's ass back into her seat. "I be late," she begged. "Please!"

Match her breathing.

"What you doing? Please damnit!"

HONK, HONK. The next asshole in line refused to pull around. He just kept honking. HONK. HONK...thinking that it would convince me to move.

"I can not stand all dees noise. Why you not move car? What is you problem?"

Breathe with her, deeply. She's starting to make eye contact, fighting it, but starting to give in. Her chest rises and falls with mine. In and out. Deeply. Slowly. SCCREETCH. The asshole behind us finally pulled around and shot past, "Fuck your mother!" Anne-Laure didn't say a word. I didn't say a word.

More breathing. More eyes.

HONK, HONK, BEEP. BEEP. "Suck a bag of dicks!" HONK. BEEP, BEEP. HONK. BEEP.

Hold it. You've almost got her.

SCREETCH.

SCREETCH.

Two more cars.

Breathe in.

Breathe out.

Okay. Do it.

I pursed my lips, just enough.

Keep her now............There.

She closed her eyes and settled back into her seat. The pre-game jitters were gone. Her hand found mine. "Thank you," she said quietly.

We soon arrived at the tennis club. Getting out of the car, she handed me her tennis bag with a kiss on my cheek. I followed behind her on our way to the clubhouse and watched her ass doing the "look both ways."

A male voice called out, "There's my grand slam hottie!" It was another tennis pro, Troy. He had the unkempt Peace Corps hair, yet he wore white shorts and a white polo shirt. The whole get up said, *"Fuck you. You aren't pompous enough wear white on white."*

"Tloy!" Anne-Laure took a swan dive into his arms and I stood there next to them until he was finished groping as much of her as he could. When I set the tennis bag down to shake Troy's hand, it was a cold, *"yeah...I see you"* kind of greeting. Meanwhile, Anne-Laure had bent doubled over at the waist and was fishing something out of her tennis bag like an old lady weeding in the garden. The way she bends over is a quirk of hers. Her legs are straight and stiff, folded at the waist. Her hair droops to the ground, and her ass points in the sky for all to see. Troy snuck up behind her like he was going to mount her, *"fuck yeah...look at me"* was the expression on his face. Then he mimicked dry fucking her.

"Butt sex is wild—don't cause no child," I crooned.

Anne-Laure shot upright. "Tloy!" She giggled, turning around to face him. "You so crazy Tloy."

"I know you French girls like it in the butt." He buried his white crotch in hers and started humping her again. She laughed her head off like it was the funniest thing in the world.

Later I was watching Anne-Laure warm up with her coach. I viewed them from a mezzanine area overlooking a bank of indoor tennis courts underneath a canopy of fluorescent lights. When she plays "teenis," everything from the neck down is a real thrill, her legs, butt, and breasts, are all kept nicely in place with tight fitting tennis apparel. But her sweet little face becomes a terror. She bites her lip and scolds the ball with her eyes, and *grunts*. Girls don't grunt, but girls that play tennis do. They *grunt*. And this was only her warm up session on a practice court. What would she look like during the actual match, I wondered?

93

I heard someone approaching me from behind, "Look at that little dick machine go, man." It was Troy. Now he was standing next to me. "I'd like to stuff her sausage wallet and knock that furry box out."

I was completely insulted. I could have lost it right there. Yet, I decided to act unbothered and continue the vulgar discussion of Anne-Laure's private parts. "What makes you think it's furry?"

He mounted the railing and started dry humping it. "FUCK, FUCK, hairy French beaver…I'm gonna fuck that little dick box. FUCK."

This guy is a certifiable sex addict.

"Yo bro, you live next to her, right?"

"Yeah."

"Dude, I think she likes you. She said you're some sort of spy or something."

"Something like that," I mumbled.

"Chicks love that shit. It makes 'em all wet."

"Sure it does, Troy."

"Yo, so like why don't I come over and we'll do a little spying and watch that dick toy get naked."

"That's not the kind of spying that I do."

"Well you should do something, bro. She wants it. You should just walk over there one day, knock on her door, and be like, 'Hey Anne-Laure, it's your neighbor from next door and I'm gonna slay your pussy!'" He started humping the rail again. This time lifting one leg over it, straddling it. "Yeah, you filthy little French whore. Your neighbor's gonna jam his pussy dart in that tight little cock snatcher. FUCK. FUCK. PUSSY. FUCK."

I wandered off to a racquetball court to get away from Troy. Racquetball: you can hit the ball as hard as you want and you don't have to chase after it like in tennis. You can just keep swinging and swinging, and it keeps coming back like a ho to her pimp.

But then *he* reappeared. "Yeah bro, so if you're like not going to hit that, do you mind?"

"Hit what?" I slammed the ball so hard it almost popped against the wall.

"Anne-Laure, bro. Are you going to hit that, or what?"

I ignored him and served a racquetball against the wall. Troy just stood there grabbing himself through his white shorts. "I only rented the court for one player, Troy. You're going to have to go whack off somewhere else."

"Seriously bro, if you're not going to hit that then I am." The ball came bouncing back. I redirected myself and surgically precisioned a shot right at his nuts. He jumped back and swatted at the ball. "What the fuck's your problem, man?"

"I'll beat your ass, tennis queer."

"I think you're the queer. You going to hit that or not?"

I dropped my racquet, kicked it away, and took off my watch.

He stood firm, "I swear to you, bro, if I weren't at work right now, I'd pound you like I'd pound that pussy." Then he backed down and turned around to head towards the tiny door that you had to duck through to get off the court. He started to duck and I pegged him in the ass with a blue ball.

"You've got a shit stain on your white shorts, bitch."

Like a shot putter, he came out of his crouched stance and spun around, delivering a speeding blue ball right at my face. I dodged. The door slammed. Apparently he'd decided to stick around and scuffle.

There were at least a dozen balls scattered on the floor. We started scooping them up and firing at each other, going for the face shots mostly. "You throw like a tennis bitch," I shouted.

"The spy can't hit shit without his laser sight!"

The air was streaked blue with balls bouncing in every which direction. I pegged him in the center of the chest as he wound up to throw. The impact caused his arms to fly out to both sides like a crucifixion. Winded, he hunched over, presenting his face for a nice square shot. Contact. Right on the nose.

I was dry. All the balls were near his feet because I'd been going haymaker crazy. It was my time to dance for a minute. He served them right back. He fired twice and hit me once in the ear.

EAR!

Fucking stings the worst.

Racquetball POPS and SNAPPS drowned the room as balls kept finding targets, missing targets, and bouncing off the walls. It was starting to turn into fun. I almost didn't hate the guy anymore. The fight wore on: eventually we both wound up in opposite corners of the court, doubled over and sucking air. Troy peered out from behind the wavy hair in his face, "Dude, Anne-Laure's match. You're going to miss it."

I went back to the mezzanine area overlooking the tennis courts where there was also an attached bar and grill. The carpet was a plaid; it was trying way too hard to be East Coast. I was the only person hanging around and the only person watching the boring match other than Anne-Laure's perverted has-been coach. He was standing below, courtside, making the best use of his time by stuffing his hands in his shorts, like I noticed Troy would tend to do. *What was it with these tennis guys sticking their hands in their shorts?*

Anne-Laure was burying the other girl. It was just a qualifying match and wasn't that important, but this didn't stop the Tiny Tornado. And there she was, *grunting*. For me though it was a much-needed quiet time to observe something more than just tennis. I watched the two girls sock the tennis ball from one side of the court to the other. I could sure relate to that ball. I felt just as wavering as it must have: being beaten in all directions by unrelenting pressures and questions with no answers. I didn't know what I really wanted out of all of this. It was just a fucking bank. But it had me trapped.

About twenty minutes into watching the match I heard "FUCK, FUCK, PUSSY, CUNT," coming from behind me. That was it. I lost my temper, and now Troy had a nice black eye creeping up. The match was over, and we had gone out to the parking lot to try and cool it. Anne-Laure stood between us. Troy iced his face, I popped some Valium, and Anne-Laure was in hysterics, "I look up an I see you fighting een club house!" she almost cried. "I almost forfeit match!"

Troy pulled the ice pack away from his face. "Yeah dude. I just wanted to sit down and talk it out, but you go bat shit crazy...What the fuck's your problem, man?"

"You."

Anne-Laure got in my face, "Well eef you can't be fren wiz my fren, den we cannot be fren!"

"Watch out for this guy, Anne-Laure."

Troy took offense. "Yo, fuck that noise, bro."

"You're just a scumbag with a permanent hard on, Troy. So why don't you go and give tennis lessons to some cougars and work on your stroke with them."

"Don't hate the game, man."

"Stop dees. Tloy eez my friend."

That I'd like to fuck, he whispered under his breath.

I shoved him. "Fuck you."

"Stop eet!" Anne-Laure punched me in the arm and pulled me back. "You looking so ugly right now."

"He just wants to fuck you, Anne-Laure."

She snatched her tennis bag off the ground and turned away to hide her face from me, "Tloy, weel you drive me home?"

Troy shrugged, "Good going bro, you made her cry," and they walked off together.

The Vomitous Horrors of a Public Library

I couldn't check out any of the books. Everything had to be read *at* the library because if the walls ever came down I wanted to avoid having to explain to a jury why I'd checked out a stack of bank robbing books. But the latex gloves were just because of all the syphilis on everything. Dirty. Public. Everything. An Asian guy studying rocket science was wearing a facemask for the same reason.

And yes, Reader, the library does have books about robbing banks. There is a whole section called true fucking crime.

I sat behind a stack of books three feet tall. That's a bad smell. A three-foot pile of public library books smells like a three-foot tower of hot, day old vomit. And from that stack of vomit came a bit of wisdom that made me want to vomit. The security system portion of this extravagant project was going to be impossible.

Alarm systems are techie gadgets that improve faster than the books at the library can explain them. With the information available to me, I could rob a bank in 1989—at best. For a guy my age, that would mean riding up on my Hot Wheels and shooting off my G.I. Joe cap gun.

Tearful, I left the books and left the library.

A few blocks from the Main Library is Pershing Square, an outdoor park-like setting that is technically the center of downtown Los Angeles. The damned aren't ice skating in Hell, but they're ice-skating in LA—in Pershing Square—outdoors—in sixty-five degree weather—a sign of the coming apocalypse that will erupt in Westlake Village—out from under the floor—in Katie's office. Worse yet, ice-skating is like having sex when you were fifteen. It never lasts long and is always embarrassing. The only difference is that at the end of ice-skating you have stinky feet. The person before me must have re-routed his asshole to the bottoms of his feet.

Somehow I managed not to think about losing my feet to some terrible infection and booted up anyhow.

Another comparison to sex: you never forget how to ice-skate. But I was never that good in the first place, so I struggled a bit. Center ice, unable to perform, I was a member of the lowest species of recreational skaters. We were the ones that would skate a few feet, stop, stand a bit, try and turn around, and then fall flat on our asses. And the falling down was infectious. A friend of the fallen would cautiously approach to help the friend back to his feet. Then the sidekick would lose balance and fall flat on his ass. Center ice was like a couch: there were more butts on it than skate blades. But I stood there anyhow. It was time to make an important phone call.

Her name was Marci, and she was presumably hot, naked, and ready to party. Her ad in the adult newspaper said that she wanted to confess about how she liked to bend over in frat houses and get spanked.

"Marci, let's rob a bank...Let's rob a bank, and then hole up in a motel room and do a bunch of coke."

"That sounds like a nice fantasy, baby. But let Marci fuck you real good first." Chat line bimbos always want to fuck first and skip the party. *"We don't need to do no coke to fuck good."*

"But we have to do this big time, Marci. We gotta lick this bank, meet up with some Columbians, and jam some major blow. Then we'll hang together for a few weeks until the heat dies down. I want you to be my ho, Marci. I need you to run off with me. Every bank hit has gotta have a ho. And we gotta sniff lots of yip too."

"But I don't blow coke, baby, I just blow cocks."

"Of course you don't do drugs. What was I thinking? Not a Hot and Horny Gangbang Grandma. Of course not. But you'll still be my bimbo won't ya?"

"Honey do you want me to suck you off or what?"

"Marci, I'm in public. At an ice skating rink. The general public is skating around me counterclockwise. No Marci, I'm sorry, I don't want a blowjob right now."

A shocked mother scooped her fallen son off the ice and pierced me with a dirty look. The mother reeked illegal, but "blowjob" translates to *blowjob* in Spanish. So I covered the receiver on my phone. "Go ahead and call the goddamn cops. Then you can get yourself a free Christmas trip back to Mexico...Feliz Nave Fucking Dad." I returned to my phone call. "Sorry about that, Marci."

"You have a partner? You and your partner want pull a team job?"

"No Marci, you're my partner. We're in this together, baby. It's just you and me. We're going to knock down this bank and then run off with a whole bunch of money. You and me...then we can fuck forever."

"Sure, baby. If that's your fantasy, Marci's with ya."

I had to move a bit. Two bratty prepubescents almost knocked me over. "Sorry, about that, I almost got trucked...So Marci, baby, let's talk about how we're going to take down this bank? We're breaking in at night, but we have to crack the security system. How are we going to do that?"

There was pause. I could hear her shifting around on the other end of the line. She was probably thinking—Robbing banks? What kind of sick fetish is this?

"So you're saying we gonna rob this bank at night, right?"

"That's right Marci. We're going to break in at night. But we have to disable the alarm first because we need to have enough time to screw before we take the money and run."

"You want to fuck me in a bank vault?"

"You ever get all hot and sweaty and roll around in a big pile of money!"

"Now this is the kind of fantasy I like, baby. We can get all hot in a bank vault and you can rub stacks of money all up on my tits and ass."

"That sweaty cash' ll stick to ya...But Marci, baby, there won't be any cash unless we figure out how to get into that vault. We have to kill the alarm."

"Well, shut the damn power off and pack a flashlight."

"The alarms go through the phone lines"

"Then blow the damn thing up, honey."

"Blow what up?"

"The damn phone company."

"The phone company?'

"Yeah. Blow the damn thing up and it won't be in the way no more. What's so hard about that?"

WEEK FOUR

Anne-Laure's convertible was parked, and she was sitting in it, top down, facing the tennis courts at our complex. I had been laying low since the tennis club disaster, but I didn't have a choice in this matter.

She was completely zoned out. Her face was blank, an expression that I'd never seen before. Usually her face was filled with something vivid from her bottomless scroll of expressions. But a blank face could mean anything. I proceeded with caution.

"I jus start car and drive! I go away from dees place. Dees eez stupid place."

"It *is* stupid. You're right." I compacted myself into the tiny red convertible and sat down beside her. She looked me in the eyes and it appeared that she was actually relieved to see me. There was no vestigial awkwardness from the club. "Tell me what happened."

"Dees judge eez fucking stupid guy."

"Screw him."

"Americans think French people are so whining all the time. But he is so stupid bastard. The ball is on one side of line or *other* side. He too stupid to see so he just make decision with heez prick. He want pretty American girl win because she not whining all de time.

"And if it's *on* the line it's in too!"

"No...The ball go *out*. Thees eez what I tell you. But he say eet was on line. The ball go out. I no hit it back. Stupid judge say eet was in. He say eet was in and I lose match."

"It was that close?"

"I will be stupeed tennis instructor for stupeed kids, rest of my stupeed life. Dees life eez shit."

"Anne-Laure..."

"No! Leesin to me! Why eez life worths leeving if you can't be happy?" She wiped some tears away and gazed over the dashboard at the empty tennis courts. "I want to be professional teenis player, but I wan to be happy more. I need to decide what eez more eemportant...teenis or life."

Cattle Call

Imagine this scene from a late nineteenth century novel: A pack of starving immigrants brave wintry Chicago gusts to fight for what few jobs remain on the other side of a meat packer's gate. As a reader, you feel sorry for them; their lives are hopeless. But unlike starving immigrants, a cattle call for starving actors is hopelessly *nauseating*. It, too, is a scene of the poor fighting over scarce resources. A cattle call is an open audition for a theatrical production. The cattle were actors, and most of them were annoying and sucked.

However, on this morning, I too was a struggling LA actor. I was out to destroy Will Williams, so I was auditioning at the Powerhouse Theater on Main Street in Santa Monica. Specifically, I was reading for the part of Caliban in the *Tempest*. Caliban is the ugliest of all the

Bard's characters, making it the perfect part for Will. Too
bad I was going to ruin it for him.

Fitting in amongst these people was difficult. The room
was like a mental ward during a medication shortage. They
were all talking to themselves. Some cowered in corners,
while others talked right out in the open in the middle of the
room. An unabated human drone filled the small lobby
space of the theater. The building had been a sub-station
power plant at one point in its history, and the low-level
hum sounded as though the power plant were still alive and
well. A classically beautiful brunette spread herself out on
the floor, acting out her own demise. I imagined poison to be
the cause. A balding ex-hippie didn't look a bit strange
practicing his Tai Chi because right next him was a militant
lesbian pounding out pushups. A Caesar-ishly looking
gentleman leapt and dashed about. He projected loud booms
of *doth* and *woe is me*. In his dashing he slammed into the
two young men that were tickling one another. A spat broke
out between Caesar and the Pansies.

"Cut your nonsense!" I scolded. "Other actors are trying
to prepare!" This attempt at regulation gave me credibility
amongst the other actors standing nearby. That was all I was
willing to do to fit in, though—talking to myself and doing
Tai Chi were out of the question.

It was much more crowded than expected. An LA cattle
call swarms with more frantic people than a run on a bank,
and time was of the essence. Will would arrive soon, and I
needed to be finished with the audition before he showed up.

"I need a favor," I said to a young lady standing near the
front of the line. "I need your spot, and I'm willing to
bargain."

"My number's about to be called," she whined.

"That's why I'm prepared to make this worth your while,"
I smiled.

She was in her early twenties, and she was a cute little
blonde with just a smidgeon of baby fat. Little love handles

crept out over the top of her jeans and poked out just enough to reveal an even tan.

"See, that's just the thing," I continued anyway. "I have to be at my rehearsal before my scheduled audition, so I need to trade spots with somebody."

"You have a slotted time?" she asked me with a new level of interest.

"Yeah, the director invited me, but I misjudged the time.

"Really?"

"Yeah, but here's the thing...Todd won't be here until twelve, so if you take my spot, you'll get to audition in front of Todd, the director. But if you go next, which is in your cattle call slot, you'll just be auditioning for the casting director."

"You mean the real director isn't even here right now?"

"Exactly, so it would be in your best interest to switch spots with me and get face time with the actual director."

"How do I know you're not full of shit? And what is that?"

She noticed the rubber fish mask I was holding. "This is a prop. Todd likes way over the top, and Caliban is ugly as a fish."

She cut a girlish laugh, "Oh I get it"

Ignoring her flirtations, I narrowed my eyes on her. "Now tell me, what part are you going for? Maybe I can give you some ideas before your noon audition."

"Miranda."

"Super! I know exactly how to approach that one...You want to play it as if you were completely drunk!" I took her by the shoulders like a coach. "My Theory and Motion mentor played Miranda...for the Royal Shakespeare Company...at Stratford-upon-Avon," I breathed.

"Theory and Motion?" she asked.

"Yes, T.M. It's a post-classical, pre-modern technique that artists can apply to their motion palate. Think of it as method acting, but for Bio-Mechanists"

"Wow, how long have you been in the business?"

"Years." I breathed. "I've been at this for many years." I offered my hand. "Isosceles Octagonopolos. I was born in Greece...Theater was born in Greece." She accepted my hand. "So we have a deal, right?"

In addition to the rubber fish mask, I'd also brought along a bullhorn. However, getting out of the Volvo, I was sidetracked by a pair of fake tits and forgot the bullhorn on the seat. But the bullhorn was completely spectacular and would be entirely unprofessional. So I just *had* to retrieve it—quickly. I was expected to be on stage in twenty-five minutes.

I burst out of the bathroom where I'd been inside preparing for my audition—drinking a flask of liquor—and re-entered the realm of the actors in the crowded lobby. That's when I spotted Will. He had arrived earlier than expected and was nervously rattling off lines to himself in the middle of the room. So being extra careful, I ducked off to the left side of the room and worked my way between the wall and the crowd of actors, maneuvering my way towards the front door. Everything was going well until I approached a large opening in the crowd of people between me and the exit. It would be necessary to cross through this opening if I wanted to get the door, and ultimately to the bullhorn. Sadly, it came down to this: forget the bullhorn or risk being spotted by Will.

Then I heard a familiar voice, the girl from earlier! She was practicing her lines within arms reach of me. "You know what, I just remembered something." I put an arm around her and promenaded her through the lobby, burying my face into her hair as if whispering a secret into her ear. The fish mask covered the other side of my face. "I apologize. I didn't get your name earlier," I said.

"It's Bri, but I go by Bri Bri cuz it's cute." I continued shuffling her along towards the door. "Do you have a card?" She asked.

"I don't carry cards."

"Then how do you network?"

"Do you want my information?" I asked.

"Yeah."

We made it to the door, undetected. "Here." I dug a matchbook out of my pocket and handed it to her. "I don't have to network. I own that bar." I turned to walk out the door, "Just remember to play the part as if you were really drunk...completely hammered."

I retrieved the bullhorn from the Volvo and returned to the theater, deciding to try the back of the building. A loading dock opened to the alley. They'd left the overhead door raised to let a cool breeze steal into the stuffy theater— my way back inside. Leaning against the frame of the open bay door was a lonely mop standing upright in a bucket. I plucked the mop out of the bucket, and mounted the stairwell leading to the crew area above the stage.

"Ladies and Gentlemen, Will Williams..."

I introduced myself over the bullhorn using a low rumble like the narrator in a horror movie, "I present to you, ladies and gentlemen of the jury, Caliban, the ugliest incarnation in Shakespeare's catalog of work." Then I activated the *AMBULENCE* sound effect on the bullhorn. A metallic shrieking filled the room.

But the stage was empty. I had not yet made my entrance.

The cacophony of mumbles ceased in the lobby, and the room became dead quiet. The actors abandoned their preparations and gravitated towards the door. Will pushed his way to the front of the crowd, "I'm auditioning for Caliban. Excuse me."

SSHHHH!

"But I have to hear what's going on."

SSSHHH, asshole. Nobody cares.

106

He pushed through anyhow, and placed his ear against the door.

I grabbed hold of the stunt cord and began my slow descent to the stage. The shrieking of the *ambulance* sound effect filled the room. From my high vantage point on the cord, I could see out into the tiny, darkened theater. There was nothing between me and the four Theater Snobs in the audience but a head full of whiskey buzz and a mission to ruin Will Williams.

What the Theater Snobs saw was a spectacle wearing a rubber fish mask and being lowered onto stage. What I saw where four noses turned upwards—not because that's where the action was, but because these were stuck-up people. They were people that tend to enter *any* situation with a slant towards the critical, and I hoped to give them something to criticize for days to come.

When my feet touched the ground, I killed the *ambulance* effect. Then, I waited a moment until all was still and silent. The hot rush of booze-courage hit me. It was time to perform.

My first lines called for melody. I sang them into the bullhorn and plotted my way around the stage with my co-star, Mop.

No more dams I'll make for fish,
Nor fetch in firing
At requiring,
Nor scrape trencher, nor wash dish.
'Ban, 'Ban, Ca-Caliban

For Mop's line I dropped to a knee. I drew the attention towards him, kneeling before him and changing my voice to a high pitch, *"Oh brave monster! Lead thy way."*

I continued my performance including some physical comedy and acrobatics. Delivering a line to Mop: *"I'll swear upon the bottle to be thy truth. For the liquor is earthly"*—something about the word "earthly" made me decide to add live human flatulence.

The bullhorn's acoustic capabilities surpassed my expectations.

I delivered my last line, tossed Mop aside, and took a bow. Returning upright, I breathed deeply and calmly. My audience was stunned. Silent. There wasn't so much as even a tiny stir in the room. They were in horrified shock. So I took another bow...

"Ladies and gentlemen, Will Williams...You have my fucking number."

Meltdown at the Powerhouse

Santa Monica bicycle cops can't physically take people to jail. There are inherent limitations of their transport. But they can sure as hell handcuff someone and hold them down until a cruiser arrives. Will Williams, the real Will Williams, learned this lesson the hard way.

I fled the theater through my back alley entrance. I felt thoroughly proud of myself because I had not demonstrated one bit of theatrical competence and, what's more, I had managed to offend everyone. It was a landslide victory in my books. But as I turned the corner and stepped out onto Main Street, I found a heap of commotion surrounding my Volvo. It was Will Williams and he was swinging a microphone stand at my vehicle.

The first shot I witnessed took a mean bite at the quarter panel, denting a deep wound. The tires were already sliced, all four, and the scratches from where he had keyed the green paint made the vehicle look like it was draped in a massive cobweb. "Somebody call the cops!" I screamed. "Arrest this man!"

Shoppers, mothers with strollers, and patrons of the Coffee Beanery became common gauwkers at the sight of this upheaval. Commerce came to a halt. Traffic stopped, and time stood still. Dogs quit pissing on lampposts, and bums stopped begging for change. Every living creature stopped what it was doing to witness the troll with a microphone stand lose his shit on a Volvo.

Will acknowledged me when I made my presence known. But my presence did not scare him or appease his insanity; he gave me curt a nod and continued his work.

"You are out of line, Will Wilson!" I screamed at him.

"You fuck with me—fuck up my shit—I fuck up yours." He took a swing at the passenger side door and took the rear-view mirror off with it. "You're a fucking piece of shit!"

"It wasn't even a real audition. It was a cattle call!"

"Why the fuck would you do this to me?" Will wound up with the microphone stand and came down with a crash. "Ugghhhh!"

"It's not like it was for the London Symphony Fucking Orchestra!"

An angry Alpha-male marched forth from the Coffee Beanery's patio area, "Hey, watch your mouth! There're children out here!" Towering over Will, he snatched the microphone stand out of Will's grip. "This is a public street for families."

I warmed up to my new supporter, "Arrest this man! For destruction of property! And public indecency!"

The huge, preppy man gave me a scolding look like I was some foolish child. "You go and wait by the coffee shop!" he ordered.

"What about the police?"

He pointed and angry finger at a bench in front of the Coffee Beanery. "THERE! Now GO!" Without further resistance I did as told and went to the bench. On my way there I crossed paths with the guy's wife. She was on her way to check on the situation. She pushed one baby in an expensive stroller—the other was still a bump on her belly. "Honey, is everything okay over here?" She asked her husband.

"Everything's fine sweetie," he said in a much softer tone. "It's all safe now. So why don't you go back inside with the baby and wait for me, okay?"

I had to admit to myself the sad turn of the situation. The whole drama concerning Will would ultimately be arbitrated by a couple of nauseating Santa Monica yuppies.

The angry prep-man had cornered Will against the car. Every time Will would try and break free, the preppy father would cut him off. This gave me the choice between waiting around to chat with the cops, or hopping on the bus that had just pulled up in front of me. I accepted that I'd probably have a parking ticket stuck to my smashed windshield when I returned for my car and hopped on the bus anyway.

Cre-*old*

A congestive mob of ladies in wide brim hats and stranded pearls crowded the ancient sidewalk that cut its way through Main Street, the exact meridian of the old Southern town. Thirteen strong, their affluence peeped through the blur of their flickering oriental hand fans, which beat furiously at the hot Southern air. Predisposed by the boisterous magnetism of their important gossiping, the women were aloof to their surroundings. Passers-by had to step down onto the street to pass by this obnoxious crowd of chatty *bitches*.

The *Po Boy Brass Band* followed closely behind, weeping a sad funeral dirge. Their sinewy hands wrapped around worn, tarnished instruments, but their minds could not quite wrap around the purpose of this employ. *These rich white women wanted a jazz funeral. But it didn't look like nobody had died!* Yet the *Po Boys* nodded and wore on as they were paid to. They dutifully counseled their horns and kept up the pace behind the noisy bunch of women—that didn't seem to have a care in the world.

The funeral home was a converted Greek Revival mansion and the former home of a Confederate general. He built it just after the Great War, as the town re-birthed itself out of the ashes of its former glory—after being mowed down by Northern Aggression and his flickering torches. A post-war nod to the South's riposte, the mansion rises above Main Street and sits snobbishly upon an elevated foundation. Its sparkle of whitewashed brick bursts with ethereal whiteness. Eight massive Corinthian columns, the girth of Northwestern pines, stand guard against the commoners of Main Street. Topping each column is a uniquely carved capital crafted to look like a heap of tobacco leaves resting on a dais. If you look closely, you will find tiny Indian chiefs peeking out from behind broad leafy bushes.

The *Po Boys* lugged their hulky cargo up the steps without missing a note. One by one, they stepped off the granite stairs and continued marching to the center of the front lawn. There, on the plush carpet of grass, a garden party fit to be the cover of *Southern Living* was set. There was a full bar, a lavishly decorated banquet table stood under a brilliant white canopy. The table was dressed with fine linens, silver, chinaware, and floral arrangements. Close by was the bounty, a lavish spread of delicacies warming in silver chaffing dishes, and the cold dishes were plated on elegant silver serving trays. An abundant staff of waiters stood idle for service. But the band saved their awe. Working professionals, they continued their song, a solemn exchange of wheezing saxophones pitting against shrill cries of trumpets. Once all of the musicians were collected at center lawn, the band leader directed them to continue their march and gather under the leafy green shade of a blossoming Magnolia, away from the party, yet not out of mind. The garden area was clear of nothing but rich ladies, smoothing out their suits and raking their hair because of the sticky noontime haze. It was about the time for the most sobering of rituals that takes place during a jazz funeral. It was time to *cut the body loose.*

Mrs. Moffat stood by at her honorable position at the key table and poured herself a glass of ice water from a frosty pitcher with slices of cucumber and lemon dancing in the ice. With a devilish grin she said, "I say, ladies, it's hot as a bitch out here."

The commotion caused on Main Street by the elegant ladies and their jazz band had attracted the attention of a *Second Line*, a small company of passing strangers, interested in the affair. They gathered at the foot of the great set of granite steps, playing at paying respects to the deceased, but hoping to get a free drink. Smoking long cigarettes and quietly gossiping amongst themselves, they too, like the faithful jazz band, were wondering what on earth was at the root of these eccentrics.

Mrs. Moffat, still stoned silly in the face by her own dirty joke, retrieved a dark amber cocktail awaiting her on the starched linen tablecloth. She gracefully presented it to signal the oncoming of a toast. The twelve other ladies stood at attention behind their chairs and a tuxedoed servant made his final few stops with his bar trolley of Sazerac cocktails.

"*What in the hell are they waitn' fo?*" A weather beaten hobo asked of the other Second Liners. "*Muss be some kinda stuck up thang,*" another replied. The hobo shrugged and shook his head, "*Maybe they waitn' for that old one at the head of the table to drop dead?*"

"Does everybody have a drink?" Mrs. Moffat asked of her associates. She soon realized her error. After an inefficient mumbling of mixed forms to the affirmative, she realized that she should have asked, *Does anybody NOT have a cocktail?* "Very well, without further adieu, let us have our first toast and begin our funeral party. Here is to us, ladies both young and old. To those fairer in their years, may all the moisturizer and all the procedures in all the world not make you think that you can outwit old age. And to those of us that have seen all there is to be see, we have learned one thing... That saying that age, like wine, gets better with age, is complete fooey. Because that would be like saying that our old husbands were still useful *before* Viagra...Today is about getting old! Cut the body loose!"

After a resounding clang of crystal cocktail glasses, the band struck up a happy tune and each of the ladies took a healthy dip into their cocktails. An over-abundance of servers soon emerged onto the lawn to attend the ladies with sterling silver platters of appetizers, both hot and cold. The buttery rich smell of oysters Rockefeller absorbed into the air, rich enough for a Rockefeller, and the earthen aroma of the herbs in the shrimp and grits spread it around.

The regal bartender cleared his throat, indicating that he wished to make an announcement. "Mrs. Moffat's wondrous frozen Hurricane's are ready for your enjoyment." There was an immediate run on the bar, a clamor of ladies uprooted from their seats to delight themselves to the finest Hurricane in the area. It was the hostess' secret recipe for fun—served in a tall glass with a cocktail umbrella.

The ladies returned to their tables, proudly clinking their glasses and showing off the pampered privilege of their gigantic pink cocktails. At their tables awaited the salad course, Bermuda Onion salad. Chatty, oiled society talk bargained its way to the table once everyone was reseated and ready to continue. I came with it.

"Elizabeth was expecting him for dinner."

"The boy just up and disappeared!"

"*How awful.* And after all that education."

"The boarding school...tutors...that enormous northern tuition."

"He was supposed to go to law school. They had already donated to Richmond."

"Poor Elizabeth. She's been through so much this year."

"It's just so awfully sad."

"I heard he was consumed by the narcotics."

"Oh dear..."

"Oh my..."

"But we mustn't jump to conclusions."

"Well he didn't leave an address. He doesn't write. He just disappeared. What is one supposed to think?"

Ellen was a childhood friend of mine from the neighborhood. She came to my defense. "SO IT ALL ADDS UP, DOES IT?" She turned up her nose to the ladies and with moxie politeness excused herself from the group. Mrs. Jones addressed her from behind, "Ellen, be a dear and ask your mother where her treats are."

Ellen obliged by not uttering a word. Without saying no, she was saying yes. So she walked towards the funeral home, where inside, in the staff's break room, was a freezer that held the desert. Her chore required her to pass by the downtrodden Second Line. They were still huddled in confusion at the bottom of the steps, anxiously awaiting a handout from the abundant cache of food and alcohol. "You shouldn't have voted for Bush last time around, should you have?"

Ellen continued up the wide steps that led between the eight massive columns and onto the mansion's veranda. She let herself through the intimidating front double doors and blushed. A little tipsy, it was a strange feeling to enter premises such as these in search of frozen deserts. She entered into the foyer where a funeral director met her. "How are you ladies coming along out there?"

"It's a wonderful time. I do think this was a great idea."

"It's a very interesting application of our facilities," he laughed. There was a short uncomfortable pause, no doubt chilling. Ellen understood that this gentleman had probably just stepped away for a short break from preparing a corpse in the basement's mortuary. "Ladies room?" he asked.

Ellen's face flushed. "Oh no, I've come inside to pick up my mother's desert."

"Mitzi Margarella's Whiskey-sickles? Let me guide you, dear."

The undertaker led Ellen through a cramped, dark hallway that led out of the foyer and into the depths of a creepy, poorly lit chamber. She could hear the hushed whisper of a woman's voice coming from beyond, where along the far wall was an outline of light marking a door. The woman's hushed whispers were coming from behind that door. Ellen suddenly shrieked, *"Aaggh!"* Something had run across her foot.

The lights came on and Ellen found herself standing in the middle of your typical family owned business' cluttered office space.

"So now you've met Mortimer," the undertaker said. Hiding under a secretarial desk, scratching its back on a paper shredder, was an obese housecat, Mortimer.

The door, which was not so mysterious anymore, opened. "Oh Ellen, what are you doing in here?"

It was Mother. She had her cell phone to her ear. Ellen later told me that Mother was on the phone with a lawyer.

"Oh there they are!" The ladies rejoiced. Ellen returned a success, having brought along with her Whiskey-sickles and Mother (frozen Bourbon and the honorary guest of the party—in no respective order). Mother took her place at the head of the table and Ellen relieved herself of the tray of Whiskey-sickles by handing them off to a tuxedoed waiter. The waiter then made his way around the table distributing the desert, self-aware that it was an awkward sight to see a group of middle-aged women lopping away at penis-shaped Whiskey-sickles like a crowd of drunken sorority sisters at a bachelorette party. Mrs. Jones, one of Mother's dearest friends, found her way to the head of the table and placed her hands on Mother's shoulders. With blitzed blue eyes, as sparkling as the Great Lakes, Mrs. Jones announced, "Happy fiftieth birthday Elizabeth!"

The Pokey

There are three things that I fear in life: God, my mother, and the pokey. I also have two goals: to become rich and powerful, and to get there in my pajamas.
Alexander Barnett—Chicago, summer 2008.

The next afternoon after work, I went down to the Santa Monica courthouse to check on Will. I also had some interesting news.

He was outraged. "I don't owe you shit!" he screamed through the vented glass.

"You owe me for damages to the Volvo," I escalated. "PLUS the one thousand dollars you stole from me. PLUS interest. Which will be assessed at FOUR POINTS above the Fed Fund rate, which is a GREAT fucking bargain." I looked around the visitation area. It was a mob of the worst form, trannies, pimps, and perverts. "Maybe I ought to leave you in here! It looks like you might finally have a shot at getting laid."

"You'll not see a penny from me, asshole. You fucked up my audition, so you can just press the charges and let me do my sixty days."

A tranny on Will's side of the glass suddenly exploded into a fit. It began beating the glass, kicking air, and screaming obscenities at the person it was talking to. "Hoe, you fuck with my man I fuck with you." The tranny tore off its wig and waved it around in the air, "I be all man, bitch."

A corrections officer arrived on Will's side of the glass and removed the hostile tranny. Making use of this time, I dialed up my voicemail for the message I wanted Will to hear. "You might want to listen to this, Will. Your life doesn't have to continue sucking."

With the tranny removed, it was quiet again. Will placed his fatty ear against the sound hole in the Plexiglas to hear the message: *Hello, Will, this is Judie Tallmans with Powerhouse Productions calling for Will Wilson... Will, we had a wonderful time watching your performance for the part of Caliban. So we want to offer you the role. It pays twenty-two thousand dollars paid bi-weekly over the course of the production. So it works out to about a thousand dollars a week. Once again, thank you for your exciting audition and please let us know what you plan to do at your earliest convenience. You can call the office and ask for me, Judie.*

I withdrew my phone from the ear hole and settled into my hard jailhouse chair. "They've not seen my face at that theater," I said. "I was wearing a mask the whole time. So they don't know that I'm you." I studied the surprise on his face. "To make us even, you're taking the part...and I'm taking fifteen percent."

WEEK FIVE

Guilt is the Birth of Desire

It had been a long time since I'd seen her, since I'd lived with her, San Diego. That northerly concubine split us apart. And though you never really love the concubine, you stay with her until the fun goes away. So what's that make Tijuana then?

A shameful hookup. The perfect place to forget.

I had a feeling that my weekends, my life, weren't typical of a guy my age. Stakeouts. Research. Stakeouts. Theater crashing.

Of the two types of guys in LA, I wasn't one of them. They were...

Those that need their ass to be sewn to the couch, only to be chipped loose for nightly binge drinking and intermittent trips to the restroom to avoid messes. (I've known some to substitute a nearby bottle.) Food and drink during the dormant couch periods is delivered directly to the couch by *"Come on in!"* being communicated through an unlocked door.

The extreme weekender! Everything he says ends with an exclamation point! He drinks smoothies and goes running! Handfuls of trail mix fuel him on maniacal binges of exertion that end with an early bedtime and sore muscles by Saturday night—which in many cases is spent in a damp tent, in a sleeping bag. "!"

I'm closer to a number two, but an interesting variation: I'm an *Extreme Degenerate*. I have to get broken down on Friday and Saturday and be put back together on Sunday. Sunday is my religious day when I'm swearing to God that I'll never drink again. But that's what keeps the rest of the week in balance. The guilt.

Only guilt like that can make a twenty-two year old psychopath make his bed and report to work on Monday morning. And lately, the only thing I was guilty of was hard work. Hard, honest work, day and night, put towards a dedicated goal. How many single twenty-two year olds can say they live, breathe, and die for a goal like that? None. That's how many. The rest are either beating off or camping out. My balance was off. I'd lost my ability to be guilty.

My momentum was beginning to drip. In the beginning of the robbery it ran like a shower of horse piss. But now it was starting to slow down to a pace like old people fuck. Soon there would be nothing left of me if I didn't get back in balance. It was high time to get bent down and damn near broken over, real hard, on some booze, blow, and bitches—to get guilty again—to get that Monday morning fire back in my veins.

Care to join me for the best party of your life, Reader?

Blown out and bright eyed, it was time for a booty call south of the border. But you have to wait for traffic to die down on Friday evening because the hike through Orange County can be a real bitch; a big fat bloated one, face down across all four lanes, clogging up the road and giggling at all the tiny cars lodging in her tummy.

Friday: whistle blows, rush home, shower and shave. Then bed down for a couple hours of shuteye before making the move down to the border. Sleep comes in fits and starts. The coffee sludge that I'd been fueling on all day at the office sits heavy in my stomach. My mind keeps going, though my eyes are asleep.

My thoughts are *off* the robbery: it's hookers and blow now. So far so good.

But maybe I should just chill, stay in and soak up that acid, I wonder? Watch re-runs and wig out a bit; get higher than Godzilla's asshole? What if a powdered dinner with Ernesto Gomez and a warm desert with a hooker named Yesicca—who'll do anything—isn't the best idea right now?

But of course it is.

TJ.

Donkey Show.

Hookers and blow...

Go, Go, Go.

I explode out of bed and bolt for the front door. I've got my TJ Jams Mix for the stereo. I've got a full tank of gas and pocket full of cash because my credit card is paid, rent's paid, and I got paid today. There's just 176 miles between me and mind erasure. In Mexico.

Out the door.

Keys?

Wallet?

Passport?

Good decision making skills? DON'T NEED THOSE.

But before I take you to Mexico, Reader, let's get a few road rules straight.

Ain't nobody stopping you from going *into* Mexico. Less than five hundred feet from the free parking lot at the border, there's a little ramp leading to a rusted metal turnstile. Once you're through that turnstile, that's it, you're in another country.

There isn't a Mariachi band. There isn't a poster of a smiling Mexican president happy about the dollars you're bringing in. There isn't even a gathering of crooked Federali to go ahead and start taking them. You pass through the metal structure, making sure not to touch it (you could get chlamydia), and you step out just three feet away from where you started. That's it. You're in a new country now. No big deal. You're still on Earth. Except on this patch of Earth, it's easy to get jacked up on blow and take your pants down in front of a stranger.

The first thing to do when you get to Mexico is to stock up on enough Mexican cigarettes to get you through the night. They're not exactly bargains, but Senior is willing to sell you straight North Carolina tobacco for about two bucks less per pack than in America, and still fresh. Three feet means two bucks denominated in cigarettes. Senior crowds the exit on the other side of the gate with his tray of smokes, so whether you want to or not, you'll bump into him, making him your first body-to-body Mexican experience.

Then you're on your way, smoking your first Mexican cigarette of the night, heading to the fuck fest of cabs not but another hundred feet from Senior. There're probably two hundred Crown Vics parked there, engines running, awaiting American butts to hop in the seats and be whisked off to a night of drinking and whoring. The cabbies have their own little system to decide who gets to pick up the next fare. It's called chaos. But it seems to work, as much of Mexico near the border is chaotic. The cabbie system works like this: he pulls up and waits in line for the next American fare to come jonesing through the gate. Then, the cabbie jolts into a hysterical fit of physical marketing, going absolutely crazy and wigging out, running up to the American screaming.

"Dancing girls! Party party. Tequilas! Sexy dance!"

Do they think this is my first time? I shoo them off.
"Fucking assholes! Sweaty fat fucks!" I scream.

The biggest tub of mole that can push his way to the front gets the fare, but that doesn't mean that he has the *information*. See it's the information you're after. Unlicensed brokers of sleaze, a well-informed cabbie can put you in contact with the provider of the entertainments you seek. And I'm not talking about hookers. I just said that so you'd come to Mexico with me, you pervert.

"Can one of you fucking morons take me to the donkey show?" you scream. *"Which one of you fucks wants to get off his ass and take this rich Gringo to the goddamn donkey dance?"*

Count on it every time, a tubby fellow with a dirty Oakland Raiders sweatshirt will come running up, "I know very nice girls. You come with me, I take good care."

"Fuck you, you pussy!...Somebody's got two seconds to grow some balls and hustle me over to watch some bitch fuck a jackass."

The pussy cabbies clear away like cockroaches under a flashlight. Then you see him, the St. Peter at the Gates of Filth, the cabbie with enough balls to drive you to the donkey show. He's the shadiest sleazebag of the entire bunch. He has two gold loops in each ear, missing teeth, a moustache, and a ponytail. Tattoos creep up over his collar and climb up his neck. Topping it off is the crown of sleaze: the leather baseball cap; the sleaziest of headwear honoring sleaze.

You don't walk around in TJ. It's a guaranteed bad time. Always take a cab, and always sit in the front. If you sit in the back, the drivers think you're a huge pussy in which case they'll rob you, or, they'll just think that you're a sicko and they'll kick you out of the cab. If you want to sniff some drugs, don't ask. Just casually pull out the bag and look the cabbie in the eye. Await his approval.

He'll nod "Fine."
"Hee Haww!"

St. Maximilian Kolbe

We were sitting in the neighborhood Catholic Church when my cell phone *beeped*. It was a text message, and I decided to take a look.

Anne-Laure snapped under her breath. "What you doing?"

"It's Will," I whispered. "I have to text him back."

"You can't be doing zat een here."

"Should I just call him then?" I escalated. I pressed *call back* on the phone's menu and put the phone to my ear.

Anne-Laure's face emboldened with fury, and she ripped the phone loose from my grip. I shrugged her off, reclaimed my phone, and walked out of the church.

It wasn't a text from Will, but I knew that all along. I'd rather sit in church and listen to a priest than reply to a text from that sonofabitch, Will, on my Sunday Funday. The text message was an automated message from my online sports book. It was an alert that the line had moved on the halftime spread, and if I wanted more action, it was mine for the taking. I sat down comfortably on the church steps and had a cigarette while I figured how much I wanted to get in for. It was a beautiful day, much too beautiful to waste inside a church when one could be smoking and gambling elsewhere on church property.

I returned to our pew after placing a hefty bet and noticed that a chubby kid was sitting next to us. His mother was shapely and strung out on pills. Father was agitated; he wasn't on the golf course or betting on football.

But this child! He was worse behaved than me!

He was dancing about, pantomiming the church music. The program involved woodwinds, stringed instruments, bells, and keys. This musical variety provided my neighborly menace ample opportunity in choosing which instrument to pantomime. Air guitar. Air flute. Air piano. He was also playing drums, even though I didn't hear any. He banged his head wildly. His mismanaged locks whipped around his excited, fat face as he pounded his imaginary piano keys with his fat little fingers. He had no visible wrists. There was just a crease between his hand and forearm where two fatty appendages met like conjoined links of sausages.

In the choral loft above, the ensemble's flautist went into a tear. This gave our fat little friend a new harmony to play, and heightened his vigor and intensity. His fat fingers danced along his imaginary melody maker, playing wildly out to the side of his fat face. This kid was awesome. He was a complete mess. So I decided to stay in church and continue to watch instead of stepping outside to place more bets.

Next, I noticed that the mother was somewhat coherent. She would intermittently glance down, inspect her duckling, scoff, and look away. My mother, *Mother*, would have smacked my imaginary flute out of my hands and beat me with a bible, right there in front of Jesus. But Cream Puff's mother was playing the passive California Mommy. She was attempting to outwait the little rascal and see if he would tire, or, self-recognize the absurdity of his monkey business and practice some self-imposed self-control. But this particular mother did not realize that five year olds don't tire and don't get embarrassed over their own absurdity— especially when they have knowingly won the adoration of a Deranged Young Professional.

I engaged my new friend with a slight nod of approval. Then I removed my imaginary conductor's want from my breast pocket and began conducting the air flautist. Anne-Laure smacked me as soon as she realized what I was doing. It provoked a giggle out of the fat boy and a hearty laugh out of me. The boy's mother looked up from balancing her checkbook. I anticipated a dirty look, but instead, in her Demerol-induced coma, she didn't seem to mind. She looked right through me. I winked at the fat boy to let him know that we were still in this together, partners in crime. It was me against Anne-Laure and him against his jaded mother. Both of us were against being locked in a church on a beautiful Sunday Funday.

I contributed by using the back of the pew in front of me as a piano keyboard. Anne-Laure pinned both of my hands against the wood. But this setback didn't kill my partner's spirits. His broad smile revealed a few missing teeth, a testament to his age, and he continued banging his head, and pounding imaginary keys with the maniacal, yet sophisticated polish of a trained classical pianist. It filled me with a great robust pride that only a master music instructor will feel when a talented student performs at the height of his ability.

The music continued as communion began. *Drinks. Appetizers.* I got up to join the free wine line, but Anne-Laure sat me back down. "Not you."

"What?" I was confused, and a bit offended.

"You are not in communion."

"Well, bring me a doggy bag then." She ignored me and joined the line. I watched her glide down the aisle and her butt doing the "look both ways" behind the thin fabric of her dress. I'd been raised Catholic but had since given it up. It's a faith based upon guilt, and I usually already had enough guilt without being Catholic. So I got wise to their game.

See, if you're Catholic, you can do whatever mischief you want all week long. Then you go and *apologize* for it at Saturday's confession. Simple as that. You can be a pervert, a drunk, and a bank robber all week long. Then you go say "sorry." That makes you aces in Jesus' book until you screw up again.

But, there is *one* major caveat. Habitual offenders like me cannot escape the endless cycle of guilt, and they can get us hooked for life. The only way out is to quit being Catholic altogether. Confession itself is on Saturday for that very

124

reason: to snare the repeat offenders like me. See, they *want* you to have a clear conscience by Saturday night. They *want* you to go out on Saturday night and screw up again. They *want* you to down that fifth of whiskey and bang two fat chicks. They *want* you to take a dump in the urinal at Dunkin Donuts. They want you to get hooked on confession. That way, you'll have to come right back the next week for a do-over. You have to run back to the church with your threadbare dignity and speak to the priest about getting it all patched up. It's like shaking up the Etch-A-Sketch. A clean slate. No matter how putrid the abomination that is your wickedness, you can always shake up the Etch-A-Sketch and start over. The only drawback is that you have to live with the guilt for a whole week, and that's the way they know they can get you back...

"PPPPPPTTTTHHHHHHHHHTTTTTTTTT!"

I heard thunderous fart noises. They were coming my way! Fat Body McGee had broken loose from his mother and was running down the aisle with his hands across his face—blowing fart noises! They always get the best, slappy wet sounds when they get going off pudgy hands. He had those fat little legs churning and was charging at me with a smile that said he was happier than a pig in shit.

"SSSSSPPPPPPPTTTTHHHHHHHHHTTTTTTTTT!"

I leapt up from my seat to welcome my friend with open arms. He was also glad to see his big buddy. Like a drunken Irishman at a wedding, I started dancing a jig. "Let's make a dance!" I sang.

We met at center aisle and he resumed playing his air flute. With the intensity of my Irish jig, together we had a good thing going. The spectating crowds seemed to agree; their stoned gazes indicating sheer amazement. That is, until the blitzed out mother emerged from her fog. She, along with Anne-Laure, charged at us with the molten disciplinarian fury of a thousand angry Catholic school nuns. But I didn't care. I just kept dancing, because like a five year old, a Deranged Young Professional rarely self-realizes the absurdity of his monkey business. I sure was going to miss that little fella. With Anne-Laure grabbing hold of my ear and dragging me for the door, that was the last I'd ever see of him.

Golf Lesson

I decided to be a real ass towards Anne-Laure for dragging me to church and then ruining my fun with my new friend. So I bought myself a stinky cigar. Then, I showed up for and an expensive golf lesson at the driving range adjacent to the courts where she gives Sunday evening lessons. My golf instructor's name was Pete, and he was helping me work on my bad slice. There was no hope for my personality.

Pete stood back and watched me take a swing with a five iron. "You're dipping your damn hips" was his immediate conclusion.

"I don't usually get complaints."

"This isn't the damn bedroom." He kicked the toes of my cleats in an effort to adjust my stance. "We need to work on your foot placement until we can find out where you're comfortable. That way you won't dip so damn much." He kicked the back of my knee by hooking around with the top of his toes. "Okay, relax those damn knees and try again."

I took another swing and the ball went sailing off to the right. Yet another slice.

"Okay, I see what's going on." Pete laid a club across my feet. With this straight reference, I could see that my back foot was too far back in my stance. "That's causing you to settle back on that damn right foot and you're dipping your damn hips to over-compensate." He removed a felt tip marker from his pocket and knelt down to draw some hash marks on the shaft of the club. Then he plotted a small dot on the tops of either of my cleats. "When you're practicing,"

126

he began, "lay down this club, aimed at your target, and line your feet up on the marks. This ought to get you going."

"You gotta be kidding me, Pete." It felt like a weird stance to me. But thirteen years of bad habits can become a part of you.

"No shit," he said.

"I'm paying how much for you to stand here and draw dots on my cleats?"

"You just see. Take a few swings."

"I want the video equipment. I was told someone would video tape me."

"So you want to watch yourself doing it the wrong way then?"

"No, I just want the full treatment. Where's the technology?"

"Swing the damn club."

"You set up a camera first."

"Swing."

"Camera."

Pete looked at his watch. "Session's over."

"But we've only..."

"Swing."

I swung. That ball sailed straighter than a fast trip to the liquor store.

Pete left me with a large bucket of practice balls and a shit eating grin on his face. I lit my stinky cigar to get in the practice mood. The courts where Anne-Laure was teaching were just yards from the driving range, so she had undoubtedly seen me enjoying an expensive lesson. Now too, she had no choice but to smell the stench of my expensive cigar.

My shots were long and straight. My arc was perfectly pitched for the longer shots, giving me nice rolls when they set down on the mock fairway. My short game could stop on a dime. The ball would meet the grass, and plop, it would stop like a lump. I was enjoying this Phoenix of my golf game.

The air was refreshing and warm, and the sky was streaked with pleasant hues of pinks and orange. My cloud of cigar smoke hung gently around me, a masculine haze of rustic fragrance; a bouquet of roasted spices. The sun slowly retired behind me and its tender light colored the fresh grass a majestic hue of dark blue. Every living thing in my range of sight was meticulously babied and beautiful. This was what Anne-Laure got to consider her office. No wonder she could stand to be cooped up in a boring church on such a beautiful day.

After my practice, I met Pete lingering in front of the clubhouse with his arms folded across his chest and a friendly smile spread across his face. He was greeting golfers coming in from their relaxing Sunday rounds and happily anticipating his routine Sunday Italian dinner with his wife at Mediterraneo, the club's fine dining offering.

"G'night Pete. Great lesson tonight."

"So, how did you hit?"

"Knocked the tits off. But I'll have to get in a few more rounds to see if the cure takes."

"Sounds like a damn plan," he said.

I nodded towards the 19th *Hole*, the clubhouse bar, Bogies Bar and Grille. "Pete, you know where I'll be."

A lush collection of bushy green shrubbery, myrtle, rock rose and Manzanita, dressed the walkway between the clubhouse and the tennis courts. Beyond the courts was a lagoon with swimming black necked swans and floating lily. I strolled through this enchanting spread, puffing the last of my cigar and half-heartedly reflecting on my day's game.

A tennis ball landed at my feet. I scooped it up out of the Bermuda grass.

I looked right at her. She stared back, standing there anxious and silent, waiting to see what I would do. Her clients, a group of teenage girls and boys, echoed the negative energy by staring back at me like I was AIDS behind a cloud of cigar smoke. The boy who'd hit the ball over the fence gave me a dumb look and was surprised that I hadn't already tossed the ball back over.

I waited a beat or two longer.

There's no doubt about it, I thought, as I sat there waiting. Georgia O'Keefe's paintings are of flowers that look like big flappy vaginas. And I? Well, I looked like a gigantic prick. So I sucked it up and did the right by the kid. I threw the ball back over the fence. "Be a good boy for your pretty teacher," I said.

The Wrinkle Room

I perched myself at a pub table on the covered patio overlooking the lagoon. The big screen televisions hanging over the bar I ignored. I wasn't there to relax and watch the games. I was there to work.

Bogies had been a Westlake Village squeeze since the seventies. The trendy décor had obviously been updated over the years, but the clientele had not. Hence, among the local Young Professional crowd, it was known as the *Wrinkle Room*. The home-wrecking barfly that was going there in seventy-seven was still showing up today. But now she was divorced, tanned, tucked, and ready to fuck.

Her name was Susan, and I had no plans to sleep with her. So when I approached her, I acted gay. "Oh I love your shirt," I said for starters. "Those are so my colors..." She swiveled around to get a look at me. A natural brunette, she had red highlights and the tightest body any forty-five year old could have. She must have been about a leggy five-ten, dynamite tits—bolt-ons—wanting desperately to jump out of her tight, sleeveless mini-shirt. It was the fashionable kind of t-shirt with glittery skulls and roses on it, expensive, yet meant to make an older gal feel young and cheap. She leaned forward, offering me a flimsy, delicate hand, but it wasn't going to work with me.

"Pinkies!" I said. She giggled and we locked pinkies, automatically becoming friends. But at the same time I casually peeked around back and caught a glimpse of a black thong riding up over the waistline of her designer jeans.

We began talking about interior decorating, which led to tales of cohabitation.

"I haven't lived with a guy since my ex-husband. That was years ago," she said. Everything in my house is so girly."

"Cheers!" I said. "It goes with you—*girly*." I poked her on the breastbone, just above the boob.

She laughed, "Oh, I'm such a bitch!"

"Stop it...you're a *huge* bitch."

"Why do you have to be gay?" She whined.

"Because Jesus screwed my nuts on backwards." She about peed her pants with laughter, almost spilling her drink. *I had her.*

"But tell me," she said. "You still think I'm hot, don't you?"

"You have one hell of a body, sugar. Keep getting me drunk."

"Do you think I look bulimic?"

I paused for a moment. "YES!" I boomed.

We both cracked up. She hugged me and squeezed so tightly that droplets of whiskey got lodged in the back of my nose. The heat caused me to start coughing—hacking.

"You're so great," she said. Then she over-exaggerated licking her cologen lips, seductively. "But what I swallow doesn't come back up."

Anne-Laure was bound to walk into the bar and see this foxy cougar eating it up. She'd erupt with jealousy, I hoped. She would not even make it past the door. I was anticipating the very moment, so much, that I was beginning to get butterflies in my stomach. But then I heard a familiar voice from over my shoulder.

"Thought we'd find you in here."

It was Troy.

"Come on," he said. "I'm having a party at my house."

"Where's Anne-Laure?" I asked.

"She's getting ready." Troy then caught sight of Susan. He did an exaggerated once over, "Hey, hey…" Susan ate it up. Then he asked me, "Where're your manners, man? Aren't you going to introduce me to the nice young lady?"

I introduced them, getting a weird look from Susan. "I'm not actually gay," I said. "It's a long story."

Troy laughed, "I knew it!" He pat me on the back and explained to Susan, "This guy had the hottest French girl in the world crazy for him, and it took him forever to do anything about it."

Susan smiled in sarcastic pity, "Oh he's such a cute little boy."

"Now come on," Troy said. "We're going to a party. And Susan, you're coming with us."

The three of us walked out of the bar in single file, and Troy naturally lined up behind Susan. "You should hear about what this guy did at church today—absolutely hysterical—every chick at St. Max wants this crazy stud." He discreetly grabbed my attention, *"Fuck. Cougar. Fuck. Ass. Tits. Fuck. Dick Machine!"*

House Party

We entered through the front door of the house, and a guy about my own age came crashing head-first down the steps. He landed at our feet in the foyer, a broken, booze-addled mess. The party was raging, and nobody seemed to notice. He pulled himself up off the ground and hollered, "This here party needs more gyrating!" Then he ran off into the crowd in the living room and penetrated a group of dancing girls. "Gyrations!" he screamed. He fumbled around underneath the collar of his t-shirt and produced a whistle. He blasted it and everything but the music silenced.

"MORE GYRATIONS!" He screamed at the top of his lungs. "*Whhheeeewwww!* THIS IS A GYRATIONS CITATION." The party returned to its raging levels, and Troy projected over the noise, "That's Party Bob," he said proudly. "That crazy motherfucker is my roommate!"

Troy took Susan and me to get drinks from the kitchen, and then we went outside to the patio for some cocktailing. A pair of chaise lounges surrounded the steaming hot tub, and Anne-Laure sat on one of them. She looked stunning. She wasn't wearing anything special, and she hadn't put on much make-up. She was just natural and young and mine. And knowing that something so beautiful is yours makes it the most beautiful thing in the world.

I walked over and sat down next to her, holding eye contact the whole time. She accepted me into her lap, and I sat down, waving to the people in the hot tub.

Among them was a chiseled sales guy type, flanked on either side by girls. "Welcome to the office." He opened his huge arms to welcome us, mindful not to lose an opportunity to pose. "Don't mind Party Bob's mess," he continued. An over-flowing coffee tin of cigarette butts sat on the deck next to one of the lounge chairs.

"No worries," I said laughing. "What a character." I leaned forward to shake Paul's hand. "Nice to meet you."

Susan set her drink on a patio table and stretched. Her big, fake breasts poked through her tight shirt like two bald heads pressed against a window pane. "Ooh it's been a long day. I'd like to get in."

Just as she'd hoped, Paul was paying attention to her. "I have an extra suit in my room," he said. "*But it's tiny!*"

Susan and Paul left to get the suit, and Anne-Laure wanted me to go inside and meet more of the people. "Let's go into the party," she said. "I want you to meet Party Bob."

We found him inside, bouncing around the room. Everything he said, he screamed. "GLOW STICKS!" He was guzzling beers and running around the dance area passing out glow sticks.

I eventually managed to catch up with him hovering around the bar area. "Party Bob, help me out." I extended my empty cup. "Dump some of that whiskey in there."

His head recoiled, and his eyes lit up. "Fuck dude, I've seen you over at Justine's." He was right. Those days I was eating a weekly average of three Justine's breakfast burritos. It was the only thing to shake me loose from bed in the morning when the cigarettes weren't working. "I'd fuck a dead cow for one of those burritos," he said.

"Do you work in the business park?" I asked.

"Yeah, I work at Uncle Milton's."

"What's that?"

"Ant farms. I'm an entomologist and I take care of the ants."

"That's fucking crazy."

"It gets me more pussy than a tampon sale," he laughed. "I even have a pick up called *Ants in the Pants*."

"Let me hear it."

He laughed and took a drink. At first I thought his whole story would be a put on. But he took a big gulp from his drink and dove right in before I could make up my mind.

So what I do," he began, "*is I get a bottle of wine and I take them over after everybody's cut out for the night. I show them around for a little while and I let them play with the ants. Girls get really stoked about feedings. Deep down they're all a bunch of carnivores. It's just like that wildlife shit on TV with lions and zebras. It's primal as fuck and gets the ladies horny as fuck. But to seal the deal, I bring out this special type of fire ant, the Anaje Bombolai ant. These guys are vicious around pussy because of the pheromones. One whiff of vagina and these guys are going off. They'll attack the girl and then she'll start trying to brush them off, but these little fuckers are fierce. So what you have to do, is jump in. You start swiping and brushing and grabbing and tickling as much as you can. Next thing you know the bitch will be screaming, 'Oh my god, I think they got in my pants. There's fucking ants in my pants.' That's when you just go ahead and rip her pants off. The girls are so freaked out they don't even care. So then we have this emergency shower for chemicals and shit. So you point to it and say, 'Over there! Hurry. They hate water.' You yank her in the shower and let it rip. Next thing you know, she's quit freaking out because the ants are off, but there's an awkward silence. She's dipping wet and naked, but the ants are gone. So you just nod and drop trou right there. Then you go at it. It's fucking hot. Swear to god."*

I left Party Bob in the kitchen with his whiskey and women and found myself back at the hot tub. The zest of Party Bob lingered in my spirits. Meeting him had been quite an experience. Anne-Laure was sitting on a chaise lounge talking with some other tennis pros. Susan and Paul, as well as the two other women he had been with earlier were nowhere to be seen—probably upstairs. Anne-Laure saw me and got up. She came towards me and did the *come hither* with her index finger. "I want to talk to you," she said in almost perfect English.

We went deep into the backyard and found some empty wicker furniture in the shadows. We settled onto the love seat together. "Isn't eet nice?" Anne-Laure said.

"Yes," I said. "It's been a good day."

"It's such nice weather. I so relaxed." We kissed, and I played with her hair the way she likes. The party was at a distance. Ambient music found its way to our private corner. There was the chatter of people and the smell of BBQ with Troy at the grill. I could hear him raising his voice about how great his special sauce was. *"Troy's Hot Wet, Great on Breasts and Thighs."* It was just a nice, relaxing house party at a Southern Californian pace. It doesn't get much better than that.

"So who is the pretty teacher you talk to my student about?" she asked. She was referring to the boy from earlier that evening. The one I'd thrown the ball back to and told to behave.

"I don't know, Anne-Laure. It must have been that hot British one that works over there."

She elbowed me, "No eet was me."

"Aren't you supposed to be upset with me?" I asked. "Didn't I ruin church this morning?"

"No," she breathed. "I not mad at you." She kissed me. "At least you are good wis children."

WEEK SIX

A Footloose Pig with a Case of the Hinkies

I was on my way to another miserable Thursday night shift, and I stopped off at a Starbucks near Staples Center to get a coffee lift. I went ahead and decided to use their parking lot to swap out the plates on my van. Before each shift, I'd stop and get coffee somewhere and switch out my legitimate tags with some temporary tags I'd gotten from a dealer. I was doing this in the parking lot of the Starbucks when a Barista came outside and lit a cigarette next to the dumpster. The dumpster happened to be Starbucks' designated smoking area, situated out-of-sight from the customers. I hoped to get some insight on this *Smoking Area* matter from the nice, young Barista.

"Do they really make you smoke back here?" I asked.
"Yeah."
"Why?"
"I don't know," she replied with slight agitation. "Why are you back here?"

"I wanted some fresh air without having to hear James Taylor."

She exhaled smoke from her cigarette. "They don't want smoke interfering with the coffee smell, I guess."

"That's the reason?"

"My shift leader just freaks if we smoke near the door, that's all I know."

"Who gives a fuck about the smell? I come here for the caffeine, right?"

"No shit!" she said.

So later that night, about half-way through my shift, I wasn't a damn bit surprised when I saw that stupid cop in my monitor. He'd probably had a triple-tall latte earlier that evening, so now he suddenly had excess energy to go patrolling around Vernon proper in search of illegally parked vans. But apparently this copper hadn't consumed enough Starbucks to give him the energy to fully investigate. Instead, he just called a tow truck and drove away.

It was not a city-owned tow truck but an owner-operated rig. The driver appeared to be intoxicated and dirty. He spilled out of his truck, almost falling to the ground before he caught himself on the doorframe. But he was functional.

After what seemed like an eternity spent tilted at thirty degrees while being towed to the impound lot, we finally stopped, and he unloaded me. With over thirteen hundred dollars worth of cameras at my disposal, I still couldn't get an adequate make on my surroundings. But I did know one thing: I was wedged between other impounded vehicles on at least three sides—front, back, and to the right.

I let myself out through the rear doors. Feet planted, I collected a real make of the lot and the situation. The impound lot was run down and welfare-grade. The fence was patched in various places with rotten boards—these were possible escape routes. There was a shanty office that had old seat cushions lined up along its outside wall for use as makeshift furniture. The LA skyline was off to the north, so at least I knew that I hadn't been misappropriated into some Hillbilly nightmare where I'd be ball-gagged and humiliated.

The place was cemetery dead; there were no signs of life anywhere. The tow truck drivers' vehicles were gone, and to the best of my knowledge there was no patrolman or junkyard dog nosing around. The drivers were probably still out rounding up vehicles, carrying out orders of their fascist overlords and buying more liquor. With a little luck, I hoped, I could get out this mess and get some pizza.

Vehicles of all types were shoved and cornholed into every hole imaginable—the ultimate clusterfuck of impound lots. There were two trucks behind me and a sedan in front. Counting both ends of the van, I had a grand total of about an inch to get out. There was also another car blocking me in from the driver's side, but that didn't matter because I had plenty of room to pull out on the passenger's side. It looked like getting out would mean "bumping" into a few cars.

I was definitely going to damage both of the trucks behind me because they'd domino into each other once I got pushing on the first one enough. I was NOT excited about damaging these peoples' cars. They had probably been late for their shitty jobs and in a pinch had to take the first spot they could find. Now their car was towed and they were out a hundred bucks. It sucked what I was going to have to do, but I couldn't risk showing my face just to buy my van out of impound.

I was thinking on a cigarette when I noticed a tow truck pulling through the front gate. It looked like a Neanderthal dragging a carcass to his cave. The driver sat in his truck and waited as the gate opened under its own power. They'd gone to the expense of installing an automatic gate; ironic given the overall condition of the place. Removing a car from this lot was a physical quandary on the same scale of trying to pleasure an elephant, yet they had an automatic gate—the fuck-tards.

I snuffed my cigarette and returned to the van, closing the door quietly behind me. In position behind the wheel, I watched the driver roll his fresh catch off the truck bed and suck down a bottle of beer he'd fetched out of a cooler by the shanty. I made up my mind. I wanted some pizza. Now.

But it looked like something opportunistic was going to happen. So I kept watching. The driver vacated his post at the hydraulic lever on the tow truck and left the automobile to roll un-monitored from the bed. He sauntered over to the clapboard shanty where he whipped out his pecker and started urinating on the worn whitewash. He began spraying willy-nilly, covering the structure with a profuse geyser of beer-piss. It appeared that he was trying to produce initials, or perhaps draw a doodle, as many drunken men will do when they are urinating on structures. Then he began to stumble.

Then he fell.

He fell flat on his back where the last remains of his bladder drained back upon his body pursuant the forces of gravity. He was rolling around at this point, deliriously drunk, and trying to get to his feet. I put the van in gear and apologized for what I was about to do to the trucks behind me.

Objects in Mirror are Closer than they Appear

I was a few blocks away from the lot, laying rubber for the distant LA skyline, and laughing hysterically about the sap tow truck driver. He was rolling around in his own piss when I drove out the gate. Trying to get up, he just fell right back down as I sped off. I was doing about fifty, not paying much attention. Just hungry, laughing hysterically, and sort of hoping for a road sign to appear and direct me towards an interstate.

Instead there was a STOP SIGN—and I missed it. Slamming my brakes, I also almost clipped the front end of a new Dodge Charger. It was about to pull through, and I didn't see it until just before it was too late. Luckily, I was able to swerve and miss it. I could smell the burning rubber from my fat van tires as I hit the skids. I jerked back into my seat as the van came to a stop and my gut dropped into my lap.

I could hear what sounded like some pissed off Mexican guys yelling at me from the Charger, scolding me for being an idiot. As they had every right—it would have been completely my fault had we hit. I did the *I'm Sorry* wave, hoping they would understand that I accepted blame. Their windows were tinted so I could not see if they were satisfied. So I slowly inched forward into my proper lane at the stop sign. They swung around behind me. I pulled through and proceeded driving, cautiously this time. After a few blocks it was obvious that they were following me.

Keep cool. Just find the interstate and keep going. They're just fucking with you.

But I couldn't find an interstate, and it didn't seem as though the LA skyline was getting any closer either. Being that far away from it, going a mile or so only made it appear a tad bit bigger. I had been driving for about ten minutes, and they were still behind me. If I went a little faster, they went a little faster. I went further and further, through quiet South Side streets, industrial, sad streets. The skyline only got a tiny bit bigger as the minutes clicked by. Still no signs for an interstate, and still they were on my ass.

More minutes went by, and they still followed after me like a dog, blinding me with their xenon headlights. But at least they weren't cops—I hoped. Their tricked out Charger was orange with lots of chrome and tinted windows. They couldn't be cops, I thought, and if they were, they'd have pulled me over already—I'd blown that stop sign! My stomach wanted to be fed, and I wanted to get home. This playing it cool thing obviously wasn't working, they were still on my ass. That's when I got the greatest idea ever—car chase practice—a great chance to test my driving skills in case they were called upon during the robbery. Now at least I'd have some experience under my belt.

Fucking Fat Van! Let's move it!

I punched my accelerator. The pursuing driver punched his. His vehicle pounced right on my back. My monitor went out. I no longer had a camera visual on what was behind me. Then I heard the damp clank of a bullet piercing the metal frame of my van. Then another.

These sonsabitches are shooting at me!

It was the first time in my life I'd been shot at. Boy becomes man—a precious moment. But I was irritated.

You wanna fuck with me, asshole! You wanna ruin my pizza time?

The rear window shattered; the sound of glass spilling onto the floor sounded like a bag of marbles exploding on linoleum. The wreckless bullet plopped dead next to me somewhere in the cushions of the passenger seat.

Missed, asshole!

Instinctively, I thrust my arm below my seat for my piece.

Cranked the wheel.

Kicked the E-bake.

The van spun around, tires screaming silly. I kicked open the door and dealt three rounds from the thirty-eight.

Dink, Dink, and Dink.

The pursuers took the slugs in their door and skidded past my van to avoid collision.

I tossed my weapon onto the passenger seat.

Slammed the door.

Pulled the van around.

Laid Rubber.

Now *I* was chasing *them*. I'd been able to maneuver my van and get behind *them*. The decision was theirs to end this nonsense and speed off. Fate was in their hands, and I sort of wished they would retreat at this point. My heart was racing...I'd just shot at people, I realized. Shot at them! I wasn't a soldier in a war. This wasn't Iraq, but I'd shot at people. Defending myself, I'd actually shot at people! That's scary, but the overwhelming feeling was brief, because all too soon one of the hostiles poked his head out of the passenger side. He turned around and faced me, a baldheaded thug just as I'd pre-judged. He took his time to line up a shot. He was going for my tires.

Get ready motherfuckers.

I punched the accelerator. The thug's eyes opened wide and he quickly jerked back inside the vehicle. I buried my bumper into their wheel well. The maneuver came with the sacrifice of losing my windshield. The glass sprouted a thousand cracks and I could no longer see. So I wound my hat around my fist like a glove and cleared as much glass away as I could. I could see again and saw that the Charger was in the pits. It must have spun out and jumped the curb because it was slammed up against a street light about a block back. It looked like the thugs were hung up pretty bad and would need a tow, at least.

I got my eyes back on the road, felt around in my pocket for a Valium, and drove. My gut grumbled. It knew that it was pizza time. It begged. It wanted food, instantly. I'd been chased, shot at, and almost shot at again. But now the ordeal was over and I just wanted some pizza and some sleep. I chewed the Valium in the meantime. My windowless van let a cool breeze steal in from the empty South Side street, and that cooled me down a bit. I tried a deep breathing exercise. I focused on navigating the street and breathed in and out calmly. My heartbeat slowed, and the wind whipped my face as I hit a larger street and could speed up. I began hitting some busier intersections. The street became two lanes on either side. A sign for the interstate had to be coming soon.

I found the 101 and hopped right on. The traffic was smooth, and my Valium kicked in. I was coasting now and felt like you do when you roll off a woman. That post-coital calm, when your thoughts are everywhere but there. You begin thinking positively about the future, perhaps that vacation you've been talking about. Everywhere but there in the moment, and definitely not in the past. I found myself thinking about those random things. Vacations. Pizza. Burritos. I was in another realm of conscience like after a good first-time fuck with a new chick. But this time it was after a car chase and a shootout. The first ever on my resume.

Now why was I here again?

I went back in my mind to the impound lot, right before all of this had started. I remembered pulling out confidently like I was supposed to be pulling out of the lot. I laughed at the tow truck driver and waved goodbye as he rolled around in his own piss. It was the same fucker that'd towed me. Then I remembered pulling out into the street and not knowing where I was. So I decided to just head for the skyline. I couldn't go wrong. It was just like the night when I first got lost in Vernon with Will. That night we both decided to just head towards the skyline. We knew that would get us back home. But I had decided to take one last look at the impound lot. That was where I went wrong. That one last look had gotten me into this mess. I'd just wanted one last look so that I could laugh hysterically at what had happened. Holy shit, wouldn't it have been a funny story to tell my friends—if only I could. That's when I just about broadsided the Charger. That's when I got to learn that I had the balls to shoot at people.

The next morning, Friday, I completely expected to get to work and find a gigantic, throbbing pink slip stuffed into my in-box. All I found was a reminder about the Christmas party. Cash bar. *Those cheap bastards.* But nothing changed the fact that I had been out all night and was over two hours late for work.

I began with what would be the first trickle of an endless river of daily coffee. At 10:29 AM I sat down at my desk and tore into my breakfast burrito. By 10:32 Katie hovered over my shoulder.

"Good morning Katie," I said.

"Those are good, aren't they?" She was referring to my *Depth Charge*, the breakfast burrito from Justine's Deli next door. A well known hang-over remedy for alcohol dependant IPD employees, the burrito wasn't helpfully complementing the fact that I was late. She was making me for a drunk.

"Is there a reason you're late today?" she asked.

"Oh, you know...alarm –"

"Late night last night?" She leaned in towards me, hoping to scent a miasma of lingering alcohol. But I didn't look or smell hung over, I was just late. Late, because I presumably had a medical condition that affected my sleeping, Ondine's Curse. She deflated and backed off when it registered. "Given your circumstances," she continued, "if you need to come in a little later, that's fine. But just as long as you're able to put in a full eight hours a day. You've been doing good work, so we want to treat you like a professional."

"Okay," I said, biting into the burrito. "I appreciate your understanding."

"How are the treatments going?" she asked.

"Katie, I didn't get much sleep last night... as you know." She nodded. "It was a real late night, and I appreciate your understanding." Then I smiled widely and said congenially, "I was actually involved in a car chase until past four in the morning. I went out for a slice of pizza, and the next thing I know, I'm being chased and shot at by armed thugs. It really affected my sleep and I'm glad that you understand."

She slapped my back and cracked up laughing like we were old buddies. "You're so funny! That made my morning!"

Katie wandered off, still laughing, and left me alone with my burrito. But I was still faced with the reality of the eight hours that remained in my work day. Some days, even two and three cups of coffee weren't enough to get me through them. And more than once I'd fallen asleep in my car during lunch and not come back to the office until late in the afternoon. But no matter how much I worried about it, *not once* did anyone say anything about it. What the fuck was wrong with these people? Better yet, what the fuck was wrong with the business school that deviously fictionalized the lofty demands of entry level work. "Introduction to Nobody Cares," that should be a new mandatory class!

Days like this, my mind was completely shot. Friday mornings in the office after the Thursday night stakeouts were blurs. But it was imperative that I show up and clock in. It was of utmost importance to keep a low profile and not give anyone a reason to get suspicious. I had to appear five days a week for my eight hours and maintain a reasonable level of output to avoid questions. My mind refused to operate on those Friday mornings, but I didn't bother pushing. So to play catch up, on the following Monday, I'd do actual work, real work, for about four hours instead of the normal two that I put in on most days. I even had Katie fooled. She had made that clear earlier.

IPD, like most companies, monitors internet traffic. So on my mindless Fridays I was forced to pass time the old fashioned way: doodling. My sketchbook portrayed the sweeping story of my struggle as a doodle artist developing his craft. A full body of work, it starts out crude and rudimentary. In the beginning I am an immature daydreamer so horribly spoiled by the overabundance of free drawing paper and ink pens that I would impulsively doodle the first blip of imagery that crossed my mind. Many examples of my early works are free-form squiggles and unobsolved depictions of strange lunchtime nap nightmares: disfigured stick people and lollipop-shaped trees with manifestations of evil. But gradually, a thematic content emerged, and a story develops of the Stick People's cultural advancements. They eventually begin riding horses with four legs across, in a row, rather than in depth-oriented sets of pairs. We learn of the stick peoples' mating practices in my most sophisticated segment, *1000 Ways to Stick It*. Sadly, the fate of the Stick People, their eventual demise, is a tragic visual narrative. They perish in a horrific prairie fire.

After a few sweeping movements in my early work, we start to see the emergence of my experimentation with a subject that would lead me to find my soul—my artistic voice—Krissie's boobs. Drawing boobs is no groundbreaking achievement. Similar brilliance liberally adorns public bathrooms and dry-erase boards in golf course locker rooms. Art historians will refer to this early period of experimentation with the candid subject as the *First School*. During the *Second School*, also referred to as the *Spring School* because of its playful flirtations with human sexuality, I venture beyond the realm of nude tits and dive right below into the world of naked ass. The *Spring School* was brief, and original productions from this period are rare and valuable if verified to be authentic. An important white paper by notable art scholar Chase S. Cox dictates a hard look at the potential cause for this weak, almost drip-like amount of doodle. He suggests that, because the artist kept his studio in a professional workplace requiring a tucked shirttail, the boners caused by the subject matter caused the artist to hastily flee the *Second School*. However, the unfinished *Spring School* opened the doors to the artist's final home and the resting place of his style, the *Making Fun of People by Drawing Funny Pictures of Them School*.

Touchdown Mary

Unanimously lauded by art historians as my finest work, *Touchdown Mary* introduced the art world to an unforgettable pear-shaped heroine.

Outfitted in a never-ending rotation of faded stirrup pants, circa the mid-nineties, and baggie sweaters, this insurance claims processor is a holy terror when she builds speed in any office hallway.

Legs churning, her peeled eyes dart, examining the landscape for both prey and predators. Chugging puffs of breath extort from her agape mouth. Like a snake's rattle, the wheezing communicates *"halt, danger."* Her head is oversized and confident. Deranged Young Professionals standing in her merciless path should stand tall and erect, backs flat and stiff against the nearest wall. Clear up as much hall space as possible. Avoid being trucked down by Touchdown Mary as her heavy footfalls unmercifully beat the floor. As soon as the message is dispatched that baked goods are available in the break room, the hallways are not safe. The unstoppable juggernaut is loose.

Someone had brought doughnuts on the late Friday morning of December 16th. Upon immediate dispatch of this news, an intense front between indecision and sloth bit its way between the thoughts and minds of the workers at Independent Plumbing Distributors.

Temptation:
"There're doughnuts in the kitchen!"
"Doughnuts? Oh that sounds great. I'm starved."
Indecision:
"You know... I shouldn't. All those carbs and all that fat. I really shouldn't."
"You know what? You're right. I think I'll pass too."
Acquiescence:
"Oh why not. One won't hurt."
"You're right! Hurry, let's go before they're all gone."
Then comes the stampede. Sloth. Touchdown Mary and her swarming pride are tipped off by their highly evolved ability to discover baked goods. They transmit to others of their kind, via pheromones, the precise coordinates for the feeding.

I was lingering in the hallway, acting like I was waiting to use the copy machine but in fact just lingering. Mary was under the spell of her instinctual predatory pursuit. She exploded around the corner with me standing in her path. She did not make eye contact but somehow her stiff arm blindly found its way to stuff itself sternly against my sternum, knocking the wind out me.

Out of my concussion came the most surreal flash of artistic enlightenment, *Touchdown Mary*. I crawled back to my desk across the carpet. Severely winded, I had to fight for my life against the charging herd, trampling me as I struggled against their charge.

I was soon safe, at my desk and alone; a comfortable distance from the feasting and probable elbowing. The slapping sounds of lips and tongues found its way back to my desk as the predators devoured their catch. I relished the primal aspect of the sounds. They added vigor to my work environment; the heathen feasting bolstered my muse to create my masterpiece.

I immediately got to work on sweaty, puffy, pear-shaped Mary. I drew her juking around the hallway's corner. She wore an old timey leather football helmet and clutched a chocolate cake like a pigskin football. Bits of crushed up entry level office workers were mashed between the damning spikes of her sharp cleats. Drool ran down her chin. Her jagged teeth bit down firmly against the tender flesh of a young doughnut.

I, the Deranged Young Professional, frantically sketched in safety behind the three walls of my tiny cubicle. The vehement grit of my artistic output was, however, not done solely for the sake of fine art, but for a just corporate cause. For I truly hoped that, through my art, the hopeless could have hope. I hoped for a new corporate policy to ban baked goods and make the work place safe once again.

WEEK SEVEN

Merry Fucking Christmas to you and yours, Reader. I hope your holiday plans are more substantiate than mine. I wish you a wonderful weekend and a fabulous Christmas holiday on Monday. Since the holiday falls on a Monday this year, it affords me the opportunity to celebrate something I actually care about, which is getting sloppy drunk and disorderly on a Sunday.

With the robbery plans, I did not make it home for Christmas to see what was left of my family. My only hope for a decent meal, Anne-Laure, was in San Francisco consorting with other French socialists with whom she shared relations. My parents were upset because they actually wanted to see me. They had recently become proud of me. I had been estranged from their custody for over six months and had yet to ask them for any help. I was gainfully employed, and to their best estimates, not homosexual. An Italian mother and a WASPy father couldn't ask for more from their son. However, the announcement of their decision to divorce indicated that my successes had failed to obscure the family's general dysfunction.

Angry? Of course I was. No one wants to see a divorce lawyer get paid. Especially two lawyers, which is usually the case with divorces.

When two people want a pizza, they can share. But when two people want a divorce, they have to place their orders with separate vendors, which I guess would reveal an important truth about marriage. When two people can no longer share, divorce is likely. Therefore sharing the same divorce lawyer is improbable.

But the advantage in all of this for me was that it removed the possibility of an unexpected visit from the folks during the holidays. Their dropping in unannounced was something I was used to during college. I can't begin to tell you how many expensive water bongs were smashed and dirty magazines ripped to shreds by Mother during those four years of her unexpected visits.

If I had told them that I didn't have the money to fly home, or that I had to work, they would have undoubtedly insisted on Christmasing in Los Angeles. This intrusion would have gotten in the way of my strict preparation schedule. So I told them I was deeply upset by the divorce and wanted to remain neutral *and remote* during the whole affair. The reason I gave them was this: *"I don't want to taint my relationship with either parent during these proceedings. I want to keep my options open in case either of your eventual remarriages results in disproportionately better inheritance prospects for me."*

But getting salty over spending Christmas alone is only for people whose souls are deader than all the dead Christmas trees in the world. For me, there was drink.

Christmas Day

I'd heard that the oak-paneled bar had a fireplace. This made me decide that I wanted to start the Christmas Day Bar Crawl sipping peppermint schnapps in front of a hearth. I was certain this was how Jesus wanted me to celebrate his birthday. The stone hearth would be comforting like a warm, familiar bosom. It would cast the hotel bar patrons in a more wholesome light—it was Christmas, and it was a bar, so there was only so much wholesomeness one could hope for.

So there I was, seated at the bar, wearing a suit and an open collar, and sipping my first peppermint schnapps. A ragged mound of wrinkled flesh of an old lady cut her way through the thin crowd of miscreants and ordered at the bar. Her hulk hung wearily on hunched bones.

"Cutty, no ice," she ordered.

She was well-dressed in a ladies suit of heavy, expensive material. She had an ornamental pin, gold with pearls, attached to her crisp lapel. But her dreadful skin hung upon her like thick woolen sheets that had been hung out soggy to dry in a musty shack. She's been ridden hard and put away wet.

"And a Freddy martini," she added.

Interesting.

"Pardon me, but what is a Freddy martini?" I asked her.

She glanced at me, but I was caught by her bright blue eyes. They held my gaze and we locked. "Freddy used to be the bartender here," she said, looking me dead on. "In those days most people would order a dry vodka martini, shaken, and up. Up means in a martini glass. *This* was the place and *that* was the drink, honey."

"Thanks for the local history, ma'am."

Her drinks were ready, but something was amiss with her heaping bowl of Scotch.

"Sweetie," she called to the bartender, "may I have a straw?" The woman held out her glass and the bartender slid a straw into it with a no problem polish. She found my eyes again, taking note of my bewilderment and need for explanation. Through the wrinkled curtains around her eyes I could sense the no-nonsense sincerity of her striking blue eyes. They were the only exposed body part that wasn't wrinkled. "The alcohol dries out my lips, sweetheart."

"Dries them out?" I choked.

The old lady went back to join her husband in their corner booth. He was a large man and wore a well cut navy jacket with a dark red tie. And he was old. Both he and his wife were sophisticates of a time when manners, respectable clothes, and stiff drinks were appreciated. Society has taken a real dip since their day, when Freddy served martinis in this bar. Jeans have ruined this country. Jeans and divorce.

The Day after Christmas, AKA "Boxing Day" in Countries Where They Respect Jesus

I should have known that going to a hobby shop on the day *after* Christmas would increase my chances for encounters with dorks—role play gamers, model builders, and sorcerers. The reason they were at the hobby shop on Boxing Day was this: wise parents.

Wise parents are smart enough NOT to buy all that nerdy shit for their kids at Christmas. But grandma and grandpa fucked it all up when they sent money. The Christmas cash enables little Simon the Space Cadet to go to the hobby shop and spend freely to stave off sex until his mid-thirties.

So there I stood, in the neighborhood hobby shop, Taco Bell adjacent, surrounded by perhaps the lowest of all hobby shop nerds, the model rocketeers. This section of a hobby shop offers the best chance to catch the Flu and hear computer words that you've never heard before. It's the first place to go if you want to be so irritated by driveling nerdiness that you want to kick a child's face in, repeatedly. It's the rocketry section, Reader!

But first, let me clarify why I know anything about model rockets in the first place.

As a summer camp counselor during my college summers, I was relegated to supervising rocketry class. Camper safety was second on my list of priorities. Being cool in front of the female counselors was first. That's why I taught the kids to glue the nose cones onto the ends of their rockets. See Reader, once the rocket reaches its peak, the nose cone is meant to pop off so that the parachute can eject. If the nose cone doesn't pop off there is no parachute, and the rocket becomes a blunt, speeding dart, headed straight towards the campers on the ground. Usually these groundling campers are daydreaming about free swim or milk and cookies. They are not mindful that speeding darts could be directed at their heads. I thought this prank was hysterical, but the camp director did not—especially on launch day. We witnessed scores of these speeding darts raining down from the sky at one time alone.

151

I ended up getting sent to teach arts and crafts. But in the end, so much as they wanted to, they couldn't fire me. They didn't have proof as I pointed out.

"Who are you going to believe, those brat kids, or me? How could you possibly believe what they say? Half of them can't even remember the last time they wiped. And most important, who in their right mind would tell a kid to glue on their nose cone? You've got to be kidding me. That's sick!"

So this rocketry digression should explain why I was standing in the rocketry section of a hobby shop. Or at least it explains why I knew where to go find a great detonator.

WEEK EIGHT

Veggie Tray

Anne-Laure had prepared for me a list of items for our veggie tray. I was in the grocery store gathering carrots, broccoli, zucchini, celery, tomatoes, mushrooms and cucumbers. We were putting the tray together as part of a bet. I would place the tray in the break room at IPD, and we were betting on how long it could survive—before being devoured whole. Anne-Laure bet that it would be a hit, everyone would love it. It would be a much needed alternative to baked goods, she thought. I bet the opposite. "You've never seen Touchdown Mary and her Baked Good Gang retreat in horror from a vegetable like I have," I said. "Survival for the vegetables isn't a matter of how long it is before they're eaten. It's actually a matter of how long they can keep before they rot."

We chopped at her place. I'd been staying there with her most nights anyhow. Looking around her apartment, I realized how empty it was looking. "How much does it cost to ship a box to France?" I asked.

"Just my shoes costing three hundred dollar," she said. "I have so much shoes."

After that, we just chopped. Not speaking. It was sinking in for both of us. We were having so much fun together in those days. But we were young, and life is life. And home is home, to some. But I knew in my head that I would follow her. After the bank job I would follow her anywhere she wanted to go.

I had to get to work early the next morning to clandestinely install my video equipment in the break room. I set it to capture all activity at the veggie tray and I programmed the clock to run on the screen so that we'd know who won the bet. Anne-Laure bet that the vegetables would be gone after lunch, so two o'clock, because some people eat late. This meant that if anything was left after two, I won the bet.

There was some initial interest in the carrots. Probably because carrots can be used in baking cakes. Being cake-related, this may have enticed Touchdown Mary and the Gang to nibble.

At one point Winston made a play for the cucumber slices.

"Yo, check this out," he said.

"You aren't going to eat those, are you?" I asked.

"No dude, look at Lenny."

Lenny had fallen asleep at his desk.

"Watch this."

Winston placed the cucumber slices over Lenny's eyes, and tiptoed over to Katie's office. He had a shit eating grin spread across his face, "I'm going to tell Katie that Lenny's hung over again," he giggled. But I saw this as a rip off. How was I going to explain to Anne-Laure that the missing cucumber was used for a prank and not even eaten?

I returned home from work with the remains of the veggie tray and a video record of the experiment. She was stepping out of the shower when I walked through the door.

Wrapped only in a towel, compromising, her tender eyes met mine and the towel dropped. *Damn, I did not want to go even a day without her.*

We were still in bed when she asked me about the bet. "We watch video in you apartment," she said.

"No. We can't," I replied. I couldn't possibly have company because of all the robbery materials left out in the open. "We're going to have to do it at your place."

"Why can't we go to your apartment? Mine eez sad."

"Mine smells, honey! I found a dead pile of laundry this morning."

She jabbed me in the shoulder, "You so crazy. What you doing in there?"

"Eat, sleep when I'm not here, you know..." The questioning made me uncomfortable. "Oh, why do you care anyway? Let's just stay here in your apartment, okay?"

"You not even taking shower at your apartment! I used to hear you. But you not shower there now."

"I shower at the gym," I said. Which was the truth. My shower, I had cordoned off for storing finished products of my tools and supplies for the job. Anything that had been cleaned and ready to go was placed in the shower and not to be touched. I caught her looking suspiciously at my camera sitting on top of a cardboard box. "Why you have all the cameras? For your spying job?"

I attempted to change the subject. I got out of bed and walked over to the kitchenette where the remains of the veggie tray were. I removed the paper sack covering it, and presented the results to Anne-Laure—mostly untouched. "Okay," I said. "I win the bet. So you're staying in America, and I don't have to move to France."

She examined the tray closely. "I not believing you. They ate at your work and you went to market and put back in." She took a piece of the zucchini and nibbled it, smiling up at me.

"Nope, that would be cheating, honey. But it looks like I don't have to learn French after all."

"We see the video first. I know you too much."

WEEK NINE

The Two Toilets: Chuck and Bert

I was at the Home Depot conducting speed and alignment tests on their shopping carts. I chose to go to the Home Depot because they have notoriously gigantic shopping carts that are perfect for hauling a million dollars in cash money. But finding a suitable cart was difficult. The slovenly home improvement types have a knack for beating things up. This left me with a seemingly endless supply of unfit carts.

I had to find a gem. Not only for practical purposes, but also because it's not good form to transport your first million in just any shopping cart. It has to be a regal coach. I needed to find a cart that had perfect balance on its casters and bearings and a sturdy frame. I should be able to release it down an aisle without it pulling to the left or right. It should go perfectly straight before bumping into an unsuspecting shopper. I was using such shoppers as my test targets.

During a trial with a particularly gimpy cart, I knocked over a bunch of rakes in the lawn and garden area. A Home Depot crank snorted at me in broken English—"Hey, are you going to pick up those rakes?" came out of his mouth like, "*Heyew gone peek uwp derake, my fren?*"

"Sure, I got it buddy," I said. "Why don't you go work on your English, the language that we speak here, and I'll tend to these rakes." I handed him a rake. "Here, then you can go rake something too."

You'd think that when these tourists from South America come up here for vacation, they'd consult their *Lonely Planet* or *Let's Go* travel guides first. Then they'd see that

155

English is the choice communication in the USA. I don't know exactly what language this particular rake specialist was speaking, but it was definitely not Spanish or English. I concluded that it must be Latin, since he was obviously from Latin America.

These people are *Latin* for God's sake! You'd think that a people renowned for their scholarship would show a little bit more aptitude for foreign language. But they must not have *Lonely Planet, Let's Go,* or even *AAA* in Latin America. So you can't expect them to know that they're supposed to learn English when they get here and want jobs at the Home Depot. It's a shame these Latin Scholars don't have real jobs. You'll never see a Latin scholar get a good paying job other than teaching Latin.

I finally located a premium shopping cart hiding out in the paint department. But first I had to unload a shopper's items from it. Not noticing me, she stood in front of the paint chip rack contemplating Crimson over Ox Blood. To be courteous, I stacked everything neatly on the floor and got the hell out of there before catching another scolding.

My first trial was all that I needed to know that this was the cart. It sailed straight down the aisle, gliding smoothly along the surface telling me that the bearings were fresh and well greased. This was the perfect cart, a cart worthy of hauling my fortune.

All that was left was to load the cart with what I came for: two of the ugliest, powder blue, low-tank, soft seat, trailer park toilets I'd ever seen. I named them Chuck Norris and Burt Reynolds. *Chubert*, for short.

I paid in cash and went out to the cesspool that was the parking lot. It was seething with Latin Scholars on sabbatical—hardcore, dance-around-the-hat Mexicans. They were poised to attack me because the instant an American emerges from a Home Depot in Southern California, he is immediately assumed to be unknowing in the home improvement arts. An army of poor Latin Scholars swarms him, offering up their consultation services.

"Uni hell widdy toilet my fren?"

"Oo wanna me work?"

"I come whiyu for de toilay."

"Tane doolars, I make toilet, no time."

"I goo pummer!"

"I—Can't—Under—Stand—You!" I screamed. Then I thought it would be funny to misunderstand the Latin Scholars. "No! You cannot use my toilets, sirs! They aren't hooked up yet! You'll shit all over the pavement, you idiots."

I needed the mad Scholars gone—quickly. I was about to load a stolen shopping cart in my van, and though I doubted it would get my ass hauled to jail, I didn't want to find out the hard way. So I removed Burt Reynolds from the cart and placed him on the ground. He was still in his box, which I think lessened the effect, but then again, this was all about shock. I sat down on top of the box and started raving. I squeezed my face up tightly and strained every muscle so that I turned bright red. *"Long drive! Long drive, must go potty before long drive home! Somebody get me a newspaper goddamnit! We're digging in! We're fortifying men! This enemy must be out-waited. You ass terrorist. You fucking turd bastard. Come out I say! Show your face, you coward! Oh no, I can't find any toilet tissue. Hurry, somebody get me the editorials. Perhaps one of those LA Times liberals will have an opinion insulting enough to sacrifice for the sake of decent hygiene!"*

The Scholars, worried, and stunned to silence, carefully distanced themselves. Soon they had all disappeared. I guess to get burritos or something. The coast was clear, and Chubert and the premium shopping cart were safely in my possession.

But where were the Latin Scholars getting those burritos from?

157

WEEK TEN

Phone Tag

It was very early on a weekday morning, about the time I'm supposed to arrive at work. Parked in the IPD parking lot, I sat in the Volvo, sipping a piping hot Starbucks. I watched as my coworkers trickled up to the door, read the sign on the front door, and danced excitedly back to their cars. *An unexplained obstruction has fatally damaged our local telephone exchange. All phones are down until further notice. Employees may work from home or take a free personal day. Normal business is expected to resume tomorrow.*

Management had placed the sign there, but the "unexplained obstruction" to the exchange *was* explainable. At about 4:30 that morning I visited the exchange and beat the living shit out of it with a baseball bat. I beat its ass so badly, you would have thought a Kennedy got drunk and drove over it with a Lincoln. Marci had been worth every penny of her phone call. I would no longer have the alarm issue to worry about, and I had the rest of the day to shop.

Being a cheap bastard, I never really let myself have fun spending money. A voice in my head, a mysterious dickering Yiddish voice, stops me every time.

"I'll take two for a dollar," the voice says.

"Sorry sir, but they're five dollars apiece."

"Then I'll just have one for a dollar."

"If you want one, it's five dollars. They're five dollars each."

"Fine, I'll take two for five dollars."

So I decided to make my big day of shopping as carefree as possible. If I thought I needed it for the robbery, I bought it. No second guesses.

I bought ropes: nylon and fiber. Duct tape and more duct tape. A bag of nails. Two pounds of gunpowder, a block of

158

wax, a yard of fuse, a roll of heavy paper, more gunpowder, two sandbags, and a fire extinguisher. A hatchet. Deranged people ought to have hatchets.

I went to a pharmacy: I needed a syringe, latex surgical strength gloves, saline, Metamucil and aspirin. They had a good buy on pepper spray so I went ahead and bought two cans. The second can was just in case someone pissed me off before the robbery.

This was all before lunch. Pizza: two slices. Then I headed over to Best Buy and bought three extra laptop batteries, a webcam, a cellular wireless card, and another laptop (bare bones, no bells, no whistles). I bought some flash drives to backup the surveillance data from my old laptop, as I was about to destroy the hard drive.

Off to Wal-Mart. Luckily, even in Gun-shy Liberal California, Wal-Mart still has a hunting department. And in the hunting department you can find a particular green spray that smells like deer piss. Yes, people pay money to smell like they did golden shower with a deer.

I bought a lot of it. I also got a breathable PVC rain suit from the tailgate party department. In the sewing department I bought heavy nylon fabric, thread, and a sewing kit. I also went ahead and stocked up on dry goods: nutrition bars, bottled water, and a first aid kit. That way, in the event my health insurance didn't cover bank robbery injuries, I could self-treat. I knew that I wasn't going to be using a flashlight, but I went ahead and got one. And new batteries. New batteries are important. Lastly, bullets. I needed lots of bullets for my heater, just in case. Thirty-eights. They look like brass cocktail weenies. I also threw in a hunting magazine and a Dale Earnhart *"Remember the Legend"* t-shirt. This, I hoped, would lessen any suspicion caused by my paying for all my purchases with cash.

Some of my items could only be found in specialty shops. I got my night vision gear at a camera shop in Hollywood. I told the asshole salesman that I was a movie director, so then he wanted to chat about my project. With nothing to say, I confessed that I actually just wanted to spy on a neighbor. That's when the prick tried to up-sell me on a better product for that purpose.

Next I went to find my telescoping billy club like the riot police had at college. I went to an Army Navy store. To avoid conversation at *that* store, I told the guy that I was pissed off at my girlfriend. Expecting a dirty look, once again, I was surprised by a sickening reply. "Then you ought to think about a trench warfare knife," he said. "I have some with brass knuckle handles. So depending on what she deserves, you can either stab her, or just punch the shit out of her." This guy was a true disaster. I had to play along.

"I think I'll just take the beat down baton, sir. Then, if she really pisses me off, I can whack her in the vagina so hard that her ovaries fly out her asshole."

He agreed quickly and enthusiastically. "Good thinking! But make sure you crank her over the head first. You don't want her remembering where her ovaries went."

I was finally so exhausted from shopping that I could have passed out in the clothing racks. I promised myself that once I'd finished scouring for raggedy clothes at the Good Will, I would stop for latte perk-up. I still had one more important stop on my list, the comedy shop in Sherman Oaks. They would have stink bombs there.

"It's All Greek to Me": *The Will Williams Guide on how to Ass Fuck a Deranged Young Professional*

Anne-Laure and I greeted Bri Bri, my acquaintance from the cattle call, at the main entrance of the theater. So what was Bri Bri doing there you might ask? Had she gotten a part? Was she there to check out the performance? Well, let me tell you something you won't believe: she was Will's new girlfriend...that's right...Will. The guy that looks like a troll and has no money unless he steals it, Will. He now had a girlfriend.

I gave Bri Bri a hug. "Thanks for the tickets," I said.

Bri Bri and Anne-Laure exchanged hellos, and then Bri Bri returned her attention to me. "Dude, you totally landed this for Will. That's awesome."

"Jealous?"

"Yeah! I have to hand out friggin playbills."

I accepted one of the bills from her inventory. Thumbing through it, I off-handedly asked her, "You're an understudy, huh?"

"I understudy here, and I'm an EMT to pay the bills."

"Anne-Laure here knows about ambulances," I chided. "It's how we met."

"Eet was the jumping cables," she giggled.

"I caught her car on fire. It's a funny story, why don't you tell Bri Bri, Anne-Laure?" Anne-Laure looked down at the ground, embarrassed to tell the story of how we met. "Come on honey, please?"

She looked up at me and smiled, "Okay. For you," she said. "So my battery die and he give me jump. Then I driving and car catch on fire. I call police and they not leesin to me and they think someone hurt so they send ambulance. But I was not hurt! And I so embarrassed. The police, they stopping traffic and everyone giving me middle finger, and then the fire truck coming and I so scared."

"The car wasn't really on fire," I clarified. "It was just the battery melting some plastic."

Bri Bri was doubled over laughing. "That's the funniest *How We Met* story ever! You two have the worst luck with cars," she said. "Will is still so sorry for destroying yours too by the way."

Lies.

Anne-Laure was surprised. "I thought it was black people."

"Black people?" I asked. "Where did you get that?"

"You say eet was black people destroy you car. Not you friend Will."

Bri Bri cut through the confusion, "Oh my gosh, babe, you don't even have a clue why you're here tonight, do you?"

I whooshed my hands back and forth in front of my face indicating *STFU*.

"So eet was not black people?" Anne-Laure asked confused. "I been so worried of black people ever since you telling me this...But eet was Will?"

"He obviously didn't tell you the truth about what happened!" Bri Bri snapped.

"He not say anything," Anne-Laure said helplessly.

"Stop this," I said. "Can we talk about this later, Bri Bri?"

"No, because you've been lying," Bri Bri continued. "You just don't want Anne-Laure to know what a jerk you were to Will."

"Okay Bri Bri. Now's the part where you really need to shut the fuck up."

"Oh do I?" She asserted herself, stepping forward. "Your girlfriend obviously doesn't know shit about you."

"We're not official!"

"That's not what I heard!"

"You heard wrong."

"I heard it from Will," Bri Bri snapped.

"What the fuck does Will know? He can't even get his own part in a play."

"Fuck you," she said to me. Then she turned square to Anne-Laure. "Babe, you're so cute. What the hell are you doing with this loser accountant?"

"What are you doing with a troll?" I asked Bri Bri. She looked at me a shook her head. It appeared Bri Bri wasn't the cute, ditzy blonde I'd first made her out to be. She was actually a cold, troll-loving bitch. A male's voice then interrupted us, "*Did somebody say something about trolls?*"

It was Chester. "What the hell are you two bitching about?"

Bri Bri answered first, "Chester, I think this asshole should tell his girlfriend the truth about his car."

"Now how did this handsome Deranged Young Professional get his car get smashed?" Chester asked.

"Yes!" Anne-Laure said. "Everybody need to start telling me why his car is smashed." She looked around the group, probing for an answer.

"Look Bri Bri," I began. "My car got smashed because your troll boyfriend thought I was sabotaging his audition."

"That's such bullshit —"

"Why nobody telling me this in first place? I thought it was the black people."

She looked like a confused foreigner asking for directions.

But Bri Bri wasn't going to let this go. "AND," she provoked.

"*And what*, Bri Bri?" I said.

"And why did you sabotage Will's audition?"

"I wasn't sabotaging his audition! I was *trying* to get the guy a fucking part!"

"Oh who would believe that? You're not even a fucking actor! It doesn't take a genius to see that none of what you say adds up." She took Anne-Laure by the shoulders. "Honey, there's a lot you don't know about your boyfriend...I believe we need to have a talk."

"I believe we need to have a talk," I whined. "Muh muh muh...Well that's great Bri Bri. I believe that everybody ought to believe in something, and I believe that *you* need to shut the fuck up."

"Well I believe that you're a fucking asshole and your girlfriend ought to know what's really going on!"

"*What really is going on?*" Anne-Laure was about to cry.

"Fucking bitches," Chester laughed. "What's so great about vagina?" He flipped his wrist and excused himself, "Somebody come get me when something interesting happens."

I left the two girls alone. Bri Bri had obviously convinced Anne-Laure that it was time to talk. And when that female anger gets its momentum, and sides are taken, trying to explain yourself only makes matters worse. The females want to feel like they made the decision, all by themselves, and that not a single word of sweet talk or apology on your part had anything to do with it. So I stayed put, by myself, in the lobby. I was by myself in a place that I did not really want to be in, and I was at risk of losing the only thing in LA that I was happy about.

So I decided to walk down Main Street and find a liquor store. The walk under a soft pink evening sky was just what I needed. Stepping into the liquor store at the corner of Ocean Park Boulevard was even better. In the doorway I passed a wino stepping out with his own package in hand. I nodded respectfully to him.

Walking back to the theater also gave me some time to think about the play. In preparation for the audition I'd read the script a few times, even ordered a DVD of an old BBC production. Wrecking Will's acting career had been important to me. But as the story goes, he wound up getting the part, and now I was stuck here, having to watch him fuck up a good play.

We were well into the first act when I found myself wondering why Anne-Laure had come back to sit with me. It must have been the assigned seating because she was distancing herself as far away from me as possible. She had not so much as even looked in my direction the whole time.

Crawling across her to exit the aisle and go to the restroom, I heard her mumble, *"You lie. What else are you lying about?"* What had Bri Bri told Anne-Laure? Even more important, what had Will told Bri Bri that got all this mess started? Could be anything.

At his core essence, Will was nothing more than a troll. His medieval ancestors had lived in hollowed-out trees in evil forests and feasted on the tender carcasses of babies stolen from noble cradles. The trolls oozed puss from their festering boils and histamine from their warts. They combed cockroaches from knaps in their brittle hair with the skeletal remains of the dead baby hands. They drank the blood of rats and chewed the fat of the lice plucked from their hides. They had huge, square heads with wax and mucus plugging every orifice, and they went to work in parking lots until their accountant friends could get them acting gigs.

So there I was, in hot water with my girlfriend, and there was Will on stage. He was nothing more than a troll, and he had fucked me. He was out to destroy the one decent thing I had going for me, Anne-Laure. Now she thought I was liar and God knows what else. What did she think about my whole "spying" gig? She probably thought that was a con too. This whole mess had me squirming miserably. I wasn't going to be able to get to the bottom of things until after the play, and that I could not take.

In the men's room, I spread out the remains of my supplies and reminisced about the now famous audition. I'd begun that audition drinking in the very same bathroom. Two pints of Jagermeister were stowed neatly, one in each of my breast pockets. I also had three cans of sugar-free Red Bull, and a Styrofoam coffee cup, having decided that Jagerbombs were a good idea. Because when everything is all fucked up: Jagerbombs. When a troll has fucked you over and your girl wants to act like a skank: Jagerbombs. Jagerbombs. Jagerbombs. Jagerbombs.

The play had finally let out, and Chester and I were alone talking. I was being a total jerk to Chester, almost screaming. "He must have told Bri Bri that I'm some sort of monster. That I hate-fuck panda bears or something."

"Bullshit, honey, Will's dumb ass couldn't make up anything that clever."

"Chester, he's told her something. That breeder cunt, Bri Bri, went and ran her mouth about it to Anne-Laure. She told her that I'm some sort of scumbag."

Chester pat me on the shoulder, "But honey, you *are* a scumbag. You *did* misrepresent to a bunch of your co-workers, and you *did* misrepresent the benevolence of your charity to Anne-Laure and trick yourself into her pants."

"That's not the point, Chester. He's gone and supplied vicious, untrue rumors about me and now people are starting to attack me."

"You lied! Anne-Laure's just pissed off because *now* she knows you're a liar. She probably doesn't even know about the youth hostel scam. She's just pissed because you lied to her about who really messed up your car. Don't read too far into it."

"I didn't lie about anything, goddamnit! That was a profitable venture. It was just business and nothing more! But Will had to go and steal from me. He's the one that started the war."

Chester lost his patience. "Lying for whatever reason is scumbag, and bitches don't like that shit!"

"Then it makes you a scumbag too, Chester. You knew exactly what the video was for and you went ahead and accepted a fee to produce it."

"I never said I wasn't a scumbag, honey. I'm a total low-life. But this isn't about me, it's about you."

"Okay, fine. So we're both scumbags, but what about Will? How come nobody's pissed off at him?"

"Hello, stupid! Will beat you to the punch. He had to explain to Bri Bri what you were doing at the audition to protect his own ass. So you lose! He's gone and blamed the whole damn thing on you. I just hope he didn't tell her about the youth hostel."

I slumped. Chester was absolutely right. Will was just saving his own ass, as usual. But even Will wasn't stupid enough to drop the dime on the youth hostel scam. "I have to find her!" I said.

"Who?"

"You know."

"Well if she won't take you back, you know where to look, sugar."

"I'm not talking about Anne-Laure...I'm talking about the source."

Bri Bri was still running her troll-kisser mouth when I found the two girls. She was still badmouthing me and perpetuating Will's lies to Anne-Laure. When the two of them detected my approach, Bri Bri looked out of the corners of her eyes, sneering.

"It's time for you to go." I ushered Anne-Laure away. "Could you? I need a moment alone with Bri Bri."

Anne-Laure fled, and Bri Bri stayed back with me. If she wanted to stand up to me, it was her time.

I went first, "Bri Bri, do you want to know the real reason behind the audition, or what?"

"It was because of the car —"

"Whoa whoa," I said. "No it was not."

"Let me finish!" Bri Bri snapped. "Don't interrupt me."

"The car had nothing to do with why I was at the audition!"

"Well Will didn't destroy your car on purpose."

"What do you mean he didn't do it on purpose? I watched him do it!"

"Bullshit! Will would never do that."

"You obviously don't know the whole story!"

"I don't believe a word you're saying," she said. "Will told me that he borrowed your car, had an accident, and didn't have the money to fix it. So you, being the prick that you are, felt that you were entitled to ruin his audition! That's what he said, and that's what I believe."

"Read the police report. He destroyed my car AFTER the audition. So the only fact that you have straight it that Will never has money."

"You're a lying DRUNK asshole."

"Will Williams is a liar."

167

"You're a piece of shit!" She got in my face. "You're the most disgusting piece of shit I've ever met. You're a liar, a fuck face, a........"

I remained calm and removed the remaining pint of Jager from my breast pocket. I uncapped it and zoned her out, looking very cool doing so. The spectators were probably thinking: *Now there's a guy that can handle his shit when a crazy bitch loses her temper.*

She stomped off to spread her infections elsewhere. I was alone again, and left with an empty bottle of Jagermeister. There was another empty bottle somewhere else in the theater, along with three empty Red Bulls.

That was not good.

I was blitzed and cranked and unsupervised in the lobby of a busy theater. And blitzed and cranked people do really fucked up things when they get irritated. Ask anybody who knows an itchy meth head a few days before welfare checks are cut. I was basically about to skull fuck the first thing that moved. And I was in this position for one reason: Will Williams.

Pretty fucking drunk.

And pretty fucking pissed.

I found him in the back of the theater chatting it up with some Theater Types. His enthusiasm sickened me. "You dirty cock sucker!" I yelled. Then I smashed him in the nose with my fist. "You promised refreshments!" I fell on top of him, tackling him. "Where're my free brownies, you motherfucker?" We both went crashing through the swinging doors, spilling into the lobby. I sprung to my feet, towering over him. "Where're the goddamn refreshments!"

"This isn't an audition for the Chargers!" Chester screamed. He dove in and broke it up before I could really start pounding. "What the hell has gotten in to you!" he roared at me. I stared through him blankly and caught my breath. The alcohol sweats seeped through my shirt and soaked into my sport coat. There was a hole in my jeans and

a matching cut on my knee just behind it. Realizing this irritated me more. My temper surged. I kicked Will in the ribs, "fucking bitch!"

Chester wrapped me up in his arms and wrestled me away. Theater Types formed a barricade of wimpy, puffed chests to protect Will as he lay frozen stiff on the ground. I felt great. I'd beat Will's ass in front of a crowd of people and had embarrassed him. But it was time to retreat. I knew how fast cops could arrive at the Powerhouse Theater.

I stepped out onto Main Street and saw Troy's Jeep Cherokee. Reggae music blasted through the open windows. He tapped the steering wheel with his fingertips and shook his long hair to the stoned out rhythm. I decided to keep my cool and find out exactly why he'd come. I approached the vehicle slowly, and when I got to his window, a long moment expired without either of us saying anything. He eventually turned down the volume, but remained silent and collected his thoughts, staring calmly into the windshield. He finally turned face to mine and looked me head on. "Dude, she's fucking pissed at you."

His eyes stood out like beacons on his sun-burnt face. They were deep and serious, and genuinely concerned. And I was a genuine idiot.

"Thanks for coming," I mumbled.

I skulked away from the Jeep, and Troy turned his music back up. The sound rode its way into my ears on a wave of warm guitars and low-end vibrations. It filled me up with a bizarre feeling of relaxation. *Maybe that was Troy's secret to staying calm, the reggae?*

But as I distanced myself, the music faded, and so did the fleeting sensation of relaxation. I was beginning to get emotional again. The events of the night were eating at me. *Now Troy was taking her home. Troy.*

I realized then that I'd better go ahead and call in sick to work. An inviting bar was just up ahead.

Uncle Milton's

Monday. The next morning was spent nursing the hangover with a slow, steady drip of Sprite and Nyquil cocktails. Consciousness was in and out of day-time television. My weightless mind floated on the warm cushion of Doxylamine, and my comatose body was anchored to the mattress.

During my second vomit trip, I stumbled over a roll of blueprints and crashed into my bank robbery workstation. The folding card table was loaded down with metal-working tools and parts for my mini-project, a collapsible catwalk ladder. Screws, scraps, and curse words flew everywhere. I wondered to myself, what the fuck am I doing? Am I really doing this?

Back in bed, the harassing clink from the overhead ceiling fan cursed me with its every rotation. I flipped through more channels, skipping shows and stopping on the commercials. My present company in TV Land obviously included the wretched unemployed, people with a need for online criminal justice degrees, but most were retired folks. No-questions-asked life insurance. Buzzers for when you fall down. Buzzers for when you pee your pants. Buzzers for when you need to be turned. By about 1:00 PM, I felt like I needed a buzzer for when I fell down, pissed my pants, and just plain needed a hug. I imagined myself an eighty year old man, penniless, alone, and bitter about a life that had slipped by. My weekly high point would be Saturday morning pancakes in my smoke-yellowed apartment. I feared that I would never have a descent retirement tucked away, a house paid for, or even a nagging old wife and a couple of distant kids. It'd just be sour old me. Alone with nothing.

I lay there stiff in the drab interior of my five hundred square foot apartment. I listened to its noises, the mini-refrigerator and the worn ceiling fan. They spoke to me in a clear voice. They motivated me. They got me thinking positively again, or rather pissed me off enough about the way things were to do something about it. Maybe I didn't care if I was dead, but would others?

So I talked myself out of bed and into the shower. Then I dressed and fought my way through intense sunlight to the Volvo. I was out to change sad state of my current prospects.

I called Party Bob and told him to meet me for a burrito, my treat. When we sat down to eat, I told him about my dilemma. But he already knew. "Troy already told me about your fuck up," he said. "Don't worry, I'll set up a romantic evening with the ants and you'll have Anne-Laure back no problem."

The plan was to give Anne-Laure a surprise that would escalate our relationship to new levels of heated passion and sexy fucking. She'd always wanted a tour of the Uncle Milton's laboratory, and I was going to make it happen. After we ate, Party Bob took me over for a reconnaissance.

I imagined the laboratory would be brightly colored and reminiscent of an old sci-fi movie, like the bridge on the Original Star Trek. There would be reels of data tape and huge boxy monitors with oval-shaped screens. They would be flashing monochrome lines of output and buzzing. There would be lots of over-sized knobs, levers with flashing bulbs, and spinning dials. Uncle Milton's after all was a relic of the 50's.

But to my surprise, the laboratory was up-to-date. The monitors hanging on the walls were flat screen LCDs on swivel joints. All monitoring devices had LED displays. There were no flashing bulbs anywhere.

First, Party Bob showed me the chemical shower. It looked like a garden hose with a pull cord hanging down like an old-timey thunder box toilet. He grasped the cord, "The most important part is where you rip her pants off," he said. "You can't be holding back. You gotta own it."

Next we went to his desk so that he could check his email. I found his collection of four Misfits action heroes. The Misfits were a ghoulish punk band from the late 70's, and their figurines stood intimidating guard over Party Bob's cluttered desk. I was playing with them when I noticed the dry-erase board hanging over his cubicle. It had this equation scribbled on it:

$$PV = FV (1+ i)^{-n}$$

"What's this supposed to mean?" I asked him.

"That's my protection."

"From what?"

"Stupid questions," he replied. "People won't come to my desk and ask me stupid questions when they see that. It scares them away." Party Bob's phone beeped and he glanced down at the incoming text message. "She's on her way," he said. Then he looked up from the phone and looked me in the eye. "Are you sure you really want to do this?"

Party Bob left out the back and went home— *"to fix a sandwich and take a shit,"* as he put it. I myself went to meet Anne-Laure in the parking lot.

I had no intention of pulling an *Ants in the Pants*. Having Party Bob invite her to Uncle Milton's was a just a maneuver to get her face-to-face, as we weren't speaking. I had something *much* better planned.

"What you doing here?" she asked when she saw me.

"I thought I'd surprise you."

"Well *surprise*, I leave!" She went to put her keys in the ignition.

"No," I said, and I let myself in the car before she could drive away without me.

"I still mad at you," she barked. "Why you lie to me? You did not need to lie!"

"I understand, Anne-Laure. I wasn't honest with you and I'm sorry."

"I not care so much about the car, but what else do you lie about? And not only that, but you act like drunk asshole last night when you could have just admit you were wrong! And now you lying again! I come here to see ants, not *you*."

"It's all part of the surprise, Anne-Laure! See, look at this." I showed her the picnic basket that was inside a paper shopping bag. "That's an empty picnic basket in there. I'm going to take you to the store and you're going to put *whatever* you want inside. Whatever wine, cheese, or chocolate, whatever you want. Then we're going to a special place up in the mountains. I want to earn you back. I care about you, and I want to spend what time we have together."

"You having a lot of work to do."

"Party Bob can show us the ants whenever we want. But tonight is a perfect time for this trip to the mountains. It's the best view in Los Angeles. Please?"

"We see ants," she said firmly.

"It's a picnic, babe. There will be ants."

Piuma Canyon

A sharp turn off Malibu Canyon is Piuma Canyon, a road that whips you around on slim shoulders and narrow needles until you reach the peaks of the Santa Monica Mountains. You get tossed around a bit if you're in a tiny convertible. But the rest of the directions I can't disclose. They're secret, a verbal record, never to be written. Those knowing of the verses are sworn only to repeat them when absolutely necessary. It's a hushed, inner circle accord amongst the young, unmarried men of Westlake Village—the directions to a panty drop spot of the highest caliber—*a sure thing.*

Moonlight poured into the tiny interior of Anne-Laure's convertible, illuminating her a thousand different ways, composing her differently each time. We arrived at the gate to the private neighborhood—it blocks the rest of the road to the top of the mountain. But you can reach your hand between the bars on the left side of the gate. Near the ground, there's an outlet box with a tiny switch cover. Lift the cover. There's a button. Push it. The gate will open. Now enter The Most Beautiful Panty Drop Spot in the World.

The neighborhood is quiet, the houses dark. Moonlight dances off their facades and illuminates the mansions, making them seem like enchanted palaces in a fairy tale. A dark asphalt street snakes its way through the middle of the spread, stretching to the top of the mountain, where the pavement ends and a hiking trail begins. Drive to the trailhead and conceal your vehicle by parking it in the brush. Now it's only a short hike to The Most Beautiful Panty Drop spot in the world—hidden in LA of all places.

As soon as we set foot in the secret area, Anne-Laure took a hazardous jump onto a boulder at the edge of the cliffs. Her panties were still on, but her jaw was dropped. Stunned and silent, she gazed in the direction of the Santa Monica Pier, approximately eleven miles away from where we stood. Billions of lights blasted radiantly beneath us, spanning from the downtown skyscrapers, through Hollywood, and all the way to the ocean below. It's seventeen miles of burning lamps in a straight line from city center to the beach—a burning city—right before your eyes. And you can *hear* the breakers below; smell them; see them.

I followed carefully behind her. "You're gonna bust your ass if you don't watch it."

"I can see de Ferris wheel," she said, and she gravitated towards the distant image without concern for footing.

I took hold of her hand to steady her. "I can't have you hurting yourself, Anne-Laure. The hospital is beginning to wonder about all the girls I keep bringing in."

She jerked her hand, *"No..."* She pulled away, excited by something else. "Look!"

The Ferris Wheel at Santa Monica Pier had begun its rotation. "Eet is beautiful here," she quivered. Her sensations were high and the breeze, a little chilly. I pulled her close to me, and she settled into my warmth.

"Do you know why the first Ferris Wheel was invented?" I asked.

"No."

"It was for the Chicago Exposition."

"Oh, *Eck*-postition?"

"Yeah, to *out do* the Eiffel Tower from the Paris World's Fair."

"Well eef French are not as good as American, then you cannot have the French wine I bring."

"Then you'll just have to seduce me sober. Good luck."

We settled onto a rock where natural weathering had scooped out a perfectly shaped bowl for two people to settle comfortably into. It had room to spread out your food and wine, and rest your back against the curvature to watch the breakers below and the illuminated city to the left. Per the lore of The Spot, this was legendary *Picnic Area*.

On our way to The Spot we'd stopped at a grocery store. There I humored Anne-Laure's femininity by insisting that she arrange the picnic basket. So, French bread, French wine and French cheeses were the staples. But among other things, English crackers, Danish butter, and Belgian chocolate somehow made it into the mix. "Everything is perfect, babe. You did a good job," I said.

"You too," she said. "This is beautiful up here."

I dug the bread out of the basket. "Let's start with this." I handed her the loaf, and she immediately broke off a piece to taste. "Let me show you a trick." I set out our votive candles, surrounding them with small rocks to block the wind, and I set the tub of butter over the rocks to soften it up. "I know how you like it melted."

"Ooh, while we wait, we eat cracker with cheese." She smiled, but I noticed a shiver. So I wrapped my wool boarding school blanket around her shoulders and kissed her. "Let's play a game," I said.

"Can we do while we eat?"

"Sure, it's sort of like truth or dare except there aren't any dares."

She finished chewing her strawberry. "But I like dares," she said.

"But there aren't dares. It's just truths like this: You ask me a question. Then I ask you a question, and we go back and forth. But there are no repeats. So if you ask me, 'What's the best meal you've ever had,' then I can't come back and ask you that same question. But I could ask a similar question like, 'What's the best mixed drink you've ever had, and where was it?'"

She dove right in with an answer even though I hadn't officially asked a question.

"The best mixed drink eez the Sidecar at Harry's Bar in Paris. The first time I have the Sidecar at Harry's, I was with my father, and I was fifteen. I had three Sidecars and when my mother come back from shopping. I was complete drunkard—like you!"

She drummed my shoulder laughing at her own joke and continued.

"I was laughing at my mother because she bought the most stoo-peed sweater I have ever seen. Eet was pink with little sequins. She looked like bimbo. She pay so much for eet. My father want to laugh too, but he did not because I was drunk and he was not wanting mother to get mad, so he say, 'Now Anne-Laure, be nice to you mother. Anne-Laure, you must have such poor taste. Your mother's sweater is so pretty. She should wear eet tonight, and I should take her to fancy dinner.' Then mother make ugly face at father and she say 'I leave you alone with our daughter and now she is drunk! You are going to have to do a lot more than compliment my sweater.' So mother knew the whole time that father and I thought the sweater was ugly. So now whenever I have Sidecar, I think about that stoo-peed pink sweater that mother never wore. Not once."

I was laughing hysterically at the thought of a drunken teenaged Anne-Laure. Harry's Bar also happened to my very own favorite place for a twelve dollar beer in Paris. Paris. She really was going back to Paris.

WEEK ELEVEN

Feast

This had to be one of the hardest decisions to make during the whole planning of the robbery. Where to eat?

It was a big decision, because I was about to become filthy rich, and rich people have nice meals all the time. One after another. It's a blur, and they *forget* that it's a luxury. However, indigents like me only get to expense the luxury once in a great a while, making it a simple pleasure that holds great value. This was going to be my last meal as an entry level, poor Deranged Young Professional, so the importance of choosing wisely would affect the rest of my life.

I chose to go with sushi. My other hankering was Italian, but I had doubts that I could run up *at least* a three hundred dollar bill on boiled flour. And I just *had* to spend *at least* three hundred dollars, a quarter of a paycheck. This dinner had to hurt my wallet. It had to be irresponsible spending. Hopefully Anne-Laure's spiraling French wine addiction would help.

By my estimation, LA's most excessively priced sushi bar was a joint situated in a replica Japanese palace. Once a Hollywood Hills mansion, it was built by some rich jerk off in the early 1900s to house his Oriental art collection. Spending two days' pay on uncooked fish in some dead rich guy's living room was just the humbling experience I was after.

177

"How about we take your car," I suggested. "Mine's seen its better days." I could imagine driving up to the famous restaurant and the paparazzi scattering at the sight of my vandalized jalopy.

"Eet sold," she said.

"What do you mean? I wanted to help you sell it."

"I not care. There are more important things in life than money."

"Money has nothing to do with it, Anne-Laure. I just didn't want you to get ripped off."

"You worrying about money too much."

"Are you saying I'm greedy?"

"I just saying that you would haggle like old man in stinking Persian fruit market. I just want to sell and forget."

We arrived at the A-list sushi joint in my outdated, scratched, and dented Volvo station wagon. We turned heads for the worse when the valet took my keys. But once we got inside, things changed. Anne-Laure's toned legs exploded out her tiny dress. The musculature of her ass did its Look Both Ways as she glided across the room, attached to my hip. I was a bad boy. A bank robber with a shit-kicking grin. I had rugged stubble, and a vintage brown leather jacket, and I hadn't removed my sunglasses. People thought we were somebodies. People were jealous. I'll bet there were even a few couples wanting to swing with us.

But looking back, what I really think is that people just thought we looked like a great couple. Unfortunately, what's not clear to one's own self is often clear to everybody else—even strangers in a restaurant. It may have been the way she elbowed me, dissatisfied, when the maitre de showed us the table. People probably thought we'd been at it for years.

"I'm sorry," I said to him when we got to the table, "but my girlfriend doesn't like this table. We'll just sit down somewhere else so that I can start getting her drunk." She elbowed me again for that comment.

178

When the waiter arrived I ordered a Johnnie Walker Blue on ice. "She'll have a goose and cran...And bring a wine list too, thank you." When Anne-Laure gets oiled up things can go one of two ways. Tonight it went this way. I let her choose the wine—mistake. She was trying to be nice, a cheap date. "No...eez too expensive for a 2000 Cristal," she said. "The Brut Premier eez perfect. So when the waiter returned, I said, "Sir, I think I'm in love with the 2000 Cristal, and that's what it's going to be. Please ignore her lack of appetite and breeding."

Anne-Laure rolled her eyes, but chuckled anyway.

"Very well," said the waiter. "A bottle of the 2000 Cristal. And will we be having an appetizer?"

I had to think quickly. Appetizers. They usually have a high price to portion ratio. Higher the price, lower the portion.

"Japanese crab cakes!" I said. Those cost easily as much as an entire entrée.

The waiter left with our order and Anne-Laure settled into her seat "Good wine eez not about price. Good wine eez about the company."

"Yes, I think Louis Roederer is a great company."

"Ugh, it's the people...the company that you share the wine with. Something telling me you no like the company. You not like me."

"Anne-Laure, I care about you very much."

"The when was the last time we really make love?"

"I love you every moment of every day."

"Then why am I going back to France?"

"Because you bought a plane ticket."

She dug into her purse and yanked an Air France ticket out of her wallet. "It's just a piece of paper," she said.

"So rip it up," I said. She set the ticket on the table between us. I'd seen the ticket before, in her apartment, peeking at me indiscreetly from the kitchen counter.

"Is your *stoo-peed* spying more important than your life with me?"

"Honey, I told you. The spying is all over in a few weeks. You gotta trust me on this one. It's over and then we can have a normal life. I promise."

"You—Are—Naïve—Boy." She scooped up the ticket and shoved it back into her purse.

"It's your call, Anne-Laure. Nobody's telling you what to do."

"And that is the problem!"

WEEK TWELVE

Pint Possibilities: Debate. Fear. Indecision...Binge Drinking...Solution.

Mr. Eikenberry: "Nobody in our family drinks because it affects ones decision making."
Arthur (who is drunk): "You know what? I think I agree with you, but I can't decide."
Arthur - 1981

When I think back to that last night in the van, the absolute *last* stakeout, I picture it like a movie. A soft string section lightly whines "memories" music. The picture is scratchy and sped up because I'm remembering this, and I remember things in vintage film stock.

The last night of staking out was a model example of the data I'd gathered over the twelve weeks in the van. The trains blew by at 10:58 PM, 12:43 AM and 2:10 AM, exactly, not approximately. The cops rolled by four times in all, just as fast as the trains, and with their heads far up their asses, not paying attention to anything.

Plotted on a bell curve, four times was the exact amount of times I should expect the cops to pass with a standard deviation of 1.2. Civilian traffic crawled. I counted 32 passersby during the wide time period I had open for the heist. I should expect to see somewhere in the neighborhood of thirteen vehicles pass by during the time I needed to complete the job.

Ominous, thirteen, but I could live with it. There were no pedestrians. I had only seen two during the twelve weeks, giving me an easy estimate that no one would walk by.

Given the data my best choices were:

- Thursday night between 11:00 PM and 2:00 AM, and
- Early Sunday morning, what I'd call a Saturday night job, between 1:00 AM and 4:30 AM.

These options led to serious debate. What if a Saturday job would only yield a small sum, like a hundred thousand dollars? What if the workers all cashed their checks and took off with all the cash on Friday? What good is a pile of cashed checks? That answer is *nothing*. The checks wouldn't even make good tissues to dry my tears because they're not absorbent. But at least a hundred large would be a step in the right direction. It would be a nice down payment on a cannon to blow my fucking head off. A Saturday job would occur after the cash was picked over, and for that reason I was vehemently against it. It wasn't worth the effort.

But what if on Saturday there was still a reasonable sum of cash left in the bank after Friday's run, say *seven hundred thousand dollars?* Then would that be worth it? Probably. But there was NO way of knowing how much cash would be left in the vault by Saturday night. So I was stuck being in love with Thursday—the day I knew there would be a maximum load of cash. But what if Thursday was too dangerous? According to my data, as well as my gut feeling, it was markedly more dangerous.

But every reason I had for the Thursday job got trumped by reasons to do a Saturday job. The risk, the gut feeling. Then, after I'd settle on Saturday for a while, my cold logic would pull me right back to Thursday—going for the mega millions. No crooked job is worth doing unless done in excess, I thought. If you're going to spray paint curse words onto a water tower, why not toss poison into it while you're up there?

After the abysmal teeter-totter repeated itself about a thousand times, I had a random fascination with Friday. Then Sunday! But I hadn't even considered Sunday. I knew nothing about Sunday! I was going completely mad. I had no answers. My thinking was bat shit.

Why not call the whole thing off? That's right. Call it off, I thought. Save your ass from having to shoot a bunch of police and run to Belarus. Call the whole thing off and get rich by buying loads of lottery tickets. Yes! And *steal* loads of lottery tickets too. Venture down crowded streets striking senior citizens and take *their* lottery tickets. You're bound to hit the big one before the papers catch up to you and expose your menace—"The A-Lotto Psycho!"

No...wait! Why not just rob the bank's armored truck when it makes the Thursday cash delivery? Walk up to the truck in a gorilla costume and pull the thirty-eight on the drivers. Tap a vicious gas line on the bastards and take off down the street with all their money. Anybody witness to the scene will check into the nut house, leaving not one sane person to testify against you—a gorilla ices an armored car—they'll know that they've cracked up for good.

Add a touch of auteur. Rampage into a convenience store wearing the gorilla suit and buy all the bananas. Start throwing stacks of bills at the cashier and snort. But don't forget to steal all of *his* lottery tickets too. Then, run out of the store and cover the sidewalk with the bananas. That way that the cops and townspeople giving chase will slip and break their knees. Remember, they're chasing the money, not you. They think you're an escaped gorilla with lots of money. They think it's a free payday. They just want to get their hands on your money and that roll of lotto tickets before the zookeeper comes to haul your ass in.

Quickly, board the first cab in sight and scream to the driver, "Amazon!" Command him, "Take me back to the homeland! These crazy people done locked my ass up!"

I suddenly found myself reconsidering a Friday night job—involving a clown costume and a giant helium balloon sculpture to float away on. I *had* lost my mind. I was slipping into insanity. Clown costumes. Gorillas. Lotto tickets...what was this? All my hard work and meticulous data collection *could not* point me in the right direction after all. A sexy chat would not even suffice in this case. Even in the most dismal lows of my life, a sexy chat had always picked me up. But this time it had to be me. I alone had to make this decision. I couldn't entrust my fate and fortune in blind faith to some phone sex operator. How would I explain the situation to her? And she'd never fully understand the data because only I had the gut feeling from my experiences in collecting it. No matter how gifted and smart phone sex operators are, they just couldn't help me in this situation. No matter how much uncontestable evidence there is to show that the phone sex industry has had a profound, beneficial effect on my life—influencing many of the important decisions that I've had to make—I just couldn't do it this time.

Sexy chat operators are pros at helping you solve everyday problems. Small problems. But this was no itty-bitty problem. This wasn't like getting a girl pregnant. This wasn't like getting pulled over for DUI, and a couple grams of blow just happen to be in your glove box. No, this was a REAL, BIG problem. There were consequences and more importantly, DOLLARS on the line here. So it was time to introduce yet another important decision making tool to this situation: *booze*. It was time to grab a bottle of rotgut whiskey and sit down on the toilet. That way I wouldn't have to move until my mind was made up.

PART IV

HEIST

The pounding on my studio door ripped me out of bed. I sprang for my piece, close by on the floor. *I'm not even out the door and the goddamn pigs are already on my fuckin' ass*, I thought.

POUND, POUND, POUND.

That's pigs for sure. Pigs always knock three times. Should I just start shooting, or should I let them in, make them coffee, and then shoot them?

No, no, no. Shoot through the door! That way if they're nice guys I won't feel guilty about shooting them.

Pillows! Grab pillows to muffle the sound. Tip toes.

POUND, POUND, POUND.

Go ahead and open the bathroom window now. That'll save time during the escape.

What if they have the place surrounded?

Grab more bullets. Peek out the bathroom window.

Buzz...My cell phone rattled against the vinyl-top card table. *How did they get my number? Don't fucking touch it! Let it ring. It's tainted. Check the windows.*

I slowly peeled back the flimsy plastic slats on the Venetian blind in the bathroom. No cops in sight. No plainclothesmen in unmarked vehicles. No snipers in the palms. I checked my body for lasers. Seeing none only frightened me more. *What are the pigs planning?*

"Fuck 'em!" I shouted. "All they can do is talk me out of it. I haven't even robbed anything yet!"

I hid my gun in a pile of dirty laundry. Cops never want to look through dirty laundry, and the gun was the only thing they could pinch me for (so far).

185

Alright, get it together. Open the door. Hear their side of the story. If they have a point, 'Don't rob a bank, you're a smart kid with a bright future,' then take their advice and don't rob the bank. But if they're just here about the violent Armenian in 309, just be cooperative and forthcoming. Get them out of here before 9:30.

POUND, POUND, POUND.

I jumped, knocking a box of bullets off the card table. They spilled onto the carpet, and I quickly kicked them under a pizza box.

Buzz...

There went my cell phone again.

It must be the cops. They must know that I'm inside the Hideout. They must have trailed me when I left work. And now they won't leave—those persistent bastards! Irritating me isn't going to convince me NOT to shoot through the door and plug them full of cocktail weenies. I'd hurry up and stop this harassment if I were them. Lives depend upon it!

I finally decided to pick up the cell phone.

The name on the caller ID brought me to my knees, "DO NOT ANSWER."

Falling to the floor, I grabbed a handful of what Valium I could off the card table. It was all that was left I could do.

POUND, POUND, POUND.

Miserable, dreadful, I chewed the pills, pegged to the floor, unable to move.

"ROBERT! Your mother loves you! Now open this goddamn door!"

Mother needed ice because her foot had swollen so much that it was popping out of her shoe. She had practically kicked my door in, and I could imagine the police arriving at any minute. Having a police shootout with Mother barking orders in my ear would just be too much. I'd rather turn myself in now that she was here.

As usual, she began playing nosey throughout my studio. The swollen foot was apparently not enough to limit her snooping.

"What's all this cash doing in your refrigerator!" she cried.

"What are you doing in there?"

"I'm your mother. I can look wherever I want"

"I don't trust banks!" I answered.

"Where did you get that money?"

"Why don't you crawl in and shut the door."

She slammed the refrigerator door, "Don't wish death upon your Mother!" she hissed.

"What are you doing in LA, Mother?"

"Shopping!"

"Well I'm not selling anything here, so leave."

"What's this?" She grasped the edge of my Velvet Elvis wall hanging. It was my souvenir from the Bakersfield flea market when I bought my thirty-eight. Then she ripped it down off the wall. "What is this ugly thing? And where's your ice? Why don't you have a proper refrigerator? Why aren't you fixing an ice pack for your poor mother's foot? She spent all day traveling. Why are you sitting there on your rear-end like your father? Why don't you even have a proper chair for your mother to sit in?"

"I do too have a chair!" I pointed at my folding camping chair leaning against the wall. "There. Sit! And sit still. I have plans this evening and I have to get ready."

"One of your satanic concerts!?"

"A swinger's party...Now sit still and don't touch anything."

"Believe me, I won't, you filthy animal."

"Would you like a Gatorade, Mother? I'm going to the kitchenette."

"If that's all you have for your mother to drink!" She quipped, trying to get comfortable in the camping chair.

The syringe of rufinol was in the mini fridge. I poured Mother's Gatorade into the taller of two cups. Then I gave the tall cup a strong shot of rufinol from the syringe.

"What on earth are you doing with this?"

I turned around to see what she was talking about. Mother had discovered my thirty-eight. Using her foot she was kicking around my laundry, where she'd found it.

"Put that down!" I demanded. "You might hurt yourself."

"This thing is loaded!...You idiot! You have a loaded gun tossed in with your dirty laundry. You'll be looking for a sock and blow off your thumb!"

She emptied the bullets from the chamber like a pro, dumping them out into the palm of her hand and checking the barrel. "I'm taking this!" Then she tucked my thirty-eight into her purse and zipped it shut. "I'm taking this awful device, and I'm having it destroyed! No son of mine will own *firearms!*"

"I need that for my hobby, Mother. I joined a marksmanship club."

"Robert, if you're suicidal, tell mommy about it. Please. Mommy loves you, and mommy will pay for you to get help."

"I'm only suicidal when you're around!"

"Don't say that. You don't mean that." She attempted to loosen the shorter of the two Gatorades from my grip. But I wanted her to take the big one—the dosed one.

"No, take this one," I pushed the tall glass on her. "I'm trying to cut back on liquids to maintain good prostate health." I wrestled the short glass back into my grip.

She had the tall glass and I thought everything was going to pan out until she set her glass down on the card table, ignoring it.

"Dreadful! Just look at your sink!" She poked at my stack of plates and cups, visually inspecting the grit and grime.

She was stalling. She must have seen me poison her drink. Or perhaps it was just motherly intuition?

"For what you pay in rent, you ought to at least have a dish washer." Then she saw the dishwasher. "Oh, there it is." She opened it. "What on earth are these old clothes doing in your dishwasher?" She slammed the door. Thankfully she hadn't touched the clothes, leaving behind any traceable DNA.

"What on earth is wrong with you?" she went on. "This is not a clothes washer!" She slammed the dishwasher door.

"My washing machine is out of order at the moment," I said, "and the maid is on vacation!"

She rolled her eyes, "I have to use the potty, and as soon as I'm finished, we're phoning *another* maid, and getting you to therapy."

"You can't go in there!" I rushed towards the door to block her from going into the bathroom. "It's an absolute mess in there!"

"Oh, is that where you keep your dirty magazines?" She questioned. "Have you not grown up at all?...Well, I guess not. You don't even own furniture. You own a firearm but you don't own a proper chair."

"Did you expect a throne, Queen Elizabeth?"

"Move it. I'll just have to ignore your smut collection. I *must* use the potty."

I started wondering: do I say, *"Don't look in the shower?"* Because if I say that, she will. If I just don't say anything, there's a better chance she'll overlook it...But no dice.

"What on earth is a shopping cart doing in your shower?" She screamed. "Why are there toilets in your shower?" She screamed even louder.

I rushed in behind her to explain. "I'm watching it for a homeless person. He went on vacation and didn't have a safe place to put them...Aren't they nice?"

"What's a homeless person doing with toilets?"

"He's renovating."

Mother was wearing her rubber gloves as she often did during room inspections. Ignoring my pleas, she began digging around in my robbery ditty bag...at least because of the latex gloves she wasn't leaving behind DNA.

"What on earth would a homeless person be doing with night vision goggles?" She stormed at me with my precious goggles in her gloved death grip. "Don't you tell me you're doing a favor for some homeless person! I travel all the way to Los Angeles to check on my baby, and what do I find? You're suicidal *and* paranoid! You're a mess! I knew I shouldn't have let you move out here...with all these...these freaks! You should have gone to Virginia and gone to law school. But instead you come out here and God knows what you're doing. And what people you associate with, I hate to think. You need help! And I'm not leaving here until we throw out this garbage and get you to a doctor!"

She placed her purse on the sink and dug through its contents. She fished out a business card. "My friend Karen has a daughter living out here who *also* ran into a bad way. She was a cheerleader until they lost the Raiders. Karen referred me to this Jewish gentleman. Fink?...Finklestien? Oh, there it is. Fink. He should be able to treat you."

"Mother! For the last time. I am *not* crazy!"

"Oh but you are. You're very crazy. You're an absolute psychopath. You need help. It runs in the family...on your father's side. *But it's not your fault.* It's your father's. Don't fight me on this honey. Mother loves you. She's here to help you."

"Mother, like I've said a thousand times, I already have plans for the evening. So why don't you go and get checked into your hotel and I'll meet you there later. Say, around 4:30 this morning."

"I'm *not* leaving until we've made some progress with your mental condition."

"Mother, I really need you to save this for tomorrow night. Tomorrow night I'm free! We can go have dinner and do whatever you'd like. You can buy me whatever you want, law school, perhaps some vodka. Whatever it is. But I *have* to get ready. I have an important engagement tonight. You'll just have to understand and take a raincheck."

"Where are you going to bathe? You have a homeless person's shopping cart in your shower."

"I've been showering at the gym! Now listen, we've got to get going."

"Why couldn't you have been more like your friend Sam? He's learning how to run his father's dealership. He already owns his own home *and* rental property!"

"He's just *your* friend's stupid son! That doesn't make Sam my friend. Now *get out!*" But Mother stood firm as I tried pushing her along.

"You're going to wind up in prison, Robert! Just like that Johnson boy you ran around with. Prison!"

"*Prison?* What the hell are you babbling about?"

"What are you planning? Where are you going tonight? *And with whom?*"

"How's dad?"

"Don't change the subject on me!"

"What have you done with Father?" I asked.

"If your father finds out what kind of scheme you're into, he'll skin your hide."

"*What scheme?* What are you talking about? Tell me what it is you think I'm up to."

She pressed in, inches from my face..."You...tell...me!"

"I don't have to. You're in *my* apartment wasting *my* time! I don't have to listen to you! Not anymore I don't. So *get out!*"

"Whatever it is that you're going to rob or steal, *don't.*"

"How did you know that?" The old lead weight dropped heavily in my gut. She'd gotten me. How I don't know, but she'd gotten me figured out. So I decided to take a different approach.

"A mother knows *everything.*"

I began sobbing, *"It's just been so hard out here mother."* I needed her to get close to me. Very close. I needed to her to hug me. "*I miss you so much. I didn't expect it to be this way. I just need a hug...*"

She hugged me and stroked my hair, "There, there. Mommy's going to make it all better," she said. "Just you see."

One...two...

We're getting a maid in here, and then we're getting you over to Dr. Finklestein's, and then..."

*Three...*I buried the needle deep into her jugular, depressing the plunger as it slid in.

* * *

Anne-Laure stood outside my front door, alone. She heard the awful yelling from within and knew exactly what had happened. *Mother* had dropped in for a surprise visit. Even Anne-Laure, the Queen of Naps, could be awoken by the screaming of Mother.

But Anne-Laure did not have all evening to stand there undecided about what to do. She had her own plans for the evening. Big plans. A once-in-a-lifetime opportunity awaited her. *Mother's* inquest was now beginning to affect even Anne-Laure. But the sudden *quiet* bothered Anne-Laure even more. *Why was it so quiet now? What happened inside Robert's studio*, she wondered?

Then she heard something large being dragged across the floor. It was the terrifying low and heavy sound that only a dragged lifeless body can make. The friction against the stiff Berber carpet echoed within the tiny space of my 500 square foot apartment. It *had* to be a body, she thought. It was much too quiet to be anything else but the aftermath of a murder.

* * *

I was finally able to bed down to catch up on the sleep that Mother had so rudely interrupted. She wouldn't be interrupting me again.

I immediately drifted off, the Valium warming me and the sweats coming in bursts. Two more hours. Only two more hours were left to catch up on the much needed sleep to prepare my body for its quickly approaching demands. I also had to re-clean everything that Mother had touched.

*   *   *

Anne-Laure never made it back to her nap. The eerie quiet from next door made it impossible to relax. Not even wine would take the edge off. So she went ahead and prepared her dress for the evening, a long black dress, and put on her makeup. Part of her surprise plan was already ruined. Her date had become pre-occupied, perhaps outlaw. But she still wanted to look her best because there was always the chance that he'd come around. It was the beginning of her last weekend in America—and the beginning of the rest of her life.

*   *   *

Mother awoke. She smelled something terrible and was positive that she was surrounded by dead bodies. But she was too mortified to feel around with her shaking hands. It was a dark and cramped space. She thought that she was a dead body, too. She thought that she had been murdered. This was her afterlife—this was an out-of-body experience. A madman had killed her and stuffed her into a cellar. Her ghost, she thought, was supposed warn others, alert the police, and to lead them to the killer.

However, she was actually stuffed in my closet. And she was very much alive. And very much blitzed on rufinol. The smell of decay was my old shoes. A few pairs *she* had actually paid for. But she did not know this. All she knew was that she had to alert the police. She did not know that her son was sleeping soundly on the other side of the closet door. She did not know that I was near exhaustion and only needed a few hours to recharge so that I could rob a bank and save the life that *she* had forced upon me. That's all I wanted, to sleep and then go and rob a bank in peace. And that's why she was stuffed in a closet, and high. But she did not know this. So she *screamed*.

Mother's screaming ripped me out of bed for a second time that evening. But this time I had a better plan. I raced to the front door and swung it open. I was going to find Anne-Laure, but she was already standing there at my doorstep. "Anne-Laure?" Startled, she stood there wearing a black dress and fresh makeup. Beautiful.

"What going on in there, Bob?"

"Come with me." I took her hand, and pulled her into her own apartment. Then I shut the door and grabbed the back of her head. I smashed her face against mine—I kissed her hard. Seeing her was like sirens for a house on fire.

She tore away and slapped me. "You not een love wis me." But then she pecked tenderly me on the cheek where she'd struck. "Kiss me like that when you are really in love with me."

"I need your help, Anne-Laure. Just for tonight. I need you to chaperone Mother. *Please*."

"Not tonight. I have plan."

"I know that you *don't* want to leave America, honey. But I promise you. Spending an evening with Mother will make it much easier."

"If she anything like you, she must be complete crazy."

"Anne-Laure?" I took her hand and dug deep into her bright blue eyes, "I'm in some real big trouble, and if I don't go, I might not make it."

"Stop eet, Bob," she brushed my hands away. "If you in *beeg* trouble, jus com wis me."

"You don't know what kind of trouble this is."

"I have two ticket for us tonight..."

"Great, take Mother. Whatever it is, I'm sure she'll love it."

"But Bob—"

"But Bob will pay for everything. Just bring me the receipts."

"Would you just listen?" She hissed. "This is special night I plan for long time for us. And now you want to ruin."

"How are you going to get there, Anne-Laure? You sold your car."

She looked at me blankly like *I* had the answer.

Turns out, I *was* the answer.

"Mother has a rental car," I said. "You can have it."

She thought for a second. "What do you not understand about *special night*?"

"I don't know, Anne-Laure. I guess I just don't understand...But what I do understand is that in less than two hours from now I have someplace that I *have* to be. And if I don't make it, well, that's it. I don't make it...I *don't* make it. And I don't think that would be a very special night for either of us.

Anne-Laure: beautiful, sweet Anne-Laure. Silent, contemplative, wasting my time: Anne-Laure. She stood there like she had all night to think about what to do. As mother screamed her head off next door, attracting cops, sweet Anne-Laure just stood there thinking.

I dangled the keys in front of her face. "Mother's rental."

Anne-Laure accepted the keys into her custody, exchanging no sensation. It was her way of telling me that accepting the keys was the result of a very complex decision.

"I do eet," she finally said.

* * *

I frisked Mother's purse for my gun, found it, and re-hid it elsewhere in the hideout. "Mother? You in there?" I asked, tapping on the closet door.

"Oh thank God! The police!"

"No Mother, it's me, your son, Robert."

"Lies!...My son's is in California."

"That's right. And so are you. You're in California and you're stuck in a closet in your son's studio apartment." I opened the door. She was hiding behind my shortboard and clutching a Senior Frog's yard glass as a weapon.

"Why am I in here? Was your father behind this?"

"You were trying to organize my closet and you must have fallen asleep," I said. "I was at my job at the big law firm, and I forgot all about you...I'm so sorry...So I bought tickets to the ballet."

"Oh I'm so proud of you! You finally went to law school!"

"Alright Mother. On you're feet. Time to meet your escort, Ms. Anne-Laure."

In a few minutes, I was dragging Mother to the rental car with poor Anne-Laure following behind.

"So you're pawning me off to one of your loose women so that you can go off to a Satanist concert. Well at least she's European. I couldn't dream of one of these Philistine Californians stepping out of her jeans long enough to go to a ballet."

* * *

"Watch the road!" Mother screamed as Anne-Laure drove. *"You're not in France! You can't be fixing your makeup while you drive. Do you think this is an Estee Lauder counter? You'll get us killed!"*

"Good!"

"Why on earth is your makeup a mess in the first place? Were you partnering with the likes of my son?"

"I wish...but he go crazy because you here!"

196

"My son needs his mother and I won't have some crazy French wino sabotaging my progress! Where did he find you, in one of his filth magazines?"

"I wish he never found me! Eez been nothing but a torture."

"Let me have that lipstick, and you just drive." Mother snatched the tube out of Anne-Laure's grasp. She touched the tip to apply the lipstick on her lip. Anne-Laure jerked the car, Mother goofed. The lipstick smeared on her lips like a clown. But jaded on rufinol, Mother didn't realize the foul up.

"You looking very nice, Mrs. Casella," Anne-Laure said, cracking a devious grin.

Mother smiled warmly. Her mouth looked like a bright red puddle of spilt paint.

"Why thank you, Ms. Anne-Laure. Perhaps we should forget about all of this bitching and just enjoy an evening away from Robert."

Go Time

Any athlete or musician of superstar status will tell you that nervousness is part of their repertoire. And they're right, or else they wouldn't be superstars. Nervousness, and the symptoms of it, are physical signals that your body is preparing for fight or flight. You sweat because your body wants to cool itself. It thinks it's about to be worked beyond exhaustion. You get dry mouth because your body needs to conserve water for sweat and energy. You get the butterflies because your stomach lining is shrinking. You've stopped producing bile, and your body would prefer an empty, lighter stomach. Find a barf bag. The shaking? That's because your neurons are tweaked, powered by adrenaline. Your motor response signals are as sharp as they'll ever be.

I was fucking nervous. By 9:02 PM, I was out of my building. Minutes later, I was abiding the speed limit in the van on the 101 South towards downtown and then on to Vernon. For this portion of the trip, I wore earplugs to make it easier to think of literally *nothing*. I was so nervous that it wasn't safe to think. I just had to space out and let my body take over...work like a machine...shut off my thinking.

I threw up near Studio City, about halfway into the trip. It was mostly liquid. I hadn't eaten solid food in over twenty-four hours, just Metamucil to avoid any surprises during the robbery.

At 9:56 I parked the van and climbed into the back to suit up. Rubber rain suit, rubber gloves, and a rubber headpiece—sealed at all openings with duct tape.

"Coats" was a homeless guy that lived in my home town. It could be hot as biscuits, the middle of the summer, and this guy would be standing on the sidewalk urinating on himself through his four pairs of sweat pants, and vomiting on his five layers of coats. All the while, he'd be listening to his FM radio as if nothing were the matter. He was the basis for my character—my disguise—enough ratty clothes to conceal my PVC rain suit without slowing me down. I topped it off with a bright red hunting cap and a dirty face. Then I doused myself with stink bombs and deer piss, looking and smelling completely flea bitten and louse infested. Any cop, streetwalker, or insomniac strolling through Vernon wouldn't have any idea that I was actually a bank robber. Lastly, I tied it all together with a pink girl's backpack. It gave my vagrant character a confused identity angle to play with.

A quick check of the cameras, coast was clear: I emerged from the van and lowered the shopping cart. Hunched over and crazy, perfectly in character, I was a Deranged Young Professional dressed up as a homeless person, with a shopping cart load of brand new toilets—nothing out of the ordinary for downtown LA.

The first target was the exchange. The exchange that serviced the credit union was just about three blocks away, on the same side of the train tracks as the bank. I had until no later than 10:24 to get there. Per my stopwatch I had about nineteen minutes to do the job.

First, I placed Burt Reynolds a few feet away from the exchange. Chuck Norris was placed so that it would look like he destroyed the exchange. After all, in real life that's how it would have been done. Chuck handles the roundhouse kicks, and Burt handles the mustaches and smooth talk. I beat the toilets a few times to get the effect that they had unexpectedly escaped from a rail car. Then, the exchange.

I beat that thing like a stray dog, but not too much. The idea wasn't to take it out just yet. That's what the nail bomb was for. Tucked under the oblong vent near the top of the exchange, the nail bomb was wired to a motion sensor that would go off when the train passed by at approximately 10:58. But by 10:58, I'd already be hiding out on the roof of the bank. All this effort was to avoid having to mace and inject with rufinol an innocent phone company employee. He gets a call to inspect a damaged exchange. Then he sees a homeless man climbing onto the roof of a credit union. You get the picture.

I wanted to save telling you about the dynamite until now because it was my proudest achievement; however, getting it wasn't easy or fun. The last thing I wanted to do was travel to a shit pit like Las Vegas. The whole poker craze is for Hawaiian-shirt-wearing douche bags. I loathe the place. But it was one of these douche bag poker players that I was after, so I'd have to get over my qualms. Having heard that Las Vegas has things like "demolitions conventions," I deduced that dynamite could probably be found in the neighborhood of *Destitute*, on the same side of the street as *Poker*.

I didn't have an exact profile on my potential mark until I got to the convention. So I had to go Gonzo. I had to attend functions and sit down with demo guys at the buffets. That meant eating a plate of prime rib or two.

One thing was immediately clear: demo guys are all alike. They're *DE*-constructionists, not *CON*-structionists. They're a step stupider than alpha dog. They blow shit up for a living, if that's any indication. And I was looking for the biggest dipshit of the bunch.

I was NOT looking for someone who needed money because he was afraid to go back to his family having spent the mortgage. That kind of guy is usually a pussy, and his limit is right at illegally selling dynamite.

What I needed was a mark that was a tough guy. A guy who liked to show off and couldn't lose in front of *anybody*. A guy who got roped in by an early hot steak and then swallowed a couple of hand grenades. But instead of lying down for the night, he'd try and ride out the bad streak, coming up bust every time.

He'd run to the ATM, buying his chips from a different cashier each trip, embarrassed to be coming back. Then it'd be nothing but more busts and more booze. He'd get cash advances on all of his credit cards, even beg someone to cash a personal check. Finally, he'd pawn everything he had, down to his luggage, and just short of the TV from his hotel room (that's why they're bolted down in Vegas).

It happens at every convention. There's always that one guy that *can't* end his night on a low note. He has to stay up all night to keep getting busted and busted, hoping for a break, to the point where he's finally willing to buy dynamite for a Deranged Young Professional.

My mark turned out to be a non-Mormon from Utah. He had *limited* funds and the *unlimited* ability to give them away at the card table. He also had a license to buy dynamite and dynamite accessories in the state of Nevada.

Anyway, as planned, I scaled the catwalk and mounted the rooftop. Then I hoisted up the catwalk and the materials: two 50 lb. bags of sand and my ditty bag.

First the dynamite.

Very simple. Using my blueprint of building from the county tax maps, I placed the dynamite over the vault, connected the detonator, and covered it with sandbags. Next, I pulled the laptop out the backpack and plugged in my newest addition to the camera collection, another remote controlled camera. I set the new camera up to look out over the front street. Cops always drive up to the front when they want to get into a bloody shootout. Cops are always bold like that, and they know it's the easiest way for the news crews to approach so that they can be on TV. A second camera with a locked mount was placed behind me to monitor the train that would be passing in about ten minutes.

That gave me ten minutes to idle.

Relaxing on the roof of the bank was the closest thing to a satisfying rest I'd had since before graduation. The rooftop was calm and quiet, and the gravel cushioned my aching back better than a sandy beach. The pristine, uncluttered beauty of the graveled commercial rooftop gave the false impression that I was laid out in some Zen garden on the trendy Westside, meditating or whatever it is those loons do. It felt good. The sky was clear and expansive. I could open my mind, and it was big enough a net to catch all the clutter. Jets and air traffic dotted it, giving me something to entertain my eyes and entice my ears. I was on a bank's rooftop not fifty feet from a quarter stick of dynamite, and there was nothing between us but a hundred pounds of sand. And millions of dollars in cash just underneath me in the vault.

During the ten-minute wait for the train I didn't have to consult the stopwatch. The powerful locomotive charging its way towards the bank was my next benchmark. My attention was focused on the tiny purr. It was growing louder and would soon be a ferocious roar.

I didn't sweat, flinch, or piss my pants. I didn't think about what my guts would look like if they were ground into the pebbled roof because I'd misjudged the dynamite. I wasn't worried about the possibility of my dick being blown off. I wasn't thinking about what my friends would think when they opened the paper and saw that I had been found, mutilated on a rooftop, dismembered from head to toe, identified only by a detached eight-inch penis found lodged in a shopping cart, yards from the body. I wasn't concerned that the entire roof could cave in from the force of the blast and spill me to the floor on a heap of rubble. But I turned over to my stomach just in case. I didn't want to crack my back over a teller's window on the way down.

Check the laptop...the train. It had already passed the exchange. Prepaid cell phone...dial bank...call sending...
"I'm sorry, but the number you are trying to reach is temporarily disconnected..."
The train was being pulled by one? two? three locomotives. It would be about a three minute and forty-five second train. It would also have at least two engines pushing from the rear. The third front-end locomotive passed. Dynamite time. Ignition engaged.
One. Two. The wind from the train whipped around the rooftop gravel dust. I couldn't see through it. The noise was killing my ears...give it another second. *Three.*
It was more of a rumble. The building hardly shook. Between the dust and the train, the noise was not much of a bark, but the laptop computer jumped anyway. The last thing I saw were the two sand bags drop in through the hole. I checked myself over. No damage. I was still alive. Using a barrel roll technique, I rolled fifty feet to the smoky hole and hit it with the fire extinguisher. The dynamite burns hot when it goes up, and I didn't want my cash becoming a camp fire.
Satisfied, I rolled back to my position against the wall. I had less than three minutes until the train would be completely passed by.

...Stow laptop in pink backpack. Descend. Drag catwalk over to the shopping cart and dismantle. Regroup.

* * *

"What kind of ballet would be in a dump neighborhood like this?" Mother screamed.

"Eez a Russian ballet."

"What kind of runaround is this? What has my son put you up to?"

Anne-Laure pulled the car into the parking lot of the Van Nuys Airport, a small private aircraft and charter airfield in a dirty, industrial part of The Valley.

"I'm calling the police!" Mother stated.

But Anne-Laure seized Mother's arm as it went for her purse to dig out the phone. "Eez nice surprise, I promise."

The rental car pulled into the parking lot, and someone tapped on the driver side window. It was a tall bearded man wearing a sailor's cap. His name was The Captain. "You must be Anne-Laure," he said, opening the car door. "We're all ready to go."

Mother stepped nervously out of the car and adjusted her ladies suit. "I'm not taking another step until someone tells me the meaning of this."

The Captain grinned at Mother's smeared lipstick, "Nice makeup ma'am."

"We go without her. Eef she want to be stubborn then she can just stand here all night." Anne-Laure locked the car, also locking out Mother.

"Wait! You can't just leave me standing here! Not in this filthy neighborhood!"

"You go with us, or you stand there all night like ee-diot," snapped Anne-Laure.

The Captain smiled. He tried warming up to Mother, "You know, this airport has a lot of history. Bogie filmed the last scene of Casablanca here. In fact, right over there, near the runway, is where his character let go of Ingrid Bergman and put her in an airplane, never to see her again."

* * *

I had the perfect spot to wait. Once you breech a bank vault, you have to wait; you have to give it some time to see whether anybody comes to check out the commotion. There was a dumpster/trash pile in an alley nearby the credit union—a perfect hobo settlement. With all the rat shit and stinky garbage I could hunker down and appear to be talking out loud to myself and self-medicating—nothing abnormal. But under my rags I used my laptop to watch a web feed of Yvonne's place.

Most smalltime branch managers, including the ones I actually talked to, told me that they would rather catch fire than get out of bed to check on a lost signal warning. And the alarm companies are reluctant to call the police unless several alarms are activated. That's because single alarms are often false, and bothering the police is a bad idea because they eventually quit coming at all—even Vernon police on Starbucks. So, under most circumstances a lost signal warning will mean that a manager gets out of bed to answer the call, takes a piss, and goes back to sleep. *"Okay, let's just see if it happens again. Good night."*

But it's always the uptight people with too much respect for their underemployment that end up being big pains in the ass for Deranged Young Professionals. Yvonne struck me as just the type. I pinned her as being a person that *would* check on it. So that's why there was a rental car parked in front of her house with the peepers on her every move. Inside the rental car was the new laptop and a camera, uploading a web feed to a private web address. I was logged on using an untraceable, pre-paid cellular wireless card, watching her every move. From my laptop I could see Yvonne, as well as all streets surrounding the credit union.

It was time to re-hydrate and check to see what was on the police scanner...*dead cat pulled from an industrial heater at the UPS depot. Foul play suspected.* Then an overlooked detail occurred to me. I should have re-bottled the waters in beer bottles to add to the vagrant effect. Oh well.

Check in on Yvonne.

All clear. Her car in the driveway hadn't moved.

Have an outburst, shake violently and shout obscenities—act vagrant.

"Suck fucking pole Queen of Narnina...Cum swallowing whorebag."

No! Way too literate. Try something more vagrant.

"Eat shit! Die! Fairy dust. Fuck. Shit. Whore. Fleas. Cream Corn!"

Better.

Check printouts from Excel spreadsheet.

Ripe bank entering time in nineteen minutes. No phones. A gigantic hole in the roof. No signs of bothersome pigs. Wait nineteen miserable more minutes. Then it's time to start lining pockets.

Starving. Must hurry up and rob bank. Then go and find pizza. Beg for Anne-Laure to take me back.

Crawling into a Wonderful, Tight Hole

Jagged yes, but just big enough to fit into. The concrete and metal bank vault stopped any further structural damage to the roof, making cave-in unlikely. This delicate, freshly opened, virginal passage was the most expensive hole I had ever crawled into. This hole had cost nearly *five grand* of the community service money. But I had three canvas bags that were able to carry about thirty-three pounds each. I could handle up to four million dollars in your typical bank vault denominations.

I used the catwalk to lower myself into the vault. The floor was slippery from the residue left by the discharged extinguisher. Fragments of roof and shards from the vault crunched under my running shoes. (Never wear anything but running shoes when robbing.) It smelled like the Fourth of July because of the scent of burnt sulfur, but it might as well have smelled like Christmas because camped out behind me was millions in cash. All I had to do was turn around and start snatching it. But I wanted to savor the moment. I had all night: according to my camera, not a soul was in sight.

I peered up through the jagged hole in the ceiling. The Vernon sky was just a patch of night poking through a gaping hole in the steel and concrete ceiling. The trick now was to not explode like a retard that had just won a teddy bear prize.

Before you turn around, Bob, and before you start scooping up huge piles of money, prepare yourself. Sit here for a minute and imagine that you're somewhere else. You have nothing to be scared of, so imagine that you're NOT standing in a bank in the middle of the night. You're standing in Italy. You're standing at the bottom of the Pantheon. It's 2000 years old, and it has a hole in its roof too. Gramma is with you, and she brought biscotti. She's proud of you because you've amounted to something. You're the pride of the family. You're her rich grandson who lives in Paris, but you can't understand a damn word of her Italian. You assume she's proud because Gramma feeds you biscotti and gives you a quart of milk from her purse. She still wants you to grow up big and strong, even though you're already twenty-two. You're always a little boy to Gramma. It's just the two of you, standing alone, quietly at the bottom of the Pantheon...In Italy. Everything is fine because Gramma is with you...And yes...what you just saw was a hot air balloon. A hot air balloon just floated

past the gaping hole in the roof. You did not imagine that.
That part really just happened.

* * *

The hot air balloon clung to the low canopy of the Pacific clouds like a bright fruit hanging from a dark branch. Beneath the balloon was an immense, pulsating blanket of lights, burning at the ends of lampposts, on the fronts of cars, and in the windows of the houses and offices that were still awake so late at night.

The balloon had just scooted over the warehouse districts of Vernon and Commerce. Before that, it had bounced around in the turbulent winds at the foothills of the Sierra Madres, where the earth below is endlessly dark, where humans can't be.

Then the city began. It was the time of night when the ground below is divided from the sky by low lying fog. The hot sun has hidden itself and it isn't there to cook off the lingering moisture. The billions of lights that burst from behind the whirlpool of murky vapor cast a rising, sweeping glow, a powerful attraction that from above will invite you to pour your thoughts into it.

But in something short of twenty miles, the fantastic display of lights would suddenly extinguish. The city stops at the flat, dark slate of the ocean's surface. That journey from the mountains, over the city, and to the ocean, where the world began, is what Anne-Laure was in the sky to see. And she wondered where the tears she dropped over the rim of the basket would finally end up.

* * *

My tear drops dripped on my cell phone clutched in my hand. I waited desperately for *someone* to pick up. Anyone. Then I heard a click...

"Yeah, I'd like to speak to a horny stewardess, or perhaps a horny maid. Yes, make that a horny maid that's super slutty. Yes. That wants to talk dirty."

Click, *buzz*. Beep.

..."*This is Dawn.*"

"I'm Bob. And I'm a big loser, Dawn. A *big* loser. You got that?"

"*Okay.*"

"Dawn, tell me, are you a foxy maid? When I called, I asked for a horny, foxy maid. That's what you are, right?"

"*Yeah. That's right baby. Do you have a mess for me to clean up?*"

"I'm afraid I do, Dawn...That's exactly what I have—a big mess."

"*How big?*"

"Oh...I'd say a seven."

"*Ooh, that is a big mess...Lucky number seven.*"

"Yeah, seven years is a long time to go to Federal prison. But I don't care. I just want to be with *you* for a minute, Dawn."

"*What kind of mess are you in?*"

"This isn't a fantasy Dawn, this is real."

"*Is it some kind of sick shit? I'm going to hang up...Sorry.*"

"No! Wait...Dawn, this isn't sick shit. This is real. I need your advice. You're the only person I have to turn to. I'm in a real big mess, and I need you to promise me that you'll help me out."

"*What happened?*"

"I'm sitting in a bank vault right now. There're about..." I had to look behind me to re-estimate, "Yeah, I'd say a little over two million dollars in cash sitting not but six inches out of my reach."

Dawn laughed, "*Oh my, this is a good one! You gonna buy Dawn a new car?*"

"This isn't funny! I can't get to the cash because it's locked up in a cage."

"You're telling me that you're in a bank vault with two million dollars?"

"That's exactly what I'm telling you, but…"

"Why don't you finish up your business in that vault and swing over to my place. Cut the chit chat. Two million dollars!"

"You aren't listening Dawn, I'm in the vault, but there's another vault. The fucking money is locked up in this goddamn cage, and I don't have any way of getting to it. Do you understand now?"

"No, I don't understand. But for two million dollars, I'd sure figure out a way to start understanding."

"Alright Dawn, since you seem so keen on this, why don't you tell me how to get into this cage."

"Now how am I supposed to know that? I can get a straight guy to stick a finger in his butt, but I sure can't pick no locks."

"I could shoot at it!" I grabbed my piece out of my coat. "That's right, I could shoot it."

"Now don't go shootn' up the place makin' noise now…"

PA PA PA PA PA POP!

"Dawn, I don't think that worked."

My hand tingled from the six shots.

"Damn, you're for real, aren't you?"

"What do *you* think?"

By then I was re-loaded. I fired five more rounds.

PA PA PA PA POP!

Still nothing.

"You just heard me pump eleven bullets the size of cocktail weenies into that fucking cage, and nothing.

"Well you best be moving your ass, cause somebody musta heard them shots."

"Absolutely not! I'm standing here penniless, and there's two million dollars so close to me I can literally smell it. And it's the best bad smell you've ever smelled, Dawn.

"Money usually stinks bad."

"Smashed under people's sweaty asses in their pockets all day, it starts to smell like complete shit. *But I still want it!*"

"Well the offer's still on the table. I'm down here in Culver City if you can get to that money."

"Well then work with me dammit! If you want a million dollar screw, you need the million dollar answer!"

"Torches, welders, dynamite, a big motherfucking jackhammer, I don't know. I'm not the bank robber. I'm a nurse, a maid, or whatever the fuck you want me to be, but I ain't no bank robber."

"But I called *you* Dawn. *You* have to help me. *You* have to help me clean up this mess."

"How old are you?"

"Twenty-two."

"What do you do besides robbing banks, because it sounds to me like you're not doing too well?"

"I'm an accountant. And I guess I rob banks too."

"What do you do for fun?"

"I like to party. And I like pizza."

"Now what's a nice, normal guy like you robbing banks for?"

"I needed some extra money."

"You must have a real expensive LA woman! Most people just get a second job."

"Yeah, I like coke. But just every now and then."

"I'm not talking about that kinda LA woman, honey. I'm talking about a girlfriend. Do you have a girlfriend?"

"Well there's this one girl, I love her, but I've been too busy for her. So she gave up."

"Too busy for what?"

"For her."

"Why?"

"Because of this bank job. It's been a lot of work."

"You lost your girl over some bank job! There'd better be a damn good reason why you needed the money then!"

"Everybody needs money."

"If you're not going to be serious with me, then you're going to have to have phone sex, or I'll have to hang up. You got that?"

"I'm sorry Dawn. You're right. You're just trying to help."

"Now tell me what do you need extra money for?"

"I don't know."

"You don't know? Then why on earth are you in a bank vault in the middle of the night if you don't know?"

"I don't know. I guess I just wanted a bunch of money."

"For what?"

"I DON'T KNOW!"

"Only somebody with a damn good reason would break into a bank."

"ALRIGHT! You got me. Yes, I broke into a bank vault. And I don't know why other than that I wanted a bunch of fucking money. Is that what you wanted to hear?"

"If that's the truth. But I don't think that's the truth."

"Okay, the truth is, the reason I broke into this bank, is because when I graduated from college I set a goal for myself. I said I would make a million dollars as soon as possible."

"That's a line of BS if I ever heard one. Either you're one sick pervert, or you're just full of BS. Now which is it?"

"Dawn, I live in a studio apartment, and I eat nothing but ramen noodles and pizza. And I wear dirty clothes. And I sleep on a mattress that's just thrown on the floor. Because I *can't*...no matter how hard I try...*I can't* get this horrible, horrible idea out of my head . . . that I *have* to have a million dollars as soon as possible.

I've given up on everything...friends, girls. I'm dead until I can get this idea out my head."

"Now wait a minute. It sounds to me like you need a shrink, honey. I just help guys bust they nut, but it sounds to me like you one sick motherfucker."

"But Dawn, I just can't pull away...not now...not this close. It's a fucking goal...that's what it is...a goal. Winners don't ditch their goals. That's why it's a goal...because it's for winners. And it's all I have in my life. My goal is the only thing that keeps me going. And my goal is sitting a foot away from me, *but I can't get to it* because there is a goddamn cage in the way. And this stupid fucking cage won't open. Even after I shot it eleven fucking times. But that won't stop me. I can't quit. I *will not* quit. You're out of your mind if you think I'm going to quit. *I'm too close, Dawn!"*

"Honey, you the one that's out they mind. I may have a fucked up life and a fucked up job, but everybody's got to pay them bills."

"But I don't know what to do. If I can't get to this money, I don't know what will happen to me, and that scares me. It scares me because I don't know what I will do to myself. I'm not in control of myself right now."

Then I was silent. Dawn was silent. The vault, silent.

"Dawn, I have one bullet left."

* * *

"Why is everybody trying to kill me?" Mother screamed.

"Nobody's trying to kill you," Anne-Laure pleaded. She choked Mother by the neck, trying to keep her from climbing out of the balloon's basket. "I Anne-Laure. Remember me?"

Mother's ruifinol fog had apparently lifted. She was right back on the broom. "Then what on earth do you have me doing up here? So you can push me to my death?" Mother slapped Anne-Laure across the face. Anne-Laure slapped back. Then Mother darted for the other side of the basket. The ruckus tipped the basket from side to side. It swung wildly back and forth suspended below the gigantic balloon floating through the night sky.

"Get a hold of yourself, lady," The Captain scolded. "I knew I shouldn't have taken some crazy old wino up at this hour. This is the last time!" The grizzled mariner of the skies grabbed Mother by the collar of her ladies suit and slung her the floor of the basket, nodding his head that it had to come to that.

"This eez my special evening! I leave America in two days. Now zip mouth!"

Mother looked up from the floor, "Did my ex-husband send you? Or was it my awful son? Why am I stuck in a balloon in the middle of the night with you strange people? Is that not a fair question to ask?...Wouldn't you worry too?...I have a room at the Hilton, and I just want to go shopping!...Would one of you two crazy people please have some pity on me and take me back to my hotel?...I have a lunatic son that I must find, and I'm absolutely starving...I demand surf and turf. That's all I ask."

"Please, God," The Captain said looking up. "Please send lightning. Please send a lightning bolt through this balloon, this instant."

Mother jumped up from the floor and stared him square in the face, "If you're planning on killing me, you and the girl here had better be ready to go down with me. I'll be damned if I die in some balloon with that French prostitute!"

"Please!" Anne-Laure pleaded. She began crying. "What eez problem, you crazy woman?"

Mother grabbed The Captain's collar. "Whatever my son or husband paid you, I'll double it. Double. Now land this death trap on the rooftop of the Beverly Hilton and let me out...Double!"

* * *

"Now don't you go and turn this into a suicide on me."

"A suicide?"

"What's this 'one bullet left' business?"

"I wouldn't kill myself? I still have one bullet left! I still have one last chance to blow open this cage. I still have one chance left to reach my goal."

"Would you get off it? Give it up! You're NOT becoming a millionaire tonight!"

"What are you talking about? Obviously you've never stood next to two million dollars. You can't just walk away from two million dollars once you've gotten this close. I'll chew through this cage if I have to."

I knelt down and inspected the intrepid lock—it was daunting.

"You know what Dawn, I think you might be right. I think this lock might just be too much."

It was the sophisticated type of lock: once it was obstructed, the inner workings of the lock would permanently bolt. Sensing danger, it would self-destruct.

"But why not try, right? Why not give it at least one more shot?"

"It's your fantasy...go ahead."

"Alright. I think I'm ready. Wish me luck."

I stood back about three feet and took dead aim. Then I had a better idea. "Dawn, do you think I should stand back a few feet or should I put the gun right up against the lock so I won't miss?"

"I already told you, I ain't a locksmith."

"Come on, Dawn, what do you think?"

"Oh, I don't know!... Just put the gun up to it as close as you can."

"Good thinking."

I knelt down beside the lock to size up the job. "Dawn, I'm going to have to set the phone down for a second. Don't go anywhere...Wait, I'll put it on speaker."

I trained the tip of the gun against the lock and traced around until I felt comfortable that my last bullet would inflict the most damage.

"Alright, Dawn, here we go! I'm going to shoot. This is it. Then I'm coming over to your place and we're going to get naked."

POP!

* * *

Mother and Anne-Laure occupied opposite corners of the basket like two boxers between rounds. The frightened Captain held his position between them and was nervously attached to the burner cord.

Mother was shouting orders through her cell phone to the concierge at the Beverly Hilton, "Yes...a hot air balloon...on the rooftop...twenty minutes. No, I won't need bell service," Mother sneered at Anne-Laure, "*unfortunately my bags are missing*," she hissed. "But please send up a robe. I need something to cover me until the stores open in the morning." Then Mother dialed another number. "Hello, I'd like to report a stolen rental car and related kidnapping..."

The Captain swatted Mother's phone. It soared out of the basket and into the sky.

"They'll be expecting me at the Hilton, you know. If I don't show up, they'll call the police, and this balloon will be shot down!"

"I have no intention other than to deliver you safely and swiftly to the Beverly Hilton, ma'am. But I can't stand by and let you file false police reports."

"False police reports? Are you blind? There has clearly been a kidnapping and car theft, and this French whatever-she-is is completely responsible. As American citizens, it is our duty to report this matter and have this vicious Frog deported on the next boat!"

Anne-Laure snapped, screaming at Mother, "I despise you, evil woman. You know nothing. You can't just shut up for once in your life. You make everything mess. *You* are the crazy person. Your son needs peace and quiet. You don't know how to stop. Poor boy, you are evil woman!"

"I dare you speak to me like that! I'm his mother, and I will not stand here and be lectured to by some dirty, French...THING!"

The balloon approached the historic Beverly Hilton and set down on the rooftop helipad. A dark, handsome bellhop met Mother. Her polite side naturally materialized.

"I've never had such an interesting night in all my life. But at least I'm still alive, and at least I still have my purse."

"What happened?" He asked.

"Well I know I was drugged...I know that much. But absolutely everything after arriving at my son's flop house is a complete blur."

"My apologies."

"It's been a hectic evening...I arrived in a hot air balloon for Christ's sake!"

"I can see that."

"You'd think that a son would be happy to see his mother, but not mine. No. He disappears and sends me on some crazy night flight in a hot air balloon. With two of his criminal friends, no less."

"You weren't harmed were you?"

"Thankfully not...But did you know that my son is a criminal?...A criminal! And he owns a firearm!"

"No I didn't. Are you sure you're alright? You don't need me to call the police or anything, do you?"

"No, I don't need to phone the police...not yet. But I do need lunch reservations at *Spago*. For two...Once I can get to a phone, I'm going to try and track down my son. I'd like to see if he'd at least meet his poor mother for a nice lunch."

The bellhop placed an arm around Mother's waist in the manner that a nurse would a patient to lead them. "Let me show you to your room and I'll see the concierge about that reservation."

"Your mother must be awfully proud of you. What nice manners you have. And how thoughtful you are...But it's not the same with my son. You'd think that for giving somebody life, they'd at least meet you for lunch. Is that not too much to ask?"

"At *Spago*?...No, that's not too much to ask."

* * *

The Captain ran his fingers through his thick beard and listened to Anne-Laure's story.

"He was suppose to be in balloon with me, but he had to go work...he is investigator, he investigate criminal. But his mother is total *ee-diot*. She think he eez criminal, but he is such nice boy. He eez just not ready to be in love, or he is just scared. We are young, twenty-two. I need just give him time."

"Then why on earth are you leaving, sweetheart? Shouldn't you wait around a while?"

"I make my mind. I need to get on my life. If it is true love, then it will happen. I will never forget him. I also decide that *tee-nis* is not my true life."

"Teenis?"

"You know, with racket and ball." Anne-Laure demonstrated a backhand stroke.

"Oh you mean tennis. You're a tennis player."

"I play pro in America for two year. But I not having success I need. So I decide in my heart to quit being *see-lee* and move on with my life."

"So you're giving up tennis and moving back home?"

"I not give up. I not quit playing *tee-nis*! I just want to have fun with *tee-nis* an not make eet painful."

"And what about this boy?"

"I love him so much."

"Then why are you moving?"

"He deserve chance to miss me."

* * *

The low grade amphetamine gave me intense relief. I couldn't feel a thing. Low grade my ass. But Dawn said to get some food. "Get out of there and get some food," she said. I asked her where they had fresh-squeezed orange juice at this hour, and she said Canter's Deli on Fairfax. So I promised her that I'd get out of the vault and hurry to get some food in my belly. She said to look up at the ceiling when I got there...sit down and look up...*just look up and enjoy.*

I hoped that birthing myself from the hole in the roof would be the first thing to go right. False hope. I lost a lot of blood climbing the catwalk. Each step sent streams pumping out the gaping holes in my side. My underwear was soaked with it; the thick hot stream ran down the back of my leg like I'd pissed myself.

The only practical way down the wall was to use rope and lurch down. The wound couldn't handle another climb on the catwalk. The rope burns singeing through the palms of my gloves was a fair trade.

A mountain of coke was not far away, and cocaine was going to save my life. This was one of those rare occasions when a person can say that. It was intended to celebrate with but would have to be used instead as an anesthesia and to stop the bleeding. I'd smear a handful of it on my wounds, both the entrance and exit. It would kill the pain and zip the capillaries shut. I'd be able to sit down and have a nice quiet dinner, alone, at Canter's. Rebuild my strength and figure shit out. Just like Dawn said. Food. That's what I really needed.

I started moving away from the bank and towards the shopping cart. It was the only piece of evidence I could afford to take. But it was a desperation move. I just needed something to prop myself up on to walk.

I had to *pry* the PVC suit away from my skin. Blood and sweat, mixed up with body heat, cooked up a bitching glue. I broke loose a few layers of skin tearing off the suit. But I couldn't feel a thing. Not a damn thing—Low grade speed, my fucking ass. I was completely cranked—I was smashed on glass.

I stripped myself out of the homeless guy disguise, tearing it away and tossing the evidence into the van. A gush of my blood splashed out onto the dirty Vernon alleyway. I was down to gym shorts and running shoes, no shirt. I snatched up the first aid kit and got to work. First I disinfected, scrubbing with antiseptic, and then a shot of some antibiotic shit out of a syringe. Then, I got some dressing on the wound—Ernesto dressing—cocaine. Pouring it directly from the plastic bag onto the wound, I worked it around with my finger tip. Lot's of it. I'd be completely pain free on that half of my body for the next month unless I fell sideways onto a table saw.

I covered the wound with some gauze and then duct taped the shit out of it to keep the pressure on. That way I could drive the fuck out of there without bleeding to death. Other than the mess of dried blood everywhere, I looked pretty good for a gunshot victim.

I don't remember the drive, really, I don't. But the bright, inviting lights of a twenty-four hour Ralph's grocery store beckoned me off the soulless interstate and welcomed me to purchase baby wipes and Gatorade.

Twenty-four hour Ralph's grocery stores in Los Angeles are the most chaotic freak shows on earth at 1:30 in the morning. If customers aren't in there to buy Nyquil and vomit vodka, they're in there to buy sharp objects to kill themselves with. Or perhaps, they're just stocking up on cord and plastic bags to dispose of the corpses they've disemboweled in their basements. But this is harsh clarity:

you're wearing dried blood like a sweater, so you have to use self checkout because you don't want to scare anybody—at Ralph's—in LA, at 1:30 AM.

What this *also* means is that you've got to return to your van, get cleaned up, and make a second awful trip back into the store to buy the lottery tickets. They don't sell lottery tickets at the self-checkout. That would be just too goddamn convenient.

Moments later, I was in the back of the van taking care of myself before changing into my black, Italian designed suit and shoes. The reason for the attire was that in the event of a televised manhunt, it is always beneficial to be wearing a nice suit when captured. It will heighten your pop-culture status, and you'll garner better returns on your eventual book deal.

Rubbish. The purpose of the suit was the intended celebration. By this point in the night I'd planned to be enjoying the first hours of my new lifestyle. I wanted to do so in style, but sometimes plans change. There was no pile of money, and the eight ball of perfectly good booger sugar was uselessly smeared on my wound instead of being smell-tested. Most importantly, I had no idea how I was going to sweep Anne-Laure off her feet *now*.

So I stomped, with great fury, back into that Ralph's grocery store. Scoring was on my mind—Scoring big.

I slid my hand under my jacket, "Give me all of it." The cashier maintained her disbelief. "I mean it. I got business." She was stiff. English wasn't her language. "I'm not kidding. I want you to empty it out." Still, she didn't move. So I lunged over the counter. She shot out of my way and I scooped it out myself. "There! Now was that so hard?"

I hopped off the counter and settled back onto my feet. "Put it in a bag."

She reached below the counter.

"Nuh uh."

She froze.

"I want plastic," I snapped.

"What's going on here?" A harsh voice asked from behind me.

I spun around and found a manager standing there.

"Boy, am I glad you came." I pulled a wad of cash out of my wallet. "I want all of your Mega Millions tickets in a plastic bag. Now!"

He understood what I meant and began rapping at the cashier in a mix of Spanish and English. She soon had a total for me. "Two-a-hundred. Sirty seex."

She collected my money, and I gave her a wink as she slid the bag of tickets across the counter. Reaching inside, I grabbed a handful of tickets and gave them to her. "That's your tip." She blushed as I hollered at her manager who'd since wandered off, "Get over here buddy, I have Mega Millions tickets with your name on them."

I spent the next few minutes sauntering around the aisles, handing out tickets to other deranged late night shoppers. I approached a stoned guy in the deli watching his Hot Pocket heat up in the microwave. "Are you too stoned to figure out that Ralph's at 1:30 AM isn't exactly a great place to be?" I asked.

"Sup dude?" he said.

"Here." I handed him what was left of the tickets, but kept *one* for myself.

"What's the word, man?"

"Anyone but me is going to get rich tonight. It might as well be you."

"Nice."

We stood there a moment, both stoned on much different substances, and awkwardly nodded our heads in agreement. "Might as we be me then," he said. "But hey, you got a ticket too, man."

I looked at the promising ticket in my hand. "That's right." I ran my finger over it, hovering in sadness. "This ticket is a memento. But like I said, it might as well be you. Tonight's not my night."

The microwave sounded.

Ding.

The sound lingered a bit, triggering a Pavlovian response in me. "Hey, you think I could at least get that Hot Pocket?"

Later, I found myself finishing a cigarette outside of Canter's deli. I put it out and dialed a familiar number on my cell phone...

"Katie...It's me...I won't be making it into work in the morning because *you're fired!*

That's right, I'm firing *you*! And the rest of Independent Plumbing. Because I'm sick of the shit business. I live in a studio apartment, dammit! But a maid cleaned me up tonight. I was a complete mess two hours ago, but the maid cleaned me up. And that's why I'm so fucked up right now. Because the guy lied and said that the speed had been cut more times than a birthday cake and that it was low grade...But it wasn't...guy fucking lied. I'm totally tweekin' balls over here. So that's why I won't be at work, Katie. And that's why you're fired."

A drunk guy and his girlfriend, both smoking, passed me on their way into Canter's. I called out to them. "Say you don't happen to have another cigarette do you? I'm starting to crash like really bad." The drunk guy casually pulled a smoke from his pack and handed it over.

"Alright, Katie, I'm back," I continued. "Sorry, but I needed a cigarette...Well anyway...I want to apologize." I had to pause again...

"Hey bro, can I get a light?" I asked him before he could get away. I got lit and went back to my call. But first I took a long drag. "Sorry about that. I had to light the cigarette ...Whoa...Where do I begin? Well, first I want to say that I'm sorry that Independent Plumbing sucks and I'm sorry that I have to fire you...So I'll put this in manager-speak that you can understand. I booked a conference room for a breakout session. Our objective was to think outside the box, and we reinvented Bob's wheel. There is no circling back at a later date for a touchpoint and lessons learned session: this is it, my walking papers, Bob is checking out.

And the last thing that I want to say. Our office is completely disgraced by all of those chichi posters. Let me mention the one in the break room that says quote, 'Teamwork: there is no such thing as a self-made man. You will only reach your goals with the help of others.' Are you fucking kidding me? Do you think that I'm stupid enough to believe that? If your goal is to *never* achieve anything, then heed the advice of that poster. But if you were a real leader you'd buy a poster that says, 'Fuck Teamwork. For those of you who want to go somewhere: wreck shit and crush balls.'

Okay, so I'm starting to digress. Low grade speed, remember? Well, my ass! So here's the million dollar question, Katie? This is what I really want to ask you. Is life really worth living if you don't have at least a million dollars? Think about it. Answer that question correctly, and I might hire IPD back."

I closed my phone and took another deep drag.

Fuck you, Katie, and goodbye. (I didn't want to compromise my professionalism by actually saying "fuck you" to her over the phone.)

For reasons obvious, there is no particular haunt specifically known as a late night bank robbers' draw. Whether it was a bad day like mine, or a good one, the bank robber has to go about his night alone. Bank robber types don't wake up on graduation morning and show up in a black robe. And for the same reason, a bank robber type wouldn't have a beer at a bank robbers' bar. We don't live like everybody else, and we don't die like everybody else, because we usually don't die on our beds.

Yet as hidden from the world as thought I was that night, smoking a cigarette and casually leaning against Canter's Deli, that hot air balloon kept finding me. Behind my cloud of cigarette smoke, pegged to the sky, there it was, not but five hundred feet above my head. A gigantic cloth bag of hot air, it floated aimlessly with no purpose other than to jar my insanity at a time when I was beginning to gain a tiny shred of control over it. "Damn you, hot air balloon! You can't follow me forever, damn you! I'm moving to France! I'm heading straight to the damn airport and I'm moving to France, damn it all to Hell. Fucking France with Anne-Laure, you fucking motherfucker! Fuck you, Balloon!"

* * *

Anne-Laure darted to the other side of the basket, the side where she heard the familiar voice outbursting insanity with his predictable words. Below she saw the scattered commercial buildings surrounding CBS studios and a quaint network of lamp-lit residential streets feeding Fairfax. Then she could see him, waving his arms and screaming.

"It's nothing," the Captain assured Anne-Laure, "It's probably just some wino. They all think it's the end of the world or something."

Anne-Laure slumped back against the basket. She covered her mouth, embarrassed by her uncontrollable smile.

The Captain raised a bushy white eyebrow, "Wait, that's funny...You're from France."

* * *

Dust hung like ivy on the tarnished chandelier. It was a vintage design and looked like the planet Saturn being attacked with metal spears that poked it from all directions. The spears were tipped with ball-shaped light bulbs, and almost half of them were burnt out. This place was old. This place was famously old.

The evil old skeleton behind the cash register scolded me with her hollow eyes as she crept from the shadows of the alcove behind the register. Faceless, listless, she guided my weary body to a booth. Her brittle bones clinked as she walked. Seated, I sunk myself weightlessly into the embrace of the Naugahide cushion. Its once rigid firmness had deflated after sixty years of late night drunks and insomniacs slumping, finding refuge. But, in all those years I was probably the first bleeding gunshot victim to do the slump.

"Coffee?" the waitress asked?

I was sinking fast. The waitress was worried.

"Are you okay?"

"You know," I said, waving her off.

She laughed. "Nothing a little coffee can't fix."

I groaned. And hunched over in my booth. Clutching my wound. Pain. I was feeling pain again. It was as sharp as I had remembered when that cocktail weenie first hit me.

Waiting for her to return with the coffee gave me time to think about the menu and get my mind off my bleeding gut. They served a tongue sandwich. Gross. Two slices of rye, pickle, mayonnaise, and a beast's tongue.

"I'll just have orange juice," I told the waitress when she came back for my order.

"You sure you don't want anything else? Hash browns? Toast?"

"Tongue sandwich."

"No you don't."

"You're right. Just the orange juice for now. I can't eat."

With the thick, heavy smells of grease and lard and hot, boned meat, salted and pickled, I was already in hell, and I even hadn't died yet. But the torture kept my mind off the pinch in my side. The smell of dead animals was so strong, I could actually taste the piss and sweat of the beasts. I imagined a rubbery tongue lapping against mine, licking me as I bit into it between the sliced bread. I heard the muscles snap. I heard the ligaments explode. I thought of the deli

225

case in the front of the restaurant. It was like a catacomb for dead, mangled creatures. The gruesome thought of flesh brought me back to the gaping hole in my side, below my ribcage. A chunk of my own my own flesh was left to rot on the floor of the vault.

Dawn said to sit down and look up. But I was afraid to.

There was a reason I had ended up in bank vault on a Thursday night: a bad reason. Life is not worth living if you don't have a million dollars, and that was the reason I was in the vault. That was the reason I was shot. And a bad reason it was. Dawn was a good listener, I thought. She understood. And for that I was afraid to look up at the ceiling.

The waitress returned. "Let me know if you need anything else." She poured a fresh coffee and set down my orange juice.

"Sure."

That was it. It was time to man up and see what was hanging up there. Then get moving. I looked up at the ceiling.

It was trees, a canopy of Autumn trees. The leaves were a multitude of color, reds, oranges, yellows and everything in between, with a bold blue sky behind it. It was beautiful. A photographer had captured the overhead canopy of some magical eastern forest and pressed the image onto glass tiles with lights behind it. Then someone covered the entire ceiling, the entire diner from wall to wall with a forest canopy of natural beauty; simple, natural beauty. Lit up and bright; enchanting. The most beautifully simple thing I'd stopped to see in a long time. It was just a ceiling, but it was beautiful. I slid the last remaining lottery ticket out of my pocket, squeezed it in my hand and smiled.

Then the lights went out. The ceiling disappeared.

My head slammed against the table, spilling the fresh coffee. My face was pressed hard against the scorching puddle. I couldn't see a thing. I couldn't feel a thing. But I could clearly hear the people around me making a fuss.

"Oh my God. Look behind you."

"Shit! Did that guy just keel over?"

But my thinking was as sharp as ever. I could hear the people around me not minding their own business.

"Honey, are you alright?...Wake up...Say something honey...He's not breathing!"

I could not feel the lottery ticket in the palm of my hand any longer. The lottery ticket that I would never, ever scratch off; never rob of its gift to provide a few cheap feelings of hope. Face down, smashed in a puddle of hot coffee, with an unscratched lottery ticket in my hand, that's where I learned about true happiness: having hope.

Part V

"Lover, Player, or Fugitive?" asked the Farmer's Daughter

We call it "dropping dirt." If you ever see it, it's little clouds of dirt dancing up from the ground. Imagine walking feet—feet that aren't there—kicking up the little clouds. *We* call it that because it looks like someone is dropping dirt—someone you can't see.

Again, the gravel dust blowing off the Basketball arena's parking lot is a whirlwind. Through the dust clouds I watch stiff and upright black robed figures gliding in procession. They roam towards the massive building that towers at the epicenter of the endless field of gravel. It's Saturday, 8:00 AM—time for another class of seniors to graduate. I was *dropping dirt* on the gravel, pushing little dimples into its surface with the bottoms of feet that no one could see. I was there, exactly a year from the Saturday when I graduated, to watch over the ceremony. *We* have lots of time on our hands to do those sorts of things, *watching over*, and such.

I take a seat on one of the rafters, above the 1987 NCAA Men's Champions banner. I was four years old that year, 1987. Seated, I dangle my legs, and watch my polished Italian shoes at the ends of custom tailored suit pants. It's a black suit this year. But I have to be careful because I don't want to accidentally kick the banner. *We* have to be careful about those things, because sometimes *you* see it, and get startled. Like dropping dirt, it causes concern. And I don't want my presence known just yet.

The university's *new* president, President Herbert, climbs his large body onto stage. He's the speaker this year. I guess The Board cut spending on the graduation speaking budget, so in a pinch they hired from within. The bastards were getting so cheap they wouldn't even shell out for the Governor's make-believe wife to come back. But since the new President was black, in their homogenous whiteness, the Board probably figured that a black speaker was enough PC showboating for the right price.

I rub my hands together, warming them in anticipation, preparing to fly down to stage to ruin another graduation. Sometimes when *We* come back, *You* mistake *Us* for troublemakers. But the least I can do is save this class from a phony graduation.

* * *

I woke from my dream and fount that I was laid flat on my stomach, half naked, confused, in a vulnerable position. I could hear Bri Bri and Will speaking. *This must be Hell then.*

"Don't get any ideas back there!" Will shouted.

"Where the fuck am I?" I asked, coming out of my fog.

"Shut up, Bob!" Will snapped.

Bri Bri was stitching the exit wound on my hip. "You're in an ambulance. You're shot and you about over-dosed. Does that answer your question?"

"I thought for a minute that I was a ghost or something," I said. "I was saving graduates from horrible ceremonies. How did I end up here?"

"It's time to roll over," Bri Bri told me. An IV was buried in my arm, feeding me nourishment and slowly bringing me back to consciousness. The needle almost hurt worse than the gunshot wound and it was hard to keep my arm still to keep the needle from moving around in the puncture. "I'm going to look away while you cover yourself with this sheet. Then I'm going to stitch up the front, okay?"

"Okay." I started the roll-over, fearful the process would jostle the IV and cause pain. But Bri Bri took control of the IV. It didn't hurt a bit.

These healthcare people sure are nice. Almost too nice.
"What's Will doing here?" I asked.

He spoke over his shoulder from his seat behind the wheel of the ambulance. "I work here now! The play's over so Bri Bri got me a job driving the ambulance."

"Must be nice," I said.

"Yeah, and we can fuck in between calls!" he added.

"Will!" Bri Bri snapped.

I shivered at the thought of being laid out naked on Will's sex stretcher.

"And you," she returned her attention to me, yelling. *"You are so lucky that Canter's didn't call the cops."* She looked at me all business and dipped the needle in for its first trip under the surface of my skin.

"Ouch!"

The needle continued its trip, weaving in and out, like a serpent in water. "Hold still." She held me down with her elbow while she stitched. "You're also lucky that the waitress thought to move your face out of the coffee or else you'd be deformed."

"Given your history with the deformed, perhaps we could have coupled."

"Do you want me to help you or not?"

"Yes...sorry." She dug the needle in again, placing another stitch. "So where's Will taking this thing?" I asked.

"I don't know. We hadn't really thought about it. But I think he's just going to drive around until I'm done working on you."

"How's it looking?" I asked.

"You're going to need lots of antibiotics."

"That's it?"

"Yes, the bullet came out so, all I had to do was clean and stitch it. It's not much worse than a bad dog bite."

"But I wanted to be able to show people that I got shot!"

"I wouldn't go around telling people that unless you want trouble. I'm not even going to ask what you did, but you need to quit the drugs. The drugs are what almost killed you. You don't even realize how many people I have in here because of that shit!"

She was right. And she'd just really saved my ass. I watched her place the last few stitches. The wound really wasn't that bad looking, maybe it was just a dog bite, but from a big dog. I leaned back on my elbows and laughed. I laughed about everything that had happened so far that night as Bri Bri put me back together. "Hey Will."

He looked back from the front, "Yeah?"

"You want a van?"

* * *

I unrolled the van's title on the dash for obtaining the proper signatures. "But one last thing before I go," I said to Will.

"What's that?" he asked.

I paused for spell, for one of those moments in your life that you never forget. "How did you find me?"

"Anne-Laure called. She said to swing by Canter's and talk some sense into you."

Spago

I had the cab drop me a few blocks away from Yvonne's and I picked up the rental car. Sure enough, there were no cops and no Yvonne. She was probably at the credit union cleaning up debris and explaining to her boss why she didn't respond to a lost signal warning. In no time, I was on my way to meet Mother at Spago. I had on a nice, only slightly disheveled Italian suit. Bri Bri had patched me up pretty good, but yet I was only held together at my seams, a gunshot victim running on no sleep. The *toxins* had worn off—I was in the dumps, low, if you know what I mean.

"Where have you been!" Mother immediately asked.

"Relax. Can we just eat and be nice?

"Would you care to tell me about that crazy French girl and her hot air balloon?"

I ignored Mother and examined the menu. "What do you think about some bruschetta for a starter, Mother?"

"I asked you about the girl."

Okay fine, today is about turning over a new leaf, so I'll be honest for a change.

"That's my neighbor, Anne-Laure. She's from Paris and she's flying back this afternoon and leaving for good. She wanted to go in the hot air balloon as a send off, but I couldn't go."

"Why couldn't you?"

"Because I fell in love with her."

...Not a complete lie.

Mother grinned and sipped from her chardonnay. "Aside from the dump that you live in, you're doing okay...Was that suit for her? It looks great on you."

"Why are you even here?"

"Your Mother cares about you, Robert."

The waiter stopped by the table. *Thank God.* "We'll start out with the bruschetta," I began, "and I'll have two of whatever she's having to drink. I don't know when I'll see you again."

"Just like your father, always drunk."

"Speaking of him—"

"That's what I'm here about."

"Okay, what about him?"

"You know about the divorce?"

"Of course."

Mother reached into her purse and produced some documents. Some legal documents. "You need to see these."

"Why!"

"To settle the divorce."

"I'm not signing anything. You two are too old for this nonsense."

"You don't even know what these papers pertain to."

"I don't care. I'm not signing anything that does such a thing to our family." My drinks appeared, and I suddenly felt a little better. I dug into the first one with great appetite.

Mother looked disgusted, "Anne-Laure would probably prefer that you slow down on the drinking, Robert."

I slammed the glass down and shook my head, reaching for the second. "Don't you listen? She's moving to France. We're over."

"Why don't you read the papers, Robert? You never took a post-graduation vacation, and there might be someone waiting for you at the airport."

"I'm not in the mood for a vacation. I've lost everything. All I have is an empty studio apartment. I'm not about to lose anything else today."

"Why don't you go after her?"

"How is that possible?"

"Is all that money in your dishwasher not enough?"

"How should I know?"

"If you read the papers, you'd see that you're fine. Your father and I want you to have a comfortable future."

I bit my lip and looked down at the floor. I almost broke the wine glass I was squeezing it so hard. I didn't want to be the hand that signed this document—a divorce document....*Wait...She said something about having plenty of money.*

"What do these papers say, and if I sign them, what happens? Does this get you and dad divorced?" I had to pinch my nose and sniffle. It was starting to run from all the coke and emotion.

"Those papers have already been signed, Robert. All you need to do is read them."

My stomach knotted. I choked. Mother and Father were divorced, and it was all my fault. Law school, graduation, running away, all of it was my fault. It was the same Mother and Father that I had not seen since graduation. The day when I was too drunk to even treat them to a picture. The bond that once held them together, me, had vanished, and thus so had they.

"I haven't seen you two since graduation," I admitted.

"We know. And the whole town knows about your disastrous outfit. It's been a huge laugh at the club."

"I'm sorry. I'll straighten up, promise, and work for father, and you two don't have to get divorced."

"Honey, we've wanted to get divorced for a long time. We were just waiting until you were mature enough."

"Look at me," I recoiled. "I'm *not* mature. You have no clue what's happened. You should have been there last night to see it! You two need to call this off."

"It's too late, honey. What's done is done."

"Remember Puccini's?" I cracked. "Remember how you wanted to go there for dinner after my graduation? Well, we're at an Italian restaurant right now. But this one is even better—it's four stars! So let's call Father and he can meet us. We can wait for him and drink this wine, and when he gets here we can have a proper graduation and everybody can be happy."

The bruschetta arrived, and I shoved a handful of bread into my starving mouth, chasing it with a spoonful of tomatoes and basil. I hadn't eaten in over forty-eight hours, save some Metamucil and a Hot Pocket. I chomped with a smile on my face. "Mmm. Garlicky!"

Mother laughed. She rarely laughed at my jokes.

"Mmm. This is good. You should have some. See how fun this is?" I spooned a heap of bruchetta on a baguette and offered it to Mother.

"Robert, your Father is not coming here today. He's enjoying a well deserved rest at home, and he kindly asked that I take care of this matter. He sends his best."

"Then what are those papers?"

"Those are your trust papers, dear."

Cha Cha Musty

I was sacked out on the over-stuffed pillow top mattress. I admired the perfect quiet of the "No Tell" room, as management called it. The room was meant to look like a prairie with the theme of the hotel being a kitsch spin on Americana. The comedic purpose was to teleport the lazy isolation of the windswept heartland to the noisy interior of West Hollywood. A ceramic statue of a proud rooster sat perched on the armoire. He observed a mural of a wheat field magnificently painted on the windowless west wall. This was the perfect place to level out—a tiny slice of quiet. It was my own private, desolate prairie...and it had a fully stocked bar.

When I'd found this motel a few hours earlier, the front desk receptionist, emboldened the mischievous inside joke about the room and asked, *"Lover, Player, or Fugitive?"* as she handed me the keys.

"Tired," I replied.

I'd junked the Volvo and moved out of my studio that morning. So neither in love, fucking anybody, or being pursued for a crime, I started my relaxation with a Cha Cha Musty cocktail. Then a second, to which I added some BBQ onion rings to graze on, ordered up from the restaurant below.

I knew that I planned to be here for a few days, and that's about *all* I knew. I had a clean slate, just like the day I dropped everything at Graduation and headed out here. Once again, I was off the hook—no responsibility. I'd gotten away with another botched caper, and I was free to go. I never had to go back to IPD for another eight hour stint in a soul sucking cubicle. I never had to go back to that cramped studio in Westlake Village, or camp out all night in front of a bank. For the time being, I was safely inside the Farmer's Daughter Motel, and I was washing a barbeque onion ring down with a cool, spicy cocktail. I even had a mesquite sauce for dipping. Life was good for the moment.

But I had learned a few things about life during this adventure. I learned during my research that old Eddie Dodson had got pinched in this same motel back in 1999. He'd hit a bank in Santa Barbara for about thirteen grand and holed up in room 177. For three days straight, he slammed as much junk as LA could turn up. Too bad for Eddie, it wasn't enough junk to kill him.

His picture was everywhere in the media after the robbery, and soon enough, somebody dropped the dime on him. The detectives followed the lead to the stolen Mercedes Eddie had parked in front of the motel. Then the squadrons arrived, and the bullhorns began hissing bold orders. *"Surrender. You are surrounded."* And boy was the place surrounded. SWAT, homicide, beat cops, all the way down to paramedics. You name it. This was the final curtain on the most prolific bank robber in the history of the United States.

Eddie *wanted* to die.

He was finally about to get hauled in after a record-setting career of sixty-four hits, and he knew that his time had come. He knew that he was going to die soon, and that it would be in jail if he were to go peacefully. He was terminal with Hep-C. So why not just ride out the thrill and go down in an ambush, he thought? Why die a sick jailbird in a few months' time when a romantic death could be had today?

So he walked over to the door, stuck his head out, and told the pigs to hush. *"Wait a minute!"* Then he closed the door and dosed up one last time. When he was good and high, with his poison fix, the ten cent pistol as they call it, he put on a Fedora and bolted out the door. He aimed a decoy handgun at the crowd of law enforcement. The H couldn't kill him—a spot the size of golf ball couldn't take out this King Kong addict—but the cops sure as hell could.

So the legend of Eddie Dodson ended downstairs in the parking lot of the very motel in which I was staying, the

Farmer's Daughter—not but a few blocks away from Canter's Deli where I myself had almost died.

But this is where Eddie and I were different.

The greatest American bank robber that ever lived went down screaming like a loon, *"Kill Me! Kill Me!"* And one of the worst, me, was sipping a cocktail, healthy, free, and about to take a long nap until it was time to head over to LAX.

* * *

And as he was a bachelor and in nobody's debt, nobody troubled his head anymore about him.
—*The Headless Horseman*

Appendix: Ramen Recipes Inspired by the Deranged Young Professional

Appetizers

Irony—Seafood flavor ramen prepared with illegal Russian Sturgeon caviar and scallions.

Noodle doodle—Tapas inspired; top Ritz brand snack crackers with a scoop of fiesta ramen and picante pico de gallo. Try salsa verde for added *fiesta*. Dress with fresh cilantro.

Bingo Biscuits—Ramen noodle flavor of your choice, breaded, and deep fried in Bob's *secret* spicy batter. Served with a side of tangy saffron horseradish remoulade for dipping. When you eat 'em, you'll scream *Bingo!*

Entrees

Vita-men—Your choice of ramen noodle topped with crushed multi vitamin. AKA *Delicious and Nutritious*.

Vita-men-ium—See above. Add also, one Valium. AKA *Loopy Soup*.

Ramen Lite—Plain Ramen noodles prepared sans flavor packet.

Jesus—Shrimp flavor ramen, one can sardines, ½ cup red wine. Bake 20 min.

Rosemary Jane—Chicken flavor ramen, one tbs. rosemary, one tbs. cannabis, one tbs. olive oil. Mince cannabis, heat in oil with Rosemary until leaves are toasted. Add to ramen, and prepare noodles as per directions on package.

Absorba the Greek—Prepare chicken flavor ramen, add 1 tbs. Knorr brand creamy pesto sauce packet and let sit so that the noodles absorb any excess moisture. Reheat, toss with feta cheese crumbles and serve.

Rocket Ramen—Ramen lite prepared in Red Bull instead of water. Add also, crushed OTC caffeine pills for *Redeye Rocket Ramen.*

Gypsy Pot Luck—Whilst at the market purchasing ramen products, shoplift, without discretion, as many condiments and ramen additives as possible. Return home and combine all materials al dente style.

Hot Block Crock —Ramen prepared using an empty tin can and the engine block of a hot Volvo, years '96 and earlier. Located adjacent to the exhaust manifold is an exposed portion of the engine block that makes a perfect shelf on which to place your tin can for heating. Takes about ten minutes to cook thoroughly on a hot engine. Use tongs.

Rockn' Ramen—Your favorite ramen kicked up and *played at an eleven*, cause ten ain't loud enough, Brother. In a blender, combine crushed red pepper, one hananerro, and one tbs. of rubbing alcohol, blend. Reduce mixture using low heat and toss with ramen.

These Nuts—Heat one heaping scoop of peanut butter, one tbs. of soy sauce, one tbs. of ketchup in a pan with ½ cup of lemon juice *or* sweet and sour cocktail mix. Stir until mixture is liquidy and serve over pork flavor ramen noodles. Top with scallions.

Ramen Deserts

Party Pasta—Ramen lite topped with three crushed pixie sticks (flavor(s) of your choice), skittles, and a Snickers bar. Pairs well with Rosemary Jane, see Entrees.

Sinful—Ramen lite topped with Hershey's syrup, one crushed Hershey's bar, chocolate sprinkles, and Hostess chocolate cupcake crumbs. Hey, if somebody could make *rice* a treat?

Cocktails

Sazerac—A traditional New Orleans cocktail. Pack an Old-Fashioned glass with ice. In a second Old-Fashioned glass add a dash of Peychaud's bitters and a sugar cube. Crush the sugar cube. Add a generous shot of Sazerac Rye Whiskey to the second glass containing the Peychaud's Bitters and sugar. Empty the ice from the first glass and coat the glass with the Herbsaint, then discard the remaining Herbsaint (or drip it into your mouth!). Empty the whiskey/bitters/sugar mixture from the second glass into the first glass and garnish with lemon peel.

Cha Cha Musty—Hindi for "Uncle Pimp." Mix 3 oz. Sailor Jerry's Spiced Navy Rum with Squirt lemon lime soda in a shaker with ice. Pour into a tall glass and add a generous grapefruit juice floater. Garnish with slice of lime.

Drink Beer and Fuck!

6605946R0

Made in the USA
Lexington, KY
03 September 2010